Sirius About Murder

This Large Print Book carries the
Seal of Approval of N.A.V.H.

Sirius About Murder

A Beanie and Cruiser Mystery

Sue Owens Wright

WHEELER
PUBLISHING

A

Published in 2006 by arrangement with Tekno Books and Ed Gorman.

Wheeler Large Print Cozy Mystery.

The text of this Large Print edition is unabridged.
Other aspects of the book may vary from the original edition.

Set in 11 pt. Plantin by Carleen Stearns.

Printed in the United States on permanent paper.

ISBN 1-59722-191-0 (lg. print : sc : alk. paper)

In memory of Dolly, who rescued me.

As the Founder/CEO of NAVH, the only national health agency solely devoted to those who, although not totally blind, have an eye disease which could lead to serious visual impairment, I am pleased to recognize Thorndike Press* as one of the leading publishers in the large print field.

Founded in 1954 in San Francisco to prepare large print textbooks for partially seeing children, NAVH became the pioneer and standard setting agency in the preparation of large type.

Today, those publishers who meet our standards carry the prestigious "Seal of Approval" indicating high quality large print. We are delighted that Thorndike Press is one of the publishers whose titles meet these standards. We are also pleased to recognize the significant contribution Thorndike Press is making in this important and growing field.

Lorraine H. Marchi, L.H.D.
Founder/CEO
NAVH

* Thorndike Press encompasses the following imprints: Thorndike, Wheeler, Walker and Large Print Press.

1

A mother lode of leaves gilded the parking lot of the Haute Hydrant pet shop, despite an unseasonably warm autumn in South Lake Tahoe. The lingering heat of Indian Summer was matched by growing dissent over a proposed lakefront dog park for Tahoe's canines. For weeks, editorials in *The Tahoe Tattler* had rekindled the age-old debate about public versus private use of Tahoe's shoreline, but only a pet psychic could have foretold that the daily growls would turn deadly.

On the balmy October morning of the Howloween costume contest and carnival, dog lovers from all over the basin gathered to help raise money for Tahoe's pup playground. Vendors from Petropolis, a new pet lover's superstore, turned out to lend support and display their wares for Tahoe's tail-waggers and their owners. Rub-a-Dub-Dog offered free bathing and grooming services for the event. There was even a pet psychic, Madame Pawline, doing complimentary readings with dogs and their owners. It was a real hound happening!

Mayor Thor Petersen turned out to show support for the event, and so did Councilman Colin Grant. Even kindly Pastor Ramseth of neighboring Lakeview Methodist Church joined our furry fold, and the ladies of the congregation had organized a cakewalk. A local dog bakery, The Pawtisserie, had even made "people crackers" for the animals.

Sally Applebaum trimmed her pet shop windows in orange and black streamers for the occasion. A long-leggedy rubber tarantula surfed a wave of synthetic web as plastic vampire bats hovered over a fuzzy cluster of guinea pigs. The multi-colored cavies rooted and burrowed in their nest of fresh wood shavings, emitting shrill chirps and chutters. The Hydrant's owner had outdone herself with spooky decorations for the event she was hosting for our fur friends. Sally, along with animal shelter volunteers, and a pack of other dog lovers, including yours truly, had done a great job of promoting the Howloween event, which drew a large crowd of participants and curious onlookers.

Outside the store, a gangly scarecrow lolled against a hay bale, which was being sprinkled by a Toto imposter. Rags, a Scottish terrier, was one of many entrants in the masquerade, which was also part of the fund-raiser for Alpine Paws Park. To everyone but us diehard dog lovers and our canine friends, who had been banned from using public parks and trails, an off-leash park seemed like a long shot in a wiener dog race compared to other far more lucrative proposals for this stretch of sandlot. Choice lakefront property could sell for as much as ten thousand dollars per foot, and various commercial interests vied for the parcel.

The issue had become so contentious it now dominated the front page of the *Tattler*, as I could see through the weathered plastic cover of the paper rack in front of Sally's store. As a stringer for the Tahoe daily, I resented having to spend a dollar and fifty cents to read news I help write, but the snoop in me won out over the skinflint when I spotted the Helvetica bold headline about the park:

PAWS PROPONENTS PERSIST IN DOGFIGHT OVER PUP PARK

Hackles are raised over an off-leash dog park proposed for a prized five-mile stretch of beachfront property, part of a fifty-acre estate donated to the

Tahoe Historical Society by the Haversham family. Haversham House has long been a popular tourist attraction, but due to economic downturns and dwindling financial reserves, its fate now seems uncertain.

"It is our fervent wish to protect Haversham House from those who would selfishly destroy it," says Abigail Haversham, prominent Tahoe citizen and namesake, who inherited the nineteenth century estate from her late father, William Haversham. "Renovation plans for Alpine Haven Senior Center, in concert with Alpine Paws Park, will not only ensure that a significant piece of Sierra Nevada history escapes the developer's wrecking ball but also preserve my family's legacy to future generations."

There are plenty of seniors or seniors-to-be in Tahoe who would clamor for lodging in such an exclusive lakefront retirement community, but I'm not including myself in that group just yet. In case you don't remember me, I'm Elsinore MacBean. That's Elsie, for short, or just plain Beanie to my friends. Although I'll soon be receiving my AARP card, I'm thankful to say

I'm not one of those people who look like their dogs, especially since my Basset Hound, Cruiser, could definitely use a facelift.

Although our efforts to raise money for the park had been fairly successful thus far, we wouldn't stand a Chihuahua's chance against the big dogs of business without community support. The only thing developers cared less about than a public dog park was an old folks' home. Fortunately, not everyone in Tahoe felt that way. The Silver Lions, a militant senior group, were determined that the Alpine Haven plan would prevail over other interests.

One Silver Lion member, my good friend Rosie Clark, also chaired the fundraising committee for Alpine Paws, volunteered at the shelter, and taught in the humane education program, just to name a few of her activities on behalf of four-leggers in South Tahoe. She had organized a committee to host a Bark in the Park Ball this year to help raise more money for the canine cause. In keeping with Halloween, the ball would be held at the Haversham "Haunted Mansion."

The excitement in the languid autumn air was palpable, at least among the human contestants, many of whom, like Rosie,

11

wore costumes to complement those of their pets. Cruiser and I, alias Sherlock and Watson, were no exception. Even though I'm generally regarded as the Sierra sleuth in these parts, I let Cruiser be Sherlock this time. I had fashioned a Cruiser-sized cape and deerstalker hat and attached a miniature spyglass and pipe to the cape. The judging would be difficult, though. There were some clever contenders for the Best Canine Costume award: Frankendog, a ghoulie Puli, and a trio of extra-*terrier*estrials whose owner was outfitted in a silver spacesuit.

"Rags, come!" Rags scampered back to Rosie, who was dressed as Dorothy in *The Wizard of Oz*. He leapt obediently into the wicker picnic basket she carried.

I beckoned to my stubborn dog. He had discovered an abandoned peanut butter yummy on the pavement and was giving it a thorough sniff before sampling. As usual, he took his own sweet time responding to my command.

"Cruiser! Leave it!" I managed to extract the gummy yummy from his jaws and tossed it into a nearby waste container. I didn't like him eating things I hadn't given him, especially since there had been a number of dog poisonings in Tahoe recently. Finally, I had to leash Cruiser and drag him away from the spot where he'd found the treat; the judging of the costume contest was about to begin!

Passersby paused to gawk at the spectacle of haute-coutured canines strutting their stuff on the catwalk, or, in this case, dogwalk. Among the gathering crowd of spectators I spotted my friend Sheriff Skip Cassidy, who had come mostly for Cruiser's and my benefit, or so I thought . . .

"Well, if it isn't Sherlock Bones himself," Skip said, petting Cruiser. Cruiser had already coated his costume in drool, which dribbled onto Skip's hand. Fortunately, Skip has never minded a little dog slobber. He couldn't mind and still be Cruiser's and my friend. Besides, he's had his hands in messier things in his line of work as county sheriff.

"Hey, thanks for coming, Skip," I said, offering him a dry corner of Cruiser's jowl towel to wipe his hand.

"Did I have a choice?"

"Not really. Cruiser would never forgive you if you missed his first modeling gig."

"Speaking of modeling, where's Nona?" Skip said. "I thought she was coming up to see this."

Since I'd tragically lost my husband,

Tom, in a forest fire, Skip had become a surrogate dad, or at least a doting uncle, to my pretty young daughter.

"She couldn't make it, but she said she'll be here as soon as her latest shoot with Vicky's Secret is wrapped up. I'm surprised to see you taking time off from work for a puppy pageant."

He laughed. "Well, things are very busy at the office, but I couldn't afford to miss this dog show, considering . . ."

"Considering what?"

"I just thought maybe I should come along and keep an eye out for any trouble." Feeding me tidbits of information this way, Skip didn't realize that he was teasing me like a dog with a squeak toy.

"Okay, I'll bite." He didn't know how close that was to the truth. I hated it when he withheld news from me. "What kind of trouble?"

The sheriff's usually sunny countenance clouded. "There have been death threats," he said, hooking both thumbs in his lawman's utility belt.

"That's terrible! Who's been threatened?"

"I have!" I was startled by a cold nose nudging my elbow. I turned to face first Rags, then Rosie Clark, who was still toting him in her basket. Her ruby slippers sparkled in the sun. I gave Rags a friendly caress, and he responded by lapping my hand with his small pink tongue. "And Rags, too," she added.

"What do you mean, Rosie?" I said.

"I've been getting some malicious e-mails from someone who says he'll hurt me and my dog, if I don't back off."

"Back off from what?"

"The dog walk park. Someone is dead set against it, apparently."

"No big surprise there," Skip said. "Haven't you been reading the news?"

"Yes," I said. "Sometimes I even *write* the news!"

"I'm not the only one who has been threatened, though," Rosie continued. "Other Alpine Paws proponents have received similar threats, including Abigail Haversham. She told me she also received a vile e-mail, warning her off the project. She was quite upset about it."

"I would be, too," I said. "Poor Abby's really been taking some heat over this."

"I wouldn't worry too much about Abigail," Rosie said. "She can give as good as she gets."

"Do you know Mrs. Haversham, Beanie?" Skip asked.

"Who doesn't? She's top dog in the fight for the park."

"True," Rosie said. "Without her backing, the Alpine Paws project doesn't stand a chance. She's wealthy, well-connected, and a force to be reckoned with."

"Abby usually gets her way, all right," I agreed.

"Any idea at all who might have sent the e-mails?" Skip said.

"I have my suspicions, but it could be just about anyone who has a bone to pick on the issue," Rosie said.

"Can you think of anyone in particular?" I said.

"Walter Wiley comes to mind."

"Who's Walter Wiley?" Skip said.

"The crabby old coot who lives in my neighborhood," Rosie said. "He hates dogs. He's always cussing out any dog owner who walks within ten feet of his property, including me. His grass looks like Astroturf, accent on the first syllable."

I laughed. "Yeah, I know the kind you mean. I've never understood people who obsess so about their lawns and make enemies of their neighbors over it."

"I never have, either," Rosie said. "It's only grass, for crying out loud."

"Funny thing is, many of them are dog

owners themselves, so they should be more tolerant of someone else's pet," I said. "People in glass doghouses shouldn't throw bones."

Rosie laughed, "You can say that again."

"Did you answer any of the e-mails you received, Mrs. Clark?" Skip said.

"No, I thought it best not to."

"Smart," Skip said. "You don't want to encourage this nut."

"There were attachments, but I never open attachments from unknown senders because of computer viruses, so I just deleted the e-mails. I shouldn't even have bothered reading any more of them after the first one, but morbid curiosity got the better of me, I suppose. I printed copies of the messages first, though, if you'd like to see them."

"Good idea," I said. "It could help us find out who is behind this. They could be empty threats, or this person could really mean business."

"Unfortunately, threats like these all too often are eventually acted upon," Skip said. "It takes a pretty sick puppy to do something like this, though."

"I know," Rosie said. She hugged her bushel of unconditional love closer, stroking Rags' grizzled charcoal coat. Rags nuzzled his mistress' open palm and gazed up at her adoringly with almond-shaped, obsidian eyes. "It would kill me if anyone ever hurt my boy."

I thought of Cruiser and the discarded treat he had nearly snatched up from the pavement before I could intercede. "I know just how you feel."

"Have you gotten any more e-mails from him?" Skip said.

"No, but I haven't checked my mail yet today."

"Well, if you get any more, forward them to me." Skip handed Rosie his card. "Here's my e-mail address."

"Thank you, Sheriff. I'd rather not open any more of his nasty old e-mails, to tell you the truth."

"What makes you both so sure it's a man who's sending these threats?" I asked. "For all you know, it could be a woman."

"I know that," Skip said, an edge in his voice that I attributed to the fact that he was still worried about proving himself worthy of his new responsibilities as sheriff. "It could be anyone who wants to kill Alpine Paws."

I didn't like the sound of that one bit.

"She's right," Rosie said. "It might be a woman. I'm only assuming it's a man, but one thing's for certain . . ."

"What?" Skip and I echoed.

"Whoever it is hates dogs. I mean, *dogsbody* doesn't exactly sound like a dog lover, does it?"

"Is that the screen name the sender uses?" Skip asked.

"Yes, and he . . . or she . . . always signs the e-mail the same way."

"How's that?" I asked.

Rosie, who is no shrinking violet herself, looked frightened when she answered, "Sirius about murder."

2

Rosie's threatening e-mails from someone who signed them "Sirius," after the Dog Star, had me worried, especially since just about every dog and dog owner in South Lake Tahoe was present at the Howloween event. The murderous tagline of the mystery e-mailer seemed *à propos*, considering that a meteor shower was predicted to occur on Halloween night. Carla at the *Tattler* had assigned me an article to write about the stellar event, but I'd worry about deadlines later. At the moment, I was worried that the creep might actually be somewhere among the crowd, waiting for an opportunity to carry out his threats. I was glad that Skip was present to keep a sharp lookout for trouble.

Meanwhile, the costume contest was already under way. It was going to be a close competition. I would have hated to be on the judging panel. How could one ever choose a winner among all these contestants? In addition to the aforementioned assortment of doggy disguises, there was an Afghan hound dressed and veiled like Barbara Eden in "I Dream of Jeannie," and a bulldog with pink toenails in Harley-Davidson leathers emblazoned with "Bad to the Bones," who further tipped the judges' scales in her favor by doing a clever trick with a treat dispenser. And, of course, there was my own hound-about-town who was due for his turn in the limelight.

"And for our next contestants," the commentator announced into the microphone, "we have that famous crime-solving team, Sherlock Bones and Dr. Watson."

"Come on, Cruiser, this is our cue." I tugged on the leash and Cruiser tagged along, nose to the ground as ever, scanning for more munchies.

Onlookers were already laughing at the silly-looking basset in the Sherlock Holmes costume when Cruiser stopped short and did a head-to-tail shake, showering any onlookers within slobbering distance in dog spit. This dislodged his deerstalker, which slipped under his chin. The neck fastener on the cape popped open, and the cape peeled down his long body like skin off a sausage. Soon the costume was trailing the ground behind him like a plaid wedding train, except for the upturned deerstalker, which served as a sort of feedbag and crumb collector for an unclaimed biscuit he had nabbed along the way. There's just no stopping a land cruiser like Cruiser.

By this time, everyone was howling with laughter. We didn't win the prize for best costume, or even a consolation prize for best clown act, but at least we provided some comic relief for the spectators, who were growing sweaty and restless on the sun-baked pavement of the parking lot.

Cruiser seemed as relieved as I was that the costume contest was finally over, and I removed what remained of his Sherlock outfit. More contests were forthcoming, including the much-anticipated Howl-off, but judging from the deluge of drool spilling from Cruiser's pendulous lips, I figured he was in imminent danger of getting overheated. Between events, I led him over to one of the communal canine watering buckets for a sip, then looked for a shady spot to get him out of the sun for a while. I figured Madame Pawline's booth would do nicely. The banner, with orange and black lettering that said "PET PSYCHIC," fluttered in a welcome alpine zephyr.

"Hey, Skip, ever been to a pet psychic?"

"Pet psychic? You're kidding me, right?"

"No, I'm not. Come on. Let's go check it out. Cruiser needs some shade, and so do I."

As we crossed the parking lot, I heard loud voices coming from the direction of the Pet Psychic booth. I saw Abigail Haversham talking to Madame Pawline outside her tent. They appeared to be arguing, but I couldn't tell exactly what was going on from where I was. Then Mrs. Haversham followed the younger woman inside. By the time we reached the tent, Madame Pawline was doing a reading with portly Mrs. Haversham and her plump Pomeranian. The psychic booth's interior was a New Age haven, complete with the soothing sound of a trickling fountain, flickering candles, and calming aromatherapy scents. Pawline, also in costume for the event, was the quintessential gypsy fortuneteller with her long, dark mass of curly hair and large, luminous brown eyes.

"Lang Po says that you should stop feeding him too many treats, Mrs. Haversham. He doesn't want to die early and leave you all alone."

"Oh, dear me!" said Mrs. Haversham, giving her dog such a fierce hug I thought his already buggy eyes might pop right out of his head. "Mummy promises never to do that again."

"He also says he wants you to replace his torn cushion with a new one."

Abigail studied Madame Pawline with her piercing blue eyes. "How do you know that?"

"Lang Po told me, of course," the pretty young woman responded with far more composure than did most people under Abby's keen glare.

The tent was dead silent but for the trickling of the fountain.

"Why, that's truly amazing! You couldn't possibly have known I was planning to buy him a new bed today at the Haute Hydrant. My little Prince Po-Po must have told you that himself." Abigail gave her pet another eye-popping squeeze. "Now, we really must be running along. Say thank you to Madame Pawline, Lang Po."

Lang Po growled and bared his teeth, which was his way of saying he'd had enough of this paw reading business and was ready to go now, please, or even if you don't please. Madame Pawline appeased him with a treat from the dog-shaped cookie jar she kept filled for her canine clients. Pawline yanked her hand away, when he snapped up the tidbit and nearly a finger or two along with it.

Abigail put Lang Po down from her ample lap. "Come along, Po-Po. Let's go buy you some diet food right now!"

"I hope she buys some for herself, too," Skip muttered. I gave him a shot in the ribs as Mrs. Haversham left the tent with Lang Po, more of a large dust bunny with legs than a dog.

"What a nice Basset Hound you have there," Madame Pawline said. "What's his name?"

"I thought she was a psychic," Skip whispered in my ear. "Shouldn't she *know* his name?"

"Shhhh!" I gave him another rib shot, a bit harder this time. He took the hint, at least momentarily.

"Come here, boy," Madame Pawline beckoned to Cruiser. Her voice was like warm honey. He responded without hesitation and waddled right over to her, which was so unlike him or any other Basset Hound in existence. She offered him a tidbit, but he didn't take it.

"I've taught him not to take treats from strangers," I said.

"That's very wise of you," Pawline said.

"I'll save it for later." I stashed the treat in my pocket.

Cruiser raised one massive paw to Pawline. She took it gently in her hand.

"What's she going to do, read his paw?" Skip said.

"His name is Cruiser," I said, trying to ignore Skip's heckling. "I can see you really have a way with animals, Madame Pawline."

"She should. She's a . . . what did you call it?" Skip said.

"Pet psychic."

"I'm an animal communicator, actually," she corrected. "And you can call me Pauline. It's spelled with a 'u,' not a 'w.' Madame *Paw*line, Pet Psychic, is just for the sake of the fund-raiser."

"Nice to meet you, Pauline. My name is Elsie MacBean, and this is my friend, Sheriff Skip Cassidy."

"Hello, Elsie. Sheriff Cassidy."

"You're telling me that you read animals' minds?" Skip said.

"That's putting it rather simplistically. Most people don't have a clue what a professional animal communicator does and tend to label it as palmistry, Tarot, or even witchcraft."

"I didn't mean to say you were a . . ." Skip said.

"I prefer to say I 'connect' with animals.

26

It's kind of a symbiotic thing. You know, like horse whisperers. You've heard of those, haven't you?"

"Sure I have. Saw the movie," Skip said. "But I didn't know that what you do is considered a 'profession' per se." I wanted to pop him another good one for that put-down, but Pauline was adept at handling Doubting Thomases. Or in this case, Doubting Skips.

"Yes, it is," Pauline said. "And rapidly gaining respect, particularly in the veterinary field. You can read all about it in my book, *The Pet Connection*." Pauline handed Skip a copy. "I'll be happy to autograph that for you, if you decide to buy it. It's on special today only."

"Er, thanks. I'll think about it," Skip said. He glanced at the cover price and quickly passed the book to me. I couldn't remember the last time Skip spent more than five dollars on a book that wasn't a sports swimsuit anthology or fly fishing manual. Pauline didn't give up so easily, trying to convince skeptics, though. In her line of work, I imagined she'd had lots of practice.

"Surely you've engaged the services of psychic investigators in your line of work on occasion, Sheriff Cassidy."

"Well, uh, no . . ."

"Then, perhaps you should."

"I don't see that happening anytime soon. We use what limited budget we have on tried and true scientific methods of crime investigation, not Voodoo or hocus-pocus."

Pauline's onyx eyes glinted with vexation. "That's too bad, Sheriff, because psychics have been very successful in solving some very high-profile cases for the police. What psychic investigators do may not be 'scientific' in your estimation, but it's not Voodoo or hocus-pocus. Neither is what I do."

I could see that Skip was in imminent danger of getting an ear-chewing from Pauline the Pet Psychic, so I ran interference. "Do you do readings with animals other than dogs, Pauline?"

"Oh, yes. Cats, birds, hamsters, and horses. Even fish. One time I communicated with one of Siegfried and Roy's rare white tigers."

"And what did the tiger tell you?" Skip the skeptic tried to sound sincere, but I knew what was going through his head. So did Pauline.

"Well, I know you won't believe this, Sheriff Cassidy, but he said . . ." Pauline spoke softly. She smiled and crooked a finger seductively at him to come closer, which he did. Skip's such a sucker for a pretty face. What happened next served him right.

He turned an ear to hear her better. Skip blushed and grinned when her lips brushed lightly against his ear.

"You're grrrreat!" she shouted. Skip's head snapped aside like he'd been slapped. In effect, he had been.

"Purrrrfect," I said, laughing.

"Harummph! Very funny." Skip grimaced, rubbing the offended ear.

Having silenced her heckler, Pauline turned to me. "Now, what can I do for you and Cruiser, Elsie?"

"Oh, I thought it might be interesting to have you do a reading with him. We've never had one before. Maybe you can find out something about his past life before we adopted him."

"I can certainly try," Pauline said. "Of course, I can't guarantee he'll tell me anything. Sometimes it takes more than one session to make contact."

Skip opened his mouth to speak, but I shot him a look that said he'd better not.

"Sure, go ahead."

"I'll have to ask you both not to talk

while I do the reading. It jams my receptors." She directed her request to both of us, but I knew it was meant mainly for Skip.

Pauline leaned back in her chair, relaxed, and closed her eyes. She took several deep breaths and quieted herself as though meditating, then opened her eyes again and focused intently on Cruiser. He was not looking directly at her, and she didn't force him to. Instead, she ran her hands lightly along Cruiser's back. I noticed that Cruiser seemed at ease and aware of Pauline, although he was still not looking at her.

She talked softly to him at first, saying things like, "How are you, Cruiser? Do you mind if I talk to you?" Then there was silence again as she tuned into my canine companion, nodding occasionally as though she were receiving his thoughts telepathically. Of course, a casual observer would have assumed she was just admiring my handsome dog. Finally, after a few minutes, she gave him a gentle pat on the shoulder. "Thank you, Cruiser." Then Cruiser did something he rarely does, even to me. He licked Pauline's hand. "Is there something else you want to tell me?"

There was another long silence. Skip was

growing visibly impatient with the whole thing, and I knew he wanted to leave. However, I was keenly aware that some spiritual connection was being made between two beings of differing species. The energy in the tent was palpable. Finally, she nodded to Cruiser and said, "Good boy. Thanks."

"What did he tell you?" I asked.

Skip rolled his eyes.

"He says that he misses The Man."

My eyes instantly misted. "That would be Tom, my husband. He died a few years back."

"Cruiser also says that he loves you and is glad The Man found him and brought him home to you. He did not like his life before and was very unhappy with his former owners. He says they were cruel to him and neglected him terribly."

No surprise there, I thought. I well remembered how malnourished Cruiser was when we found him. His noble head looked huge on his emaciated body. You'd never even know he was the same dog.

Pauline continued. "He says that's why he ran away."

"He ran away? I always thought he had been abandoned."

"No, he escaped from them. He says he

likes living with you, and he also likes your friend who wears the uniform."

"That must be you, Skip."

He couldn't repress a smile.

Pauline continued. "But Cruiser says he wishes you'd take him for a run off the leash more often."

"I would if there was anywhere left to do that in Tahoe, without getting a citation from the pooch police," I said. "I sure do hope we get our dog park. Dogs need to have a place to exercise without restraint."

"The odds don't seem in favor of it," Pauline said. "There's a strong anti-dog faction in this community."

"Not just in Tahoe, unfortunately. There is a great deal of intolerance toward dogs, and it seems to be growing worse as land becomes scarcer and towns like this one become more urbanized."

"There's more, Elsie," Pauline said. "Cruiser says it's very important."

"What's that?"

"He says for you to pay attention."

"Pay attention?" Skip said. "I don't know how she could pay any more attention to him than she already does. She treats him like a king."

"Skip's right," I said. "Why, Cruiser even has his own throne, my couch."

32

"No, that's not it," Pauline said.

"What, then?" I asked.

"What he said to me exactly was, 'Watch out for the bad thing.' "

"Bad thing? I don't understand. What could it mean?" A cloud obscured the sun, and a shadow fell upon the Pet Psychic booth, where we sat with Pauline. I felt a chill zip up my spine when I heard her next words.

"Someone here is in mortal danger."

3

What had begun as a day of enjoyment at a community fund-raiser for our furry friends had taken a decidedly serious turn — first with Rosie Clark's report of death threats against her and then the message Pauline related to me via Cruiser. It wasn't every day I received prognostications from a pooch. Although Skip's unwavering skepticism about all things unseen usually annoyed me, I felt vaguely relieved when he pooh-poohed the whole idea of pet psychics, or animal communicators, as Pauline preferred to call herself.

"I wouldn't take what she said too seriously, Beanie. It's all a crock, if you ask me."

"I'd like to believe that right now more than anything, but, as a Native American, I cannot deny that there is a connection that exists among all living things. I may not be as good at communicating with animals as Pauline, but I understand that such things are certainly possible. Tribal shamans can even assume the shapes of animals."

"Depends on what they're smoking in their pipes, I guess," Skip said.

"If I didn't know better, I'd say you were insulting me and my people."

"Sorry. You know I don't mean any offense. It's just that I think this Madame Pawline would say she had Harry Houdini's ghost on direct dial, if she thought she could make a buck from it."

"She didn't strike me as being dishonest. Besides, she wasn't accepting any money for her services."

"She tried to sell me a book, and you bought one. What do you call that?"

"A writer trying to make a decent living."

"Well, I didn't buy it, or her book. If you ask me, she's just rounding up suckers for her parlor tricks."

"Oh, cut her some slack, Skip. You're just looking for any excuse to dismiss what she does as authentic."

"Come on, now. You know as well as I do that it's the old bait-and-switch tactic. Sure, her service was free today, but she was just setting you up to get suckered in for more paw-reading sessions later on. I'll bet she usually charges fifty dollars an hour, minimum. She's just a fur-fleecing fakir, if you ask me."

"Well, I didn't ask you. Her talent seems genuine to me."

"Talent? Hah! These so-called psychics are all the same. People are so eager to believe the impossible, without even realizing they give these guys all the information they need to make their predictions seem valid."

"What do you mean?"

"When the psychic does the reading, all they do is repeat what you already told them. Maybe they word it differently or embellish it, but the information is still the same."

"But she knew about Tom and Cruiser's past. How could she know about all that?"

"You forget that you said you wanted to know about Cruiser's past life before he was adopted. So she knew right off that Cruiser is a rescue dog. She could also easily assume that you were referring to your husband when you said 'we' adopted Cruiser. Since you no longer wear a wedding band, it was easy for her to infer that you're either divorced or widowed. When she told you that Cruiser said he 'misses The Man,' you confirmed this with an emotional reaction, even giving her your husband's name and the fact that he's no longer living. You see how it works?"

"I see what you mean, but . . ."

"Some of them even research their subjects beforehand or use electronic devices to receive information from someone hidden backstage."

"But you're forgetting one thing, Skip."

"What?"

"The warning of someone's death. And whose death exactly?"

"I'm still trying to figure that out. I don't know why she would tell you that, unless . . ."

"Unless what?"

"Maybe *she's* the one behind the threats to Rosie and others."

"But why would she do such a thing? She obviously loves animals, and tries to help them and their owners."

"What better camouflage than calling yourself a pet psychic? Perhaps she was also threatening *you*."

"Why would she want to threaten me? She never laid eyes on me before today."

"At least that you're aware of," Skip said.

"Why are you always so suspicious of everyone?"

"It's my job. I have to remain detached in my line of work."

"Yes, I suppose you do."

"Best hang onto some of that useful skepticism yourself, Beanie."

"I guess a little now and then can be a healthy thing. In fact, it's saved me from disaster before. I tend to confuse skepticism with cynicism."

"Lots of people do."

"But you're still forgetting something."

"What?"

"Cruiser liked her. He even gave her a lick on the hand."

"So?"

"He hardly ever does that, not even to me, unless food is involved."

"Maybe she palmed a treat, or she could have rubbed bacon grease or something on her hands. These types use all kinds of clever tricks to convince people they're genuine."

I didn't doubt that Cruiser could be easily bribed with bacon. On numerous occasions he'd nearly taken my fingers along with a Bacon Beggin' Strip, but I was certain of one thing: he is a far better judge of character than anyone else I know. And if you can't trust your dog, whom can you trust?

Skip's and my heated debate over Madame Pawline's psychic abilities was interrupted by an announcement over the microphone. "All contestants for the Howl-off, please assemble at the judging table."

"I think they mean you, Cruiser," I said. "Come on, Skip. We can't let our canine Caruso miss this event."

"Yeah, uh, sure. I'm right behind you." I could see from the worried expression on Skip's face that despite his admitted skepticism, he was just as disturbed as I was by what he'd heard Pauline say.

We gathered at the judging table with the other Howl-off contestants and their owners. The competition was going to be tough. There was another Basset Hound in an Elvis costume; a legal Beagle wearing law briefs; the "I Dream of Jeannie" Afghan hound; a *real* wiener dog, which was a Dachshund sandwiched in a hot dog bun; and a Basenji wearing lederhosen.

"Do we have any other contestants for the Howl-off?" the announcer asked.

"Yoo-hoo! Wait for us!" Her apple cheeks blushing overripe red, Sally Applebaum bustled over carrying Fabian, her yappy Yorkshire terrier and pet store alarm. The Holy Terrier was still dressed in a nun's habit from the costume competition.

"All right, everyone," said the announcer. "When I give the signal, the Howl-off will begin. And may the best dog win. Ready, set, howl!"

At the signal, owners began coaxing their dogs to sing. It was hard to tell who was really competing in this contest, the people or the dogs. Owners began howling at the tops of their lungs to encourage their dogs. Sally played the harmonica for Fabian, which set him to yipping and yapping. One woman gobbled like a turkey to get her dog to vocalize. The Afghan just looked blonde, gorgeous, and perplexed by the whole affair. I finally understood why the Basenji's owner had dressed her in lederhosen instead of an African safari outfit when the "barkless" dog began to yodel — really more of a glass-splintering screech. The wiener dog was doing his best to out-bark the Beagle, but the main contenders in this Howl-off were the dueling bassets, Cruiser and Elvis, a *basso profundo* chorus. The other canine contestants, knowing they were outmatched, stopped barking. Not the two hounds. They kept right on competing.

Rising above the crowd's uproarious laughter, in shrill accompaniment to the howling bassets, was a blood-clotting shriek.

4

The Howl-off contest was interrupted, and the day's second competitive doggie dash ensued as everyone ran with dogs in tow to see what was the matter. The scream had come from the vicinity of Madame Pawline's tent.

That was where we found Abigail Haver-sham lying on the grass. She gazed up at the sheltering pines with unseeing sapphire eyes that matched the skate rink–sized ring on her finger. A young man and a vendor or two were already gathered on the scene when we arrived. One might have thought Abby was just resting in the shade, if it hadn't been for the unnatural angle of her neck and the blue nylon groomer's leash knotted around it. Her face was bluer than the leash.

The Sheriff knelt down to loosen the leash and take a pulse, but evidently there was none to be detected.

"Is she . . . dead?" the young man asked.

"I'm afraid so," Skip said. "Looks like

her neck's been broken."

Rosie gasped. I placed a steadying hand on her shoulder.

"Who found her like this?" Skip asked.

"I did," the young man answered.

"Do you know Mrs. Haversham?" I asked.

"Sh . . . she's my aunt," he said. I noticed he used the British pronunciation, "awnt." Whether it was just an upper-class affectation or he had really spent time in En-gland was hard to say, but it made him sound almost as pedigreed as he looked. Peering shyly up at me through a wave of pale blond hair with lake-blue eyes, he said, "I'm Addison Haversham."

"Did you see anyone else in the vicinity?" Skip asked.

"I thought I saw someone disappear into one of the tents just as I arrived."

"What happened to Lang Po?" Rosie said.

"I guess he must have run off," Addison said. "He was probably scared away by whoever did this to Aunt Abby."

"Did you see who it was?" Skip said.

"No. He was in costume."

"There are a lot of people in costumes here," I said. "What kind of costume was it?"

"A long, dark robe with a hood, like a monk or Druid would wear."

"I'll go see if I can find Lang Po before he comes to any harm," Rosie said. "Poor little thing is probably scared to death."

"Go ahead, Rosie." I knew the real reason Rosie didn't want to stay. If humans, like dogs, had functioning vomeronasal organs, I would have opened my mouth to the air, exposing the twin olfactory sensory sacs in the roof of my mouth, and smelled raw fear emanating from my friend.

A crowd continued to gather and gape at the spectacle of the murdered woman. Skip tried his best to keep the rubbernecks at bay while he tied a yellow ribbon 'round the old pine tree.

"Is there anything I can do here?" said Reverend Ramseth, who had just joined the fray. He looked as horrified as the rest of the frightened flock at the sight of the victim.

"Nothing except administer last rites," Skip said.

"I'm afraid I can't help you there. You'd need a Catholic priest for that, Sheriff," the reverend said.

"Then there's nothing left to be done except call the meat wagon . . . er . . . coroner."

I winced at Skip's insensitive crime scene

blooper. I knew he wasn't accustomed to having a large audience present at the scene of a crime, but then tact has never been his strong suit, anyway.

"I'm out of tape, Beanie. Hold the fort while I get more, will you?"

That was an odd request of an Indian from a paleface, but I agreed. "Sure thing."

"And keep an eye out for anything unusual."

"Will do." I'd already seen a lot of unusual things — dogs in disguises, pet psychics, a murder victim wearing a dog leash — what could classify as more unusual than that?

"What's going on? I heard the commotion from my booth." I turned to see Pauline standing right behind me. "Is everything all right here?"

"Far from it," I said.

"Oh, my gosh. Isn't that . . . Mrs. Haversham?"

"Yes. Looks like your earlier prediction was accurate, Pauline. Someone *was* in mortal danger. Abigail's been murdered."

"Murdered? But how?"

"Strangled, with a dog leash."

"That's terrible. I can't believe it. We were talking only minutes ago, and now this. Where's Lang Po?"

"He ran off. Someone has gone to look for him."

"Looks like they found him," Abby's nephew said.

Rosie returned, carrying the Pom. The little dog hung limply from her arms, his tongue lolling from his mouth.

"What's wrong with Lang Po?" I said. "Was he hit by a car?"

"No." A tear slipped down her cheek. "I think he's been poisoned."

5

The Dog Park fund-raiser had turned out to be a dog day afternoon for all of us, but worst of all for Abigail Haversham and her little dog, Lang Po. Doc Heaton, the veterinarian who has treated Cruiser for this and that over the years, worked tirelessly to save the poisoned Pomeranian. It was nip and tuck, with Lang Po doing most of the nipping, but after a few days in intensive canine care, it looked as though the late Mrs. Haversham's pampered pooch would pull through just fine.

Fortunately, the small dog hadn't had time to ingest enough of the poison to finish him off or do any permanent damage. Whether he'd been purposely poisoned or had simply gotten into the garbage or something he shouldn't have hadn't been determined. Until the culprit was found, dog owners in Tahoe would be more vigilant for the safety of their pets and, in the wake of Abigail Haversham's murder, for their own.

Meanwhile, things had continued to heat up over the dog park issue. The debate was about to get a lot more heated. The town hall meeting to discuss the proposed dog park had drawn a large crowd of supporters and plenty of others who were not so supportive. Before the night was over, all those present would try to out-growl one another to claim this particular piece of Tahoe territory as their own.

I glanced around the room at the crowd. I saw some familiar faces, including my old rival, Sonseah Little Feather, and Tribal Elder Dan Silvernail; Rosie's grumpy neighbor, Walter Wiley; Reverend Ramseth; and several affluent Tahoans whose property also skirted the land in question. The Boyds, the Strouds, and the Menckens were among those who were vehemently against the dog park, which they feared might lower their property values. They were oblivious to the fact that their sprawling, pastel-painted mansions created more of an eyesore along Tahoe's shores than a dog park ever could. Even Diggs' Sierra Dive and Quest had an interest in this property. They planned to build a new boat dock, which opened up a whole other Pandora's Box of ecological issues. Except for the good reverend, many of those present looked angry, but none of them looked more irate than did Walter, a crusty old curmudgeon if ever there was one.

The meeting was intended to serve as an opportunity for community members to share their thoughts and for City Council subcommittee members to collect feedback, suggestions, and ideas from residents for the best and most equitable use of the property in question. At least that was how Rosie and the rest of the dog park supporters, including yours truly, hoped it would go down. The ensuing discussion turned out to be more like a pack of coyotes trying to out-mark one another on the old sugar pine in my front yard, the one Cruiser waters regularly. You'll have to excuse my canine analogy, but if the dog collar fits . . .

I must spend way too much time alone with my dog. I've even begun to think like him. It's a good thing my daughter, Nona, comes to visit with me from time to time or I'd go totally to the dogs. In fact, she had arrived from San Francisco just in time to witness the fur fly in Conference Room Number 2 at the community college that night.

Among the Alpine Haven boosters were the Silver Lions Seniors, who had broken

48

out into boisterous songs of protest: "We are lions, hear us roar, in numbers too big to ignore . . ." Dan Silvernail did his best to drown them out by beating the Washo ceremonial drum. I felt ashamed that Nona was witnessing the ugly underbelly of local politics, but I appreciated that she had come along to support her mom. Skip had come, too, although he arrived late, along with several others. I waved him over to where my daughter and I were.

"What's going on in here? This place is packed tighter than a sardine can."

"Hey, Skip!" Nona shouted over the din.

"Hi, Nona!"

"It's a good thing you turned up, Skip," I said. "You may have to referee this rabble."

"Yeah, I wish I'd brought earplugs. I heard the racket from down the hall. What's all the commotion about?"

"It's supposed to be a town hall meeting about getting our dog park."

"It sounds more like a dog fight," Skip said. "Who's winning?"

"I'm betting on Rosie, but the odds are abysmal. She hasn't made any friends here tonight."

"Order, order!" Councilman Grant pounded the gavel like a pile-driver. "I must insist on order here, so everyone can be heard."

Walter Wiley saw his chance to vent and took it. "I'm sick and tired of people who let their dogs run loose in my neighborhood to do their dirty work on my lawn."

"So am I," added Sylvia Boyd. "My gardener is constantly picking up after the neighbor's Cocker Spaniel, who seems to think my front lawn is its own personal port-a-potty."

"Me, too!" Hannah Mencken chimed in. "Dogs chase my cats and dig up my garden."

"Sylvia, you have no right to complain," Rosie said. "I've seen you look the other way while your dog does the same thing on other people's lawns."

"I've never done any such thing. How dare you? That's an outright lie, Rose Clark!"

Rosie isn't one to pour gasoline on an open flame. She's a peacemaker and proved it by trying to deflect the rising dissension in the room between the anti- and pro-canine camps. "I agree that some dog owners in the community are not conscientious about cleaning up after their dogs or obeying local leash laws," Rosie said. "Irresponsible owners give the rest of us who do obey the laws a bad name."

"Not all of the dog problems people complain about are due to locals," I added in defense of dog lovers like myself. "Many of the worst offenders are tourists. They sometimes even abandon their dogs on the streets at the end of the summer, and the results of that are far worse than any soiled lawn."

"We don't need a stupid dog walk park; we need better enforcement," Walter sniped. "Why don't the police enforce the leash laws around here?"

"Gosh, I don't suppose it could be that we're too busy catching criminals and protecting the public," Skip muttered.

"This piece of land you're all squabbling over doesn't even rightfully belong to you," Sonseah Little Feather interjected. "This land belongs to the Washo." As usual, she was ornamented in traditional Native dress for this public forum, just in case there were any TV cameras.

"That may have once been true, Ms. Little Feather," Reverend Ramseth said, "but the Havershams have owned this stretch of property for over a century."

"Stole it, you mean," Sonseah said.

A collective gasp filled the room, but implying the reverend was a liar didn't dissuade sassy Sonseah from making her point. "The Whites probably bought it from my people for twenty-four bucks' worth of beads, the same way they acquired Manhattan."

"That's a fallacy, Sonseah," I said.

"Check the history books, Elsie. It's all there in black and white."

"Then the history books are wrong," I countered. "In fact, the Canarsie Indians sold the Dutch the proverbial Brooklyn Bridge. They didn't even own the land."

For once, Sonseah was at a loss for words. It did my heart good.

"I think we're getting off track here again, folks," Councilman Grant said. "May I remind you that the purpose of this meeting is to get some constructive views on the use of the land in question. There are many issues to consider."

"The councilman is right," said Sharon Driscoll, who represented the Tahoe Basin Preservation Society. "There are endangered species of flowers on this tract of land that must be protected. The Tahoe Yellow Cress grows only on the shores of Lake Tahoe."

"Are there Spotted Owls, too?" said Ted Diggs, concerned more with profit than preservation.

"I'm happy to hear all points of view on the issue, but this bickering is counterproductive," the councilman said. "If we can't conduct this discussion in a civilized manner, I'll have no choice but to adjourn the meeting."

"No need to do that," said Reverend Ramseth, smiling. "I'm sure we can all discuss this matter peacefully, can't we, folks?" His voice was a still pond in the woods, and it had an instantaneous calming effect on the crowd.

Silence fell upon the group, and everyone suddenly looked rather sheepish about having behaved so badly in the presence of a man of the cloth. Everyone, that is, except Walter. He wasn't about to give in so easily.

"Dog park or no dog park, I'm issuing fair warning to all the dog owners here that they'd better keep their mangy mutts off my property or else!" Walter barked, then stormed out of the meeting.

The silence that had overtaken the crowd moments before erupted in renewed dissonance. The Silver Lions resumed their roaring. Dan Silvernail banged the war drum even louder, as he and Sonseah chanted tribal songs. Talk about the Dogs of War! This conflict had become neighbor against neighbor, and the poop going around was that no one was going to win. The repeated crack of Councilman Grant's gavel resonated down the hall as Skip, Nona, and I exited the Town Hall meeting into the star-stippled night.

6

It was a dark place. Dark as the grave. It smelled of rot and mold like a grave. "Let me out of here!" The captive was alone and afraid. "I want out! Please come let me out!" The pleas were met with silence. Yet someone was there. There were shadows moving under the door. Someone was definitely out there. The captive clawed repeatedly at the door, scratching until the blood came. "I'll be good. I promise I'll be good. Please open the door. Please!" Then there was the cruel laughter from the other side.

7

"Hey, Mom, you'd better be careful where you stash your Halloween candy."

"Why?"

"You-know-who found your hiding place. He almost had a Mr. Goodbar unwrapped and was ready to scarf it down."

"I'm glad you discovered what he was up to, before he gobbled up the whole thing. We'd have had a sick dog on our hands. I don't need any vet bills right now. Not with all the book promotion expenses I've had lately."

"How are sales?"

"Hard to say, honey. I won't know until I get my first royalty check."

"That's exciting! Will it be a lot?"

"I wouldn't count on it. I can barely afford the costs of traveling to the book signings and conferences I've done since the book was released. Maybe by the time my third or fourth book is published, we can make plans for that trip to Scotland to visit your dad's relatives."

"I thought you were going to use the jackpot you won at Caesar's for that."

"I was, but I didn't count on having to pay so much out of my own pocket for book promotion. At least I still get regular work with *The Tahoe Tattler* and the odd article with the wag mags."

The doorbell rang, and Cruiser sounded a baritone bark in alarm — one if by front, two if by rear. He ambled along behind me as I went to answer the front door. It was Rosie Clark, and she had Rags with her. She looked anxious.

"Hi, Rosie."

"May I come in, Beanie?"

"Sure."

"Okay if Rags comes in, too?"

"Of course. Dogs are always welcome here. Cruiser would love some canine company, wouldn't you, boy?"

"Thanks." Rosie glanced back before she came inside, as though she were being followed.

"Have a seat."

My friend sat down in Tom's old easy chair. Cruiser and Rags did a brief do-si-do of canine greeting; then Rags catapulted into Rosie's lap. It reminded me of when Tom and Cruiser used to sit together in the evenings; of course, Cruiser was a bit more of a lapful than Rags. More of a two-lap dog. I could still see Tom trying to read his evening paper over Cruiser's pointy little noggin. "Why don't you read him the funnies, Tom?" I used to tease. That always made him laugh. How I miss Tom's laughter, even more than I miss complaining about picking up his dirty socks and underwear off the floor.

"Care for some tea, Rosie? I was just about to brew some."

"Yes, that would be nice."

"I'll make the tea, Mom. You two go ahead and chat."

"Thanks, Nona." I turned to Rosie. Her blue-gray eyes were thunderheads. "What's wrong?"

"We're going to have to band together against the wolf pack that's fighting us on this dog park issue, especially now that our most ardent supporter is out of the picture. I could sure have used Abby's clout at that town hall meeting. What a dogfight that was!"

"Things were getting ugly, all right."

"Thanks mostly to Walter Wiley. What a bad-tempered old goat!"

"You think he's the one behind this?"

"I wouldn't doubt it a bit. He's never liked Abby or me, and he hates dogs. He has no proof that my dog has ever set foot on his lawn. Has he done a dog pile DNA test or something?"

"Oh, Rosie, you are so funny." I couldn't help laughing, even though I knew she was deadly serious.

"He also has a computer, or at least his wife did."

"He's a widower?"

"Yes, Dodie died a couple of years ago. Cancer. That woman was the salt of the earth. She was always doing volunteer work in the community. She used to volunteer at the animal shelter, but she did it on the sly. She knew how Walter felt about it. She loved dogs, but he'd never let her keep any. Too bad. Having a dog might have done his disposition some good."

"Too bad for Dodie, too. Dogs are such wonderful healers."

"Oh, I know. I used to visit her when he wasn't around, and then later on when she was admitted to the hospice. I always took Ragsy along. She adored Rags. Her face always lit up when she saw me come in the room with him." Rosie fell silent and stroked Rags' head.

I sensed that something else was on her mind, something more unsettling than the community dispute over a dog park. I was right. "Why don't you tell me what's really bothering you?"

"I need your help."

"Sure. Just name it."

"I got another one of those e-mails I told you about, only this one is much worse than the others."

"What did it say?"

"If you'll log onto your computer, I'll show you."

"Okay."

Rosie followed me into my office. I powered up the computer, and she logged onto her Internet account. She clicked on the latest e-mail from *dogsbody*.

Our eyes scanned the message in unison: *Make no bones about it; every dog will have his day.* "Well, that doesn't exactly sound like a threat."

"Wait, there's an attachment."

"I thought you said you weren't going to open any attachments."

"I didn't intend to. I opened it by accident, or rather Rags did. He sits on my lap sometimes when I'm typing. He hit the return key with his paw."

I couldn't help smiling when I thought of Rags, the computer literate canine. I'm just glad that Cruiser isn't a lap dog.

"Are you sure you want to see this?

You won't like it."

"Go ahead and open it."

Rosie clicked on the attachment and downloaded the JPEG photo. I watched as the image loaded pixel by pixel.

"I think I need a new computer," I said. "This thing is so darned slow."

"You probably just need to free up some space on your hard drive. I can help you with that sometime."

"It's a deal."

Finally, the entire image appeared on the screen, but it was still a bit fuzzy as the computer finished downloading. All I could make out were mottled tones of browns, tans, grays. At last the image finished loading, although I wished it hadn't. As it finally came into focus, at first I didn't comprehend exactly what I was seeing, or maybe I just didn't want to. Then it became all too clear.

Rosie was right. What I saw was shocking, but nothing that doesn't occur daily in pounds and shelters across the country — the shame of a nation that professes to be the most humane in the world. How *à propos* that this black e-mailer used the screen name *dogsbody,* because that's what we saw on the monitor. Dogs, cats, rabbits, and other domestic pets heaped in trash bins, awaiting shipment to the rendering plant.

"I can't look at this anymore. It makes me sick to my stomach," Rosie said, tears welling in her eyes.

"Me, too." I quickly closed the mail, and signed off the Internet. "What's really sickening to me is that this photo could have been taken anywhere. Even in our own town."

"I know," Rosie said. "You only expect to see things like that in Third World countries."

"You said that Walter's wife used to volunteer at the local shelter?"

"Yes, why?"

"If Walter is the one who's behind this, he could easily have acquired such a photograph. He'd also have access to the type of leash that was used to strangle Abigail Haversham."

"You're right, Beanie. I never thought of that before. Dodie fostered dogs for the shelter, in spite of Walter's complaints. He *must* be the one. I'm sure of it."

"Well, we can't be certain it's him. Not yet. But he's worth keeping a closer eye on."

"Yes, especially after last night."

"Why? What happened last night?"

"Someone was prowling around my house. I heard strange sounds outside."

"Did you see who it was?"

"No. Rags' barking must have scared off the intruder."

"Did you call the police?"

"No."

"Why not?"

"I'd rather keep this on the QT for now. I think a full-scale police investigation will just drive the cowardly weasel farther into his hole."

"I don't think we have much choice but to involve law enforcement, considering someone has already been a victim of this blue-collar criminal."

"I'll volunteer to be a decoy, then. I want to draw this creep who killed Abby out into the open."

"I don't know, Rosie. It sounds much too risky."

"That's why I came to you. I need your help. We have to find out who is behind these threats before any harm comes to me or Rags."

"Well, since you put it that way . . ."

"I can count on you, then?"

"Of course you can. We dog lovers have to pack together, just like Cruiser and Rags."

"Come here, Ragsy," Rosie said. Unlike my stubborn hound, Rags responded immediately to his mistress' command. "Isn't he adorable?"

"Pretty doggoned adorable," I said.

"I don't know what I'd do without this little guy. He's my soulmate."

"I feel the same way about Cruiser."

I saw Cruiser's ears flick ever so slightly and an eyelid flutter at the mention of his name. Rags, however, was instantly on his feet. His bat-like Scottie ears perked up as he cocked his head with keen interest, eyes glinting with intelligence. He reminded me of the RCA Victor dog listening for his master's voice. However, I wondered if he wasn't picking up on something else with his doggie radar. Something beyond the limited range of human capacities that only dogs can sense.

8

When I was young, if anyone had told me that someday I would be spying on people for a living or helping to solve a murder, I'd have said they were nuttier than that Mr. Goodbar Cruiser had almost gobbled up. Except that's exactly what I was doing hunkered down in my car at the witching hour of night, peering through high-powered binoculars as I staked out Walter Wiley, dog-hating senior citizen-at-large. I would have brought my furry partner along, but I was afraid Cruiser, the K-9 crooner, would blow my cover if he happened to spot a cat.

I was just about to pack it in and drive away when I saw Walter slip out his side gate under cover of darkness, carrying what looked like a Zip-Loc bag. I watched him stroll up the street past Rosie's house. He paused and looked around before opening the baggie and tossing its contents onto her lawn. Then he backtracked as fast as he was able to his house. Just as he slipped back in the gate, I thought I saw him glance in my direction. I ducked down so he wouldn't see me. I was probably too far away to be spotted. Besides, I suspected that old Walter's night vision wasn't what it used to be, even with the aid of a bright harvest moon.

When I saw the lights go off in his house, I drove up to Rosie's place and got out of the car. I could hear Rags barking his head off inside the house. I pulled my flashlight out of the glove compartment, flicked it on, and scanned the spot on the lawn where I thought I'd seen Walter throw whatever he was carrying in the bag. At first I couldn't see anything; then I saw several objects reflecting in the beam from the flashlight.

I heard Rosie's screen door squeak. "Wh . . . who's out there?"

"Don't worry, Rosie. It's just me."

She stepped out on her porch. Rags bounded out the door behind her to see what was going on.

"Thank goodness it's you, Beanie," Rosie said. "I was afraid it was the prowler again."

"You *did* have a prowler."

"What? You mean you saw him?"

"Sure did. And you were right. It's Walter. He's up to no good, that's for sure.

I saw him throw these on your lawn." I trained the flashlight beam on the half-dozen ice cubes nestled in the grass.

"Ice cubes? I was all wrong about Walter. He's not just mean; he's crazy."

"He's worse than that. These aren't just ice cubes. He's frozen something in them. See how they look kind of dis-colored?"

"You think they're poisoned?"

"Yes, I'm thinking it could be antifreeze. There's plenty of that in snow country. Pets are attracted to the scent, and it's lethal to them if they swallow it. I think he may have been trying to poison your dog."

"Oh, dear. Rags, get in the house, now!"

Rags dashed back into the house.

"Walter's probably the one who sent you the threats, too."

"You think he's the one who . . . ?"

"Killed Abby? Yes, I'd say it's possible Walter might be our Sirius Killer."

"Boy, you never really know who your neighbors are, do you?"

"Do you have a plastic bag?"

"I'm sure I do."

"Good. I'll put this ice on ice for the lab; then I think we'd better let the sheriff's office collect your neighbor for questioning."

"Yes, I suppose you're right. At least that

crazy old coot won't be hurting anyone else."

"Or their dogs, either."

"Thank heavens for that," she said. "Lang Po is a very lucky little dog."

"Thank goodness for Doc Heaton. The man's a magician. And it was good of you to offer to pay for Lang Po's care."

"It was the least I could do for Abby. I'm sure she would have done the same for Rags. Are you going to her funeral on Wednesday?"

"Yes, I'll come. Think you'll keep Lang Po, or will you place him in another home?"

"Oh, I'll keep him, if he and Rags can get along. Rags has been alpha dog around here for a long time."

"Well, looks like dog owners around here can rest easy now, knowing that no one is trying to poison their pets," I said.

Rosie picked Rags up and cuddled him. "And that hateful old Walter Wiley will finally get his comeuppance."

I had to admit I was pretty proud of how quickly I'd wrapped this all up in a neat little Zip-Loc bag. My pride in a job well done would be short-lived, however. This case was far from open and shut. Trouble in Tahoe was only beginning.

9

Lakeview Methodist Church was aptly named. The view of the lake from the stained glass cathedral windows was a heavenly backdrop to the service being held for Abigail Haversham. The hand-carved pine pews were filled to capacity with prominent citizens in the community. I pulled a notebook from my purse and discreetly made a quick checklist of those present, just in case not all of the mourners at this wake were Abby's friends. There were a few latecomers, including some of her society cronies, and Abby's nephew, whom I added to my list.

I accounted for most of the known dog lovers, including dog park supporters who had attended the town hall meeting and the Howloween event. Many of the event's vendors were also at the funeral, including Sally Applebaum from the Haute Hydrant and Madame Pawline. I didn't spot Rosie, though. Perhaps she was running late again. I adored my friend, but punctuality was never her strong suit. I always teased her that she'd be late for her own funeral. In this case, it was Abby's funeral.

The cloying perfume of floral arrangements of every variety, size, and shape infused the church. The music was even worse. I would have much preferred just about anything to the soap opera organ selection I was hearing. But this church was Methodist, not Unitarian.

Nona already knows that when my time comes to graduate from this level of existence to the next, I do not want to be buried in the ground eating a dirt sandwich. Even though I would have liked to rest for eternity beside Tom, who did not believe in cremation after death, I couldn't choose that for myself. I didn't want Nona to have to feel guilty if she didn't plant flowers on my grave every week or neglectful when the weeds overtook my gravesite. Instead, I wish to be cremated and have my ashes scattered in the sunny clearing at the crest of the mountain behind my cabin, where Cruiser and I have sojourned so many times. That's where Cruiser will be, too.

Much to my relief, that morose organ music stopped playing and so did the maudlin thoughts in my head. Reverend

Paul Ramseth ascended the altar. The light from the window reflected off the top of his balding pate. Before him was displayed the open casket that held Abigail Haversham's earthly remains. He opened his Bible upon the pulpit, leafed briefly through the pages, and began to recite verses befitting the solemn occasion. The reverend's placid demeanor and the measured cadence of his voice perfectly complemented the serenity of Lake Tahoe in the distance.

As the reverend sermonized, I observed the mourners. Sally Applebaum sobbed hysterically, as though grieving for a close family member. This was no surprise to me. Sally always cried over weddings and funerals and TV pet food commercials, never mind the animal emergency shows on cable channels. Those reduced me to tears, too. I noticed a few people in the group who were not dog park supporters but had probably known Abby through her other civic activities. Even the mayor was present. So was Councilman Grant.

Colin Grant was a craggy but handsome, burly fellow with a full beard of gunmetal gray and matching bottlebrush eyebrows that formed a furry tor above peat brown eyes. He was also a widower, I had heard from Rosie. The councilman was seated close enough to me that I could catch a faint whiff of his aftershave — English Leather. I was suddenly reminded of the sexy TV ads of the 1960s, where the beautiful young maiden proclaims as the handsome prince sweeps her up in his arms and onto his saddle, "All my men wear English Leather or they wear nothing at all."

I missed the pheromones of a man around the house. A male scent has the same effect on me as a Bacon Beggin' Strip has on Cruiser. I salivated like Pavlov's dog just thinking of it. I began to daydream about the councilman. *I wonder what it would be like to have those tree trunk arms of his wrapped around me in an embrace? I wonder what he's really like? Do you suppose he's dating anyone? Geez, what am I doing? Here I sit at this poor woman's funeral fantasizing about some bureaucrat. How desperate is that? Nona would laugh her head off at me, if she were here. Must be Hormone's Last Stand at Little Big Horny.* I decided I had better focus my attention on something else.

Addison Haversham, Abby's only living blood relative, sat in the pews reserved for the bereaved. His head bowed, Addison appeared to be praying. Or was he dozing?

With Ralph Lauren model good looks, the young Haversham heir surely had no shortage of admirers, I surmised. If Nona had come, I would have made sure to introduce them. She could do a lot worse than dating the likes of him. In fact, she already had, many times.

Unfortunately for her matchmaker mom, Nona decided to skip the funeral. She'd have thought it to be a major bummer, to use her own generation's turn of phrase. She hated attending funerals, especially since the loss of her father. She hadn't known Abby very well, anyway. Too bad for you, Nonie, I mused. You passed up your chance to meet the Haversham hottie.

Never much of a churchgoer myself, I feared I might start to nod off if this didn't end quickly. My head began to swim, and I felt nauseated. I could hardly wait for the service to end, so I could get back outside into the natural pine-scented air, away from all this artificiality and hothouse floral profusion.

About the time my chin dropped to my chest for a Cruiser-style snorefest, the organ music resumed, the signal for guests to file past the casket and pay their last respects. I didn't really want to view Abby's corpse; I'd already seen it at the crime scene. But I didn't want to appear rude or disrespectful, so I allowed myself to be carried along in the sea of mourners. I wish I hadn't.

I stalled as long as I could in going up to the casket. The reverend also operated the funeral parlor that had done the pre-interment handiwork on Mrs. Haversham. Abigail's face looked waxen and unnaturally pale, like she should be displayed in a Madame Tussaud's museum. Two rosy dots on her cheeks, along with the high, ruffled collar to hide the damage to her neck, made her look like a Barnum and Bailey circus clown. All dressed up for Halloween and no place to haunt. At least her face wasn't blue, like it was when I had last seen her.

I'd had enough. I flitted past the bereaved and made a beeline for the exit. Reverend Ramseth stood at the church exit, shaking hands with each of the departing mourners and offering his condolences. He stretched out his hand to me next, and surveyed me with coal black eyes. I shook his hand, which was softer than most women's hands. Formaldehyde apparently worked better than beauty salon wax dips for keeping one's hands baby's-bottom smooth.

"It was good of you to come, Mrs. MacBean."

"Er . . . a lovely service, Reverend Ramseth."

"Thank you. I thought certain that Rosie Clark would be here, too. I know she and Mrs. Haversham were good friends."

"Oh, you haven't seen her?"

"Not yet. Perhaps she's still inside. You might go have a look-see."

"That's all right. I'll just wait out here for her." There was no way I was going back into that charnel house. If I did, I knew I'd faint dead away and they'd have to bury me along with Abby. Besides, I was certain now that Rosie hadn't shown for Abigail's funeral. What I didn't know was why.

As I stood outside, making sure I hadn't missed anyone on my list of attendees, I saw Pauline exit the church. I noticed the reverend didn't extend his hand to her. I didn't think much of it, until I heard the usually gentle timbre of his voice turn sharper than a pine needle. I couldn't hear what he was saying, but it wasn't "the Lord bless you and keep you." That much I understood.

10

A walk in the woods with Cruiser was just what I needed after sitting through Abigail's funeral. I definitely needed some fresh air, and there's always an abundance of that at Lake Tahoe. Cruiser led the way up the mountain, stopping now and then to sniff a shrub or hose a pile of coyote scat. Aspen leaves shimmered like a precious cache of gold coins in the breeze that seems ever-present on our mountaintop. The wind rising among the pines murmured a tale of the coming winter and the first snows. Days of shoveling the white stuff and being cabin-bound seemed remote as I gazed at a perfect, cloudless sky of Wedgwood blue, like the MacBean family china Tom's mother had passed down to us when we married.

I still had the china but used it only for very special occasions, as Tom would have insisted. He was just like his old mum. She never used any of her good things but kept them preserved in the museum attic of her

Tiburon house for a special occasion that never came. I finally gave up sending her nice things at Christmas and birthdays, because I knew she'd never use them. It's the way of those who grew up in Britain during World War II. You never use your best for everyday.

Thinking of his mum's china reminded me of the matching teapot. That made me think about brewing a good cup of Earl Grey tea, and that made me think of Rosie. Why hadn't she attended Abigail's funeral? It seemed very odd to me, considering that she had known Abby so well. I hoped she wasn't sick or something. I'd give her a call as soon as Cruiser was finished watering the woods and we got back to the cabin.

Nona was waiting for us when we returned. "I thought you two were going to stay out there all day."

"If it were up to Cruiser, we would have. I've never figured out where dogs stow all that water. A Bactrian camel has less storage capacity."

"Are you sure he doesn't have a camel hump on him somewhere?"

"Not that I've ever noticed. Only a sebaceous cyst or two."

"Skip called while you were out. He says

to meet him down at the sheriff's office right away."

"Did he say what for?"

"Nope, only to hurry."

"Okay. Will you give Cruiser some tepid water in half an hour or so?"

"Why half an hour?"

"I don't want him to gulp ice cold water on a warm day after exercise. It could cause him to get gastric dilationvolvulus."

"What the heck is that?"

"Bloat. Bassets are prone to it. All large, deep-chested breeds are."

"Sounds serious, Mom."

"It is. An acquaintance of mine lost her Great Dane to bloat. The poor thing's stomach twisted like a pretzel. Not a nice way to lose a pet and excruciating for the dog."

"Gotcha. Don't worry, Cruiser's in good hands. You'd better get going now. Skip sounded anxious."

"I'm off, Nonie. See you later." As I headed for the door, Cruiser trailed close on my heels. "Sorry, fella. Not this time. You have a nice rest after your walk, and I'll see you later, too."

"You don't really think he understands what you're saying, do you, Mom?"

"Of course he does. Cruiser speaks

fluent Human — far more fluently than I speak Dog." Cruiser let out a robust *Roo!* I understood that phrase perfectly. The translation — *Please take me along!*

11

It was late afternoon when I arrived at Skip's office. Already, the days were growing shorter. Purple shadows shrouded the majestic peaks of Mount Tallac and her towering sisters.

"Well, it's about time," Skip said. "Where have you been all day?"

"I just finished walking Cruiser, and I was at Abigail Haversham's funeral before that. What's so urgent?"

"We just finished questioning the suspect in her murder."

"You talked to Walter Wiley?" I was feeling kind of proud of the fact that I'd cracked this case before the sheriff's office had.

"I wish you had gotten here sooner, but it doesn't matter. I don't believe that he's our perp."

"What do you mean?"

"We've got it all on tape."

"If what you say is true and there's still a killer out there, we have no time to waste.

Just give me the facts, man."

"Right, Sergeant Friday."

I grinned. Good ol' Skipper. Ever the kidder. Always ready to lighten things up, no matter how serious they might seem. I guess that's why I like him so much. His sense of humor is so much like Tom's. He never lets me take myself too seriously.

"The thing is, Wiley says he was nowhere near the scene of the crime on Saturday. He was at his doctor's office at the time of the murder."

"So you're telling me that our prime suspect has a doctor's note?"

"Evidently he was having a colonoscopy at the time Mrs. Haversham was killed."

"Sounds like a buttload of fun. My doctor has been after me to have one, but I keep putting it off."

Skip laughed. "Can't say I blame you."

"But if he's so innocent, what was he doing prowling around Rosie's house the other night? And what about those ice cubes I found? Those weren't just ice cubes. There was something frozen in them. I think he was trying to poison Rags."

"The lab did an analysis on those. It was weed killer."

"Weed killer? How peculiar. Why would he do that?"

"He was trying to kill her lawn, not her dog."

"To make it look like a dog spotted her lawn. I get it. But if he'd go to those lengths to get even for a few yellow spots on his lawn, I wonder what more he might be capable of?"

"This old guy has nothing better to do, Beanie. His wife is dead. He's got cancer. What else is there to do but sit around and watch the grass grow?"

"Wiley has cancer?"

"Colon cancer. That's why he was having the colonoscopy."

"Oh, I didn't know that. How do you know he's telling the truth, though? Maybe he's just a clever liar."

"I'm having one of our guys follow up on his alibi. He hasn't confirmed it yet, though. The office is closed while the doctor is on vacation."

"Then Walter could still be a suspect."

"Until we have positively confirmed his alibi, I suppose you're right. But I feel fairly certain he's not our killer. He seemed pretty convincing to me. I think he's just what your friend says he is, a grumpy old man."

"Who hates dogs. And so does the Sirius Killer."

"Point taken. I guess it's not over 'til the fat lady sings."

"The fat lady is dead and buried, Skip, but this is definitely not over. Not by a long shot." And neither was my work on this case. Looks like I still had a job to do for my friend, Rosie. But where was she?

12

When I drove up to Rosie's place and saw her car parked in the driveway, a wave of relief swept over me. She'd decided to skip Abby's funeral. Perhaps she wasn't feeling well. A nasty flu virus had been making the rounds in Tahoe. I decided I'd better check on her and see if she needed anything.

I got out of my car and walked to her front porch. When I rang the doorbell, I heard Rags barking, but it was a different bark than usual. Perhaps I speak Dog better than I give myself credit for, because I knew this was not your standard, "Who's that knocking at my door?" bark. After living with Cruiser all these years, I knew the subtle nuance of the dog's bark for the mailman, the cat on the fence, a prowler, the solicitor at the door, and the All Paws on Deck! bark when something is seriously wrong. I recognized Rags' frantic alarm as the latter. I knew this was definitely so when I opened the screen door and saw that Rosie's lock had been jimmied. I'd been after her for ages to get a deadbolt, but busy gal that she was; it had remained at the bottom of her To Do list.

Against my better judgment, I pushed the door ajar and stepped inside. I knew I should have gone to a neighbor's house and had them dial 911, but curiosity and concern won over common sense. Rags leapt up on my legs, barking incessantly.

"Off, Rags!" He obeyed my command and scurried off to the den. When Rosie wasn't busy with community affairs or was feeling under the weather, she could usually be found in her den, resting in her easy chair. I felt sure I'd find her there now. But when I stepped into the den and didn't see her reading or crocheting or find her sitting at the computer typing, I knew something was dreadfully wrong. Things were in disarray, as though there had been a struggle. The desk lamp had been upset, and her computer chair was overturned.

Rags hid behind Rosie's computer desk. When I called him, he wouldn't respond. That wasn't like Rags. He was usually very obedient. Something was wrong, that much I already knew. Then I heard the familiar *yak, yak* sound I'd heard Cruiser make many times just before upchucking something all over my clean carpet.

Rags finally emerged from his hiding place, staggering like a drunk in a windstorm.

"Rags, what is it, fella?"

When I stepped around the side of the desk, my breath caught in my throat like I'd swallowed a wad of bread dough. It was Rosie. Just like her friend, Abigail, she had a blue groomer's lead noosed around her neck. Her head was turned to one side.

"Rosie!" I knelt down and placed my fingers on her carotid artery. There were angry red abrasions on her neck where the attacker had tried to strangle her with the plastic leash. Apparently, he had been unsuccessful. Her pulse was faint, but it was still there.

"You're still alive. Thank God." The killer hadn't had time to finish the job. My arrival must have scared him off. Then I noticed the bloodied bookend lying beside her, one of the heavy, antique bronze ones in the shape of Scottie dogs that she displayed on her bookshelf. Flecks of red dotted the carpet. I saw blood seeping into the carpet beneath her from the wound to her skull. Time was precious. I lunged for the phone on the desk and dialed 911. I could only hope that help would come in time to save my friend's life.

While I waited for the paramedics to arrive, I stayed close to Rosie and tried to comfort Rags. I was pretty sure he'd just dumped most of the offending substance he'd ingested on the carpet, but I'd get him to the vet ASAP, just in case. I felt assured he would be okay when he kept trying to revive his mistress by licking her hands and face. She didn't respond. When I opened one of her eyelids and saw that the pupil was fixed and dilated, I feared the head trauma might be more serious than I had first thought.

I noticed that Rosie was still logged onto the Internet. She was probably attacked from behind, while researching dog parks. She'd brought up something about a new off-leash park in Manhattan. "If they can get a dog park in Manhattan, I don't know why we can't get one here," I said to Rags, who of course didn't know what I was saying but responded with perked ears to the tone of my voice. Another encouraging sign that he was probably none the worse for wear.

I was also trying to fill the eerie silence in this too-quiet room. I almost jumped out of my skin when the electronic voice announced, "You've got mail!" Using the eraser end of a pencil so as not to disturb any evidence, I clicked on the little mailbox to see who was sending Rosie an e-mail. The room was warm, but I felt ice freeze in my veins when I opened the mail. The sender was *dogsbody,* but it wasn't addressed to Rosie. The subject line said, *Open me, Elsie.*

13

I opened the mail that was sent to Rosie's e-mail address but had my name in the subject field.

As you stumble in the dark, listen for the great dog's bark. Heed the warning in this mail. Elsie MacBean, watch your tail!

Now *I* was being hounded by the Sirius Killer, but how could this creep already be sending an e-mail after having just left here moments before I arrived? It's possible that he had sent the mail from this computer and delayed the time it was to be sent, or perhaps he had sent it from a wireless handheld. Whoever it was obviously knew I was here. He probably saw me driving up to the house through the den window. My gut feeling was that he might still be close by. Not a comforting thought.

Could this be Rosie's neighbor after all? Walter lived nearby, and no one had yet confirmed his alibi. Until he was cleared beyond a shadow of a doubt, he was still on my short list of suspects. Even if it was only weed killer he used on Rosie's lawn and not poison intended for Rags, it was strong enough evidence to me that he bore her ill will. In my opinion, it wasn't much of a stretch to posit that such malice could escalate to murder.

I heard the sirens of the ERT van and went to the front door to lead them to my friend. Within seconds the team had tested her vital signs, started an IV drip, and had the patient secured on the gurney for transport to Barton Memorial Hospital.

Moments later, the sirens screamed to life. Pines lining the street flashed red in the oscillating beacon atop the ambulance as it sped down the street and out of sight.

A moment later I heard another siren, only this time it was Skip barreling down the street. His car skidded to a halt. He scrambled out of the car and raced for the door.

"I had a hunch you might already be here, Inspector MacBean."

"You're not turning psychic on me, are you, Skip?"

"You know I don't believe in that stuff. Are you all right?"

"Yes, I'm fine."

"Thank goodness for that."

"Rosie isn't, though."

"How is she?"

"Not good. I'm worried she may not make it."

Skip spotted the blue leash lying on the carpet. "Same M.O., I see."

"Yes, but when that didn't work, her attacker grabbed the nearest weapon he could find and whacked her a good one on the head."

"With what?"

"That!" I said, pointing to the Scottie dog bookend stained crimson with Rosie's blood. "How *à propos* for the Sirius Killer — if a dog leash doesn't dispatch your victim quickly enough, use a brass dog statuette."

"Where was she when you found her?"

"Over there, behind her desk. Apparently, she was attacked while she was working at her computer."

"Kinda looks that way, doesn't it?" Skip said, surveying the scene with a practiced eye from years of crime investigations. There seemed to be far too many of those in South Tahoe these days.

"She managed to fend him off, though."

"You must have interrupted whoever did

91

this before he could strike a fatal blow. Lucky for her you came along when you did. You probably saved your friend's life."

"Could be, or perhaps she saw the reflection of her attacker in the computer screen like I can see yours right now. If you see trouble coming up on you, it gives you time to react. That's more likely what saved her from being strangled."

"I think you're right. The killer probably didn't get a chance to get the leash looped firmly enough around her neck to squeeze the life out of her."

"Rosie had some training in self-defense, so she was probably able to fend him off."

"He made a bloody mess of her, though, from the looks of it."

"Can you be any more blunt, Mr. Sheriff Man? I'm the one who found her *that way*." I couldn't erase the image of my friend lying there in a pool of blood with that nylon noose around her neck. I'm not as hardened to the messy side of crime as Skip is. I'm more like Cruiser, trailing quarry to its lair and letting someone else do the dirty work.

"Sorry. That was insensitive of me. I guess I've witnessed too many crime scenes to be delicate about these things," Skip said. "Hey, what's this?" Skip had spotted the e-mail addressed to me.

"A little spam from the Sirius Killer."

He read the message on Rosie's computer screen. "I don't like the looks of this, Beanie."

"Neither do I."

"I may have to keep a closer eye on you from now on."

"Never mind about me. I can take care of myself. It's Cruiser's safety I'm worried about."

"At least old Rags here is okay." Skip reached down to pet the little Scottie and realized he wasn't quite as okay as he had thought. "What's wrong with the dog?"

"Someone slipped him a Mickey Finn is my guess." Rags staggered over to his dog dish. He started to eat more of the moist dog food in the dish. "No, Rags!" I snatched him away before he could ingest any more of the food. "And I'll bet the evidence is right in here."

"Well, the boys will be along in a few minutes to bag and tag. They'll also test the contents of the bowl. I'm headed for the hospital to gather any evidence I can salvage. It won't last long in the ER."

"I'll be there as soon as I get this little guy to the vet, just to be sure he's okay. I know Rosie would want that."

"Who'll take care of Rags after the vet checks him out?"

I knew what Skip meant, but I refused to entertain the possibility that Rosie might not survive her injuries. "He can stay with Cruiser and me until his mom's all well. She would want to know he was being cared for while she's in the hospital."

"You're a friend in a million, girl." I liked it when he called me "girl," even though we both knew I wasn't one.

"It's no less than she'd do for me, if the situation were reversed." I started for the door. "Say, Skip. After you finish up, why don't you join me for supper?"

"You sure I won't be in the way with Nona visiting?"

"Heck, no. Besides, she'll be out tonight, and Cruiser and I could use some company. You can fill me in on your findings while I fill you up with my famous chili."

"Sure. Sirius Killer nor not, I've still gotta eat. You won't forget the onions?"

"Do I ever?" I clapped my hands. "Come on, Rags. Let's go see Cruiser!"

Ordinarily Rags would be dancing his version of the Highland fling at the mention of Cruiser, but not this time. I picked him up and carried him out to my car. He seemed to understand that he couldn't go where his mistress had gone and that he would be safe with me.

After Rags was checked out and released, I took him home and hurried over to the hospital to see Rosie, but she was in surgery. I was told to go home and wait. It was going to be a long night for all of us.

14

The sound of barking dogs alerted me to my visitor before he could ring the doorbell. Rags, in spite of the drug that could have killed him had he ingested enough of it, received a clean bill of health from Doc Heaton. After a long nap, he was his old feisty Scottish self again and was at the front door in a flash. Cruiser wasn't far behind. Lang Po didn't budge from Tom's easy chair. I had sprung him from solitary confinement in the veterinary kennel, as Rosie had intended to do.

"Come in, Skip."

"Thanks." He came inside and stooped to greet the Welcome Waggins.

"Any news about Rosie?"

"She's out of the O.R. but hasn't regained consciousness."

"Why did this have to happen to a sweet lady like her?"

"Don't worry. I swear I'll find this creep if it's the last thing I ever do, and the way I've been feeling lately, it might be." Skip doffed his cap and ran a freckled hand through a sheaf of sandy hair. He looked as worn as his boot heels. The responsibility of his promotion to sheriff was taking its toll.

"You look beat, buddy. Take a load off your feet while I grab you a cold brewski."

"Thanks, don't mind if I do." Skip headed straight for Tom's chair, which was already occupied. Lang Po bared his teeth at him when it appeared he might be ousted from his newly acquired throne.

"What's this? Are you collecting dogs now? Where'd the killer powder puff come from?"

"Don't you remember Lang Po? He belonged to Abby. I'm keeping him for Rosie until she gets out of the hospital. She was planning to adopt him before . . ."

"Hmmph. Nice dog."

"Sorry. Looks like you'll have to share the sofa with Cruiser and Rags, at least until Rosie is better." I knew I was being optimistic. The chances were that I might have to find a new home for Lang Po, and maybe Rags, too. I love dogs, but I wasn't sure I had the energy or bankroll to maintain a pack of three. I'm sure people all over Tahoe could smell the burning plastic of my credit card from the bills I'd just racked up at the vet's office for Rags and Lang Po.

Skip didn't say anything when I invited him to sit on the couch with the dogs, but I knew what he was thinking. Fortunately, he was a good enough friend to tolerate with good humor the established barking order around here. Everyone who knows me and plans to spend much time around here just has to accept that dogs rule in the MacBean household. In Cruiser's case, that's *dogs drool.*

Braving threats of bodily injury from Lang Po's needle sharp teeth, Skip managed to slide the ottoman away from the chair and over to the couch. He flopped down, propped his feet up, and closed his eyes. By the time I returned from tending the chili and fetching refreshments in the kitchen, the living room was filled with the sound of snoring, from man and dogs alike.

"Here's your beer."

Skip mumbled in his sleep. "Bag 'em and tag 'em, boys. Bag 'em, and . . ."

"Skip?"

He was starting to twitch, like Cruiser when he's chasing his imaginary rabbits in his sleep, only Skip was probably chasing robbers.

I shook his shoulder, first gently, then

harder. "Wake up, Skip!"

His eyes popped open. "Huh, wha . . . ?"

"You must be really tired. You were out cold."

The sheriff sat up and rubbed his eyes. "Yeah, I've been putting in a lot of extra hours lately on this doggoned crime wave." I laughed at Skip's unintended pun. He didn't understand why I was laughing at first. When he grinned, I knew he finally got it. "I guess I'm just not as young as I used to be."

"That makes two of us. So, how'd it go at Rosie's place?"

"Well, everything's wrapped up, and we've got all the evidence we're going to get, which isn't much. This guy covered his tracks very well. Anyway, the boys have everything bagged and tagged."

"So I heard while you were snoring away. Did you know that you talk in your sleep?"

"Yeah, but only when I'm worn out, like I am now. As if things weren't bad enough, I think I'm fighting that flu. People at the office are dropping like flies."

"Don't give it to me, okay? That's the last thing I need right now."

"I'll try not to breathe on you."

"Did they manage to lift any prints from the computer keys?"

"No. Nothing." Skip stretched and yawned. "The assailant was probably wearing gloves to keep from leaving any prints at the scene."

"No doubt. That's the first lesson in Murder 101. Criminals are pretty sophisticated about fingerprints these days."

"They have to be, because our methods of fingerprinting are a lot more sophisticated. We've lifted prints from places you'd never imagine."

"I have a vivid imagination."

"Well, we went over the place with a fine-toothed flea comb. If there was anything left behind to find, we found it."

"So you didn't find anything at all out of the ordinary?"

"As I said, the scene was pretty clean."

"By the way, Skip, what did the crime lab find in the dog's food?"

"Nothing but lamb meal and rice. Rags must have picked the poison up someplace else. Anyway, the dog seems fine now."

"He was lucky. Doc Heaton said that if he'd swallowed more of whatever it was or hadn't thrown up most of what he did swallow on Rosie's carpet, he might have been one dead dog. It was the same thing with Lang Po."

Skip scratched his head, and I could almost see the gears turning.

"What's the matter?"

"I just remembered something."

"What's that?"

"There were some odd stains on the carpet where Rosie's body . . ."

"She's not dead yet."

"Er, I mean where you found Rosie."

"What kind of stains?"

"Drips of red candle wax. At first I thought it was blood."

"Yes, I recall seeing some red flecks on the carpet. I thought it was blood, too. Could be she just dripped some candle wax on the floor during a power outage. We get a lot of those during winter storms."

"Wasn't she another one of those woo-woo types who burns incense and candles?"

"Oh, you mean like me? Careful, I may rescind my dinner invitation."

"Actually, I was thinking of Pauline LeBlanc, your dog psychic."

"She not *my* dog psychic."

"You know what I mean. I just want to eliminate all other possibilities so I can identify the dirty dog who attacked your friend."

"Me, too, Skip. Me, too."

The three dirty dogs soiling my furniture no doubt agreed.

Skip devoured my killer veggie chili like it was the last bowl of beans in Bangladesh. Watching the sweat bead on his brow, I knew my chili had lived up to its fiery reputation. After dinner, he headed for home and a well-earned night's rest. I, on the other hand, was still wide-awake. I had so much on my mind: Rosie, what Skip had told me about the red candle wax on her carpet, the e-mail threat I had received on my friend's computer.

Nona sensed my anxiety. "Say, Mom, how about some popcorn and a movie? I rented one for tonight. Want to watch it with me?"

"No, I don't feel much in the mood, honey."

"Oh, come on. It will take your mind off of Rosie and everything."

"Thanks, but I think I'll do a little research on my article. Immersing myself in a writing project will help me more than anything right now. Will you be okay in here?"

"Sure. The dogs will keep me company, won't you, guys?" Rags jumped into Nona's lap while Cruiser zeroed in on the bowl of popcorn on the coffee table. Lang Po wasn't about to abdicate his easy chair throne for anything, not even treats.

"Don't let Cruiser eat too much popcorn. It'll just end up on the rug later. I've had enough of hurling hounds for one day."

"Okay."

I went into my office and sat down in front of the computer. I found the zip disk where I'd stored what I had so far on the *Tattler* meteor shower article. I even got so far as to open up the file and type a couple of words. Then nothing. I watched the cursor blink on the screen while I waited for my muse to drift down from whatever illusive pink cloud she floats on. The cursor blinked for a full five minutes, until I decided maybe I'd check to see if there was any interesting e-mail.

I logged onto the Internet and typed in my password. A string of SPAM came up, which I quickly deleted. The rest were correspondence from my online writers' and pet lovers' chat groups. I knew I shouldn't have joined so many groups. I hated scrolling down through dozens of messages but hesitated to delete them, in case there was some good bit of information contained in them. I didn't usually wait so long to check my e-mails for this very reason, but I'd had a lot of other things on my mind lately. And all our troubles started right after we had the reading with Madame Pawline at the fund-raiser for the new dog park. *Just a coincidence,* I said to myself. *Or was it?* Hadn't she used candles when she did her psychic readings that day at the Howloween event?

I decided not to get bogged down opening e-mails but do a little research instead. I found research to be an equally reliable tactic for delaying literary labors. I typed in "stars" and hit the search button. Up came photos of celebrities: Julia Roberts, Halle Berry, Tom Cruise.

"Hmmm. Wrong kind of stars." Next I tried entering "constellations." First on the recommended sites list was *outer space.* Under sponsored links I spotted something called Stellarscope: Sky Constellations Guide, which turned out to be some kind of interactive telescope for stargazing. I was getting warmer. Then I saw another site on constellations, clicked on that, and found everything I would ever want to know about stars, comets, asteroids, you name it. Just for fun, I clicked on the "constellations and their stars" link and came upon an alphabetical list. I scrolled down through the list and found Sirius, the eye of the dog in the constellation Alpha Canis Major and the brightest star in the heavens besides the Sun. There was even a sky chart of the Greater Dog, naming its position in the sky at various times of year and all the stars in the constellation: Murzim, Muliphen, Wezen, Adhara, Furud, and Aludra. Connecting the dots or, in this case, stars of the constellation created an image of a long-bodied dog that appeared to be leaping upward, although it reminded me more of a Basset Hound sitting on its hind legs begging a biscuit. I'd seen my own hound do that often enough. Perhaps the astronomers should rename this constellation Cruiser Major.

I printed out the information on Sirius and some other factoids about meteors and asteroids. "All right, Elsie, old girl," I chided myself. "You've stalled long enough. Check your e-mail, then get back to work."

I had become adept at repeating click and delete on my computer when it came to trashing junk e-mails, and there were always a lot of them. I knew it had something to do with cookies, and they weren't the chocolate chip kind. I didn't yet know how to dump the cookies that get downloaded on your hard drive whenever you visit a new website. After researching Canis Major, I no doubt had dog cookies on my computer, too. I had always intended to take one of those computer courses where you learn all that stuff about streamlining your computer's performance, but I just never seemed to find the time. I hoped Rosie would show me when she was able. These days I seemed to be involved in a whole other aspect of computer use, or abuse.

I kept scrolling down the list, looking for e-mails from anyone I recognized. Nothing from my agent. Drat! There were a few messages from Carla at the *Tattler*. I'd read those later. I kept on scrolling until I was nearly at the bottom of the scroll bar. Then I saw it. Another e-mail from the Sirius Killer.

15

I couldn't figure out how *dogsbody* had managed to get my e-mail address, unless he pulled it off Rosie's address list before he fled the crime scene. That seemed the most logical possibility, since I wasn't in the habit of giving out my e-mail address to every Tom, Dick, and Hacker. Of course, if I was getting all of the SPAM I'd spent the last fifteen minutes deleting, then I guess I could certainly also be the recipient of this even more undesirable kind of e-mail. I opened up the e-mail and read it. It was another sick poem, worse than the one before: *When all the dogs have gone away, and all their masters I shall slay, the underdog shall have his day.*

Was the killer a man? Had the last words in the poem been a slip or an intentional attempt to make me think this was a man when it was really a woman? As I'd mentioned before, the killer could just as easily be a woman as a man. That could be the reason Rosie was able to fend off her attacker.

I decided I would answer one of these mystery e-mails. I didn't really want to start an e-mail correspondence with a killer, but perhaps it was a way to get some more information before someone else became a victim of the Sirius Killer — like me, for instance.

Why are you doing this? I typed in an e-mail to *dogsbody* and hit the send button. I didn't really expect an answer right away, if I got any answer at all, so I went back to working on my *Tattler* article. I stayed logged on, though, just in case.

I was deep in concentration, as I get only when I'm writing. As I focused intently on the words appearing fluidly on the computer screen, typing away while lost in that mystical creative realm where time seems not to advance, I was blissfully unaware that the door to my office was opening . . . slowly, deliberately.

I let out a yelp of surprise when I felt a cold, wet nose nudge my elbow. "Cruiser!"

Cruiser crouched down and gave me a Sad Sack look, visibly crushed by my unexpected irritation at the sudden interruption. "Don't sneak up on me that way, boy. You scared me half to death."

Nona stepped into my office, a look of concern knitting her brow. "I heard you call out, Mom. Anything wrong?"

"It's nothing. Cruiser startled me, that's all."

Rags trotted in on Nona's heels. Even Lang Po had condescended to make an appearance. Yep, the gang was all here. Never fails when I'm really getting in the flow of writing. Next time I'd remember to shut the door after me. Maybe I needed to install a deadbolt on my office door. My dream was to have my writing space located in a high tower surrounded by a moat amply stocked with crocodiles and piranha.

"I may as well come and watch the movie with you, Nona. Looks like I'm not getting any more work done here."

"Oh, good. I hoped you'd change your mind."

"What movie did you rent, anyway?"

"It's one of Stephen King's."

"Yeah? I love Stephen King movies. Which one is it?"

"*Pet Sematary.*"

16

The first chill breath of winter blew down from the mountains. After a prolonged and sultry autumn, the sudden cold snap surprised those who were not accustomed to the caprices of nature at high altitudes. Longtime residents heeded the cues of the forest creatures that gather and store early for the long, frigid months ahead. Tourists packed up their belongings and traversed the winding trail from Tahoe to winter at the lower elevations, as my Washo ancestors had when they struck their camps. Unlike the tourists at summer's end, however, Tahoe's native people left behind no trace of ever having been here.

Seasonal residents repaired window shutters, wrapped water pipes, and secured their vacation homes in preparation for the coming snows and freezing temperatures. Those of us who regularly weather blizzards in the high country stored up firewood and stocked our larders for the whiteouts, when roads aren't passable, and we become cabin-bound.

I had stacked enough firewood to keep the home fires burning for the next millennium. I know how quickly it gets used up, especially if the power fails and there's no source of heat other than your fireplace. My woodpile also serves as winter quarters for the chipmunks and mice that don't stake their claim early enough to make a cozy nest in my attic. Often Cruiser and I are rudely awakened on winter nights by the sound of vermin in the roof tap-dancing like Fred and Ginger. I never set traps for them like most people do, although I know they are probably doing some damage up there. I'm glad to provide shelter to creatures of the forest that might otherwise perish from the cold. I draw the line at bears and coyotes, however.

I resist the temptation to feed the wild animals, no matter how sorry I might feel for them. I'm also careful to keep my garbage cans securely covered, to keep the animals from becoming dependent on humans for their food supply. Unfortunately, most tourists provide easy pickings for bears and coyotes with their improperly discarded trash and open food containers, not to mention providing them with a smorgasbord of pets. Cats and small dogs in the area are regularly preyed upon by hungry coyotes.

"A fed coyote is a dead coyote," as the saying around here goes. That applies to bears, too. I know if I feed them, they become a nuisance to people and eventually are killed, as was the case with a bear and her cubs that had a notion to homestead in a family's cabin one winter. Once a nature area becomes populated with people, a conflict of interests is bound to arise; if it's a contest between wildlife and humans, humans always win. This is the *real* reality survival show!

What I didn't know was whether Rosie was going to win her battle to survive the injuries she sustained from her attacker. The onset of winter seemed somehow to mirror the dread I felt about the Sirius Killer and my friend's dire situation.

When I went to the hospital to visit her again, I found Rosie in a coma and hooked up to life support. It was distressing to see this vital, active woman, a pillar of the community, lying in a hospital bed showing no response, not even when I called her name or touched her hand. The only signs to indicate that she was still alive were the beeps of the heart monitor and the steady *shoosh, shoosh* of the oxygen ventilator.

There was nothing to be done but wait. Wait for her to awake from this deathlike slumber. Wait for the passing of winter. Wait for the outcome of the conflict over the dog park. Wait for the Sirius Killer to strike again. But I've never been one who is content to wait for anything, which makes you wonder why I ever became a writer. Writers are always waiting for something — acceptance letters, rejection slips, royalty checks — but that's something you can't control. Finding out who was behind these attacks was something I could and would take in hand or, in Cruiser's case, paw.

We are a team, and I felt that it was up to us to find out who was behind this before anyone else was hurt. I don't know if murderers make lists, but I knew if this one did, my name was definitely in the top ten. I had the e-mail threats to prove it. After the nearly fatal drugging of Lang Po and Rags, that could mean Cruiser was in danger, too. It was time for Cruiser and me to do some serious sniffing around, starting with Walter Wiley. Regardless of what Skip said, he was still at the top of my list of suspects. Cruiser and I would hound him until he confessed to his crimes.

17

Cruiser was relishing the drive to Walter Wiley's place that cool but sunny Sunday afternoon. He hung his head out the passenger window, a spray of joyriding drool spattering the rear window of my car. Rags and Lang Po had stayed behind at the cabin with Nona. No point in carting along the whole pack on this outing, and I felt better knowing that Nona had some furry company that could alert her to intruders.

I had some doubts about bringing Cruiser along with me to a confirmed dog hater's house, but there was no way I was paying an unannounced visit to a murder suspect without my trusty sidekick along for protection. He'd saved my bacon before, and I had no doubt he'd do it again, if necessary.

We passed by Rosie's house. It seemed strange not to see her sitting on her front porch crocheting one of her colorful afghans, with Rags resting his chin on her feet. It seemed even stranger to see the yellow crime scene tape still barricading her property. Was perfect landscaping worth all this? Could someone actually be so fanatical about a patch of sod that he'd kill for it? Wars that aren't fought over religion are fought over territory, so the answer to that question was yes.

Case in point was the conflict over a vacant stretch of lakeside property, which grew more heated as voting day drew closer. Daily in *The Tahoe Tattler*, pro and con letters on the subject of the dog park continued to pour into the editor's office. Most of the letters were not in favor of it. The ones most vehemently opposed to using this land for the dog park were those who had staked their claim on it for a boat dock, a casino, a hotel, a shopping center, what have you. Everyone wanted a piece of this pie-shaped parcel, but if you try to slice a pie into too many pieces, it will crumble to bits. I feared community relations were going to crumble right along with it. Not the least of the problems choking this issue, so to speak, was the murderer whose wrath had been unleashed on Tahoe residents and their pets.

It was obvious that Walter took a lot of pride in his place. His was the neatest yard in the neighborhood — every flowerbed devoid of weeds, not a blade of grass over-grown, every shrub a topiary masterpiece. In fact, as I parked the car and led Cruiser up the driveway, the old man was busy clipping a hedge. I surmised he was a bit deaf because he didn't hear us approach. In fact, he didn't know we were anywhere within a mile of his property until we were practically on top of him. Then I noticed his bottle-lens glasses and understood why.

"Shoo! Go on, get outta here!" He brandished his shears like a machete.

I was a bit startled at his reaction until I realized he had seen Cruiser but not me. Macular degeneration, I figured. "Mr. Wiley?"

"Huh, who is that?" He peered in my direction.

"I'm Elsie MacBean, a friend of Rose Clark's."

"Yeah? What do you want?"

"I'd just like to ask you some questions. Got a few minutes?"

Walter frowned. "You with the sheriff's office?"

"No, not exactly."

"Good, because I already told them everything I know."

I thought sure he was going to refuse my request, but he set down his shears, slipped a red and white bandana from a pocket of his overalls, and mopped his brow. "This is backbreaking work when you get to be my age."

"It's backbreaking work at any age, Mr. Wiley."

When Walter turned away and walked toward his front porch, I thought I was being dismissed. Then he looked back at me and barked, "Well, are you coming or not?"

"I'm right behind you."

"Watch that your dog doesn't pee on my shrubs."

"Yes, sir." I led Cruiser straight as an arrow up the walkway to Walter's porch, taking care that he didn't decide to lift a leg on the way. He can be pretty sneaky about it, and the more you try to hurry him along, the slower he wants to go — that basset stubborn streak at its best.

"Care for some lemonade?" Walter said. "I just made some."

"Uh, sure." I was disarmed by his hospitality. I hadn't expected him to even talk to me, let alone offer me refreshments. But perhaps that was part of the plan.

"Have a seat, and I'll bring it out here."

I sat down on the porch swing. Hot chocolate would have been my beverage of choice on a chilly day, but I hadn't been working in the garden. Cruiser made himself comfortable in a patch of sun.

As I sat waiting for my drink, I shivered in a cool breeze that wafted the scent of Walter's last summer roses from the garden. I wondered how anyone could feel cranky while sitting here, but apparently that was no problem for Walter Wiley. How do people get to be so sour? What transpired in the course of one's life to make one into such a malcontent? More important, what happened to turn someone into a murderer?

The squeal of the screen door hinges interrupted my reverie.

"Here," Walter said, handing me a cold glass of lemonade. Before I took a sip, I checked to make sure there were no discolored ice cubes in the drink like the ones he'd left on Rosie's lawn. It looked safe to drink. When I tasted it, there was no sourness, like some homemade lemonade or the frozen kind you buy in grocery stores, or like Walter Wiley. It was sweet and the color of pollen on a bee's knees. It *was* the bee's knees!

"This is delicious," I said. "What's your secret?"

"It was my wife's recipe. Dodie always

made it with honey, not sugar like most folks do. Makes it a lot sweeter. And she used special lemons, the Meyer lemons off our tree. We planted it next to an orange tree. They cross-pollinate. Makes the fruit of both trees taste better."

"You sure know your plants, Mr. Wiley."

"My wife was the gardener. She loved working in the soil. I'm not as fond of it as she was, but I like to keep everything just the way she left it."

"I'm sure she'd be happy to know how nice you maintain her garden. You must miss her."

Walter swallowed hard. "Yes, I do. I light a candle for her every night. That woman was the love of my life. That's why I get upset when people let their dogs mess things up. I want to keep it nice, for Dodie."

"I'm sure you do."

"People don't understand how hard I work to keep the yard up. It gets harder when you get to be my age. I'm not as strong as I once was, especially after the heart attack a couple of years ago."

"Oh, I didn't know."

"Yep, the old ticker ain't what it used to be. It happened after my wife passed away. And now it's the cancer. Same thing that took Dodie from me."

"If you're ill, you ought to hire someone to do your gardening for you."

"Can't afford it. I'm on a fixed income. Besides, my Dodie would never have wanted some fly-by-night gardening service butchering her prize-winning roses."

I saw my opening and cut in. "Speaking of roses, you and Rose Clark don't get along too well, do you?"

"I don't have anything against her, really, except for when I caught her dog digging in my garden. She knew I didn't like that. I told her on more than one occasion to keep her dog out of my yard."

"Did you ever threaten her over it?"

"I know what you're getting at, and I already explained to the sheriff that I never threatened her. I told her I'd call the dog catcher if I caught her dog in my yard again, but I don't think you'd call that a death threat, would you?"

"No, of course not. Do you own a computer, Mr. Wiley?"

"No. Dodie had one, but I donated it to the college after she . . ."

"Did you or your wife belong to AOL?"

"No, but I belong to AARP. What's AOL stand for, anyway?"

"America Online. It's an Internet provider service." Walter looked blank. "You know, for surfing the Web and using e-mail."

"Me, surf webs? You must be joshing. Spiderman maybe, but not me." Walter laughed. I'd never heard him laugh before. It was such a startlingly pleasant sound I was shocked to hear it issue from his mouth. I wondered if a ventriloquist wasn't hiding somewhere in the rose bushes. "Heck-fire, I didn't even know how to turn the dang thing on. Dodie was the one who made me buy one of those contraptions for her. I hate the blasted machines. Them's for the young 'uns. That's why I got rid of it after she was gone. All it was for me was a hat stand. Besides, it reminded me too much of her."

"You really miss her a lot, don't you?"

Walter nodded.

"Have you ever thought of getting a dog, Mr. Wiley? I live alone, too, and they're sure good company."

"We did own a dog once. Loved it to death, but it up and died on us a few years back. Dodie 'bout never got over it. I couldn't stand seeing her grieve like that, so I wouldn't agree to getting another one. I didn't think she could take it, if something happened to it. Plus we were getting older and were afraid another dog would outlive us, you know?"

"Yes, I know what you mean." I glanced at my dear boy, Cruiser, who was dozing contentedly in the sunshine, and I understood completely. If only we could cross the finish line together. "Well, I've taken up enough of your time, Mr. Wiley. Thanks again for the lemonade."

"Sure thing. I hope you catch the guy, whoever he is. Dodie would be real upset about all this."

"We're working on it, Mr. Wiley."

I was doing as Skip had told me, exercising my skepticism, but I was thoroughly puzzled after my chat with Walter Wiley. I had a slightly different profile of him now. He reminded me of a caramel popcorn ball — hard and crusty on the outside but soft and gooey on the inside. I'd have to talk to Skip about what Walter had told me. Did old man Wiley really have terminal health problems and think the Web was something out of a Spiderman comic? Or had this whole folksy, sipping-lemonade-on-the-porch scene been a clever smokescreen to convince me he wasn't serious about murder?

As I walked back to my car, I saw Walter's garbage can on the curb for the weekly pick-up. The lid had fallen off, so I picked it up to save old Walter the effort. As I replaced the lid, I couldn't help noticing the contents in the garbage can. Resting on top of soda bottles, aluminum cans, and banana peels was a blizzard of Styrofoam popcorn and the empty carton that had recently contained a brand new computer.

18

I spent the rest of that autumn afternoon lounging on the back deck with Nona and the dogs. As I lay on the chaise in the sun, the chill in the air was barely noticeable, although I wore my sweater and scarf for a little extra warmth. I felt lower than a basset's belly after my visit with Wiley, or maybe it was something else making me feel like a hollowed-out Halloween pumpkin.

Talking with Walter about his wife had stirred up painful memories of my husband, Tom. Sometimes I forget just how much I miss him. We had spent many lazy Sunday afternoons out here on this deck, sipping wine, talking, and making plans for the trip abroad we would never take together.

I felt the coolness of grass beneath my bare feet as I stood on the manicured lawn. But it wasn't Walter Wiley's lawn I was standing on; I was among a crowd gathered at Happy Homestead cemetery. It seemed like it was Tom's funeral, only there were no firefighters assembled in their dress blues or bagpipes playing for a fallen comrade. The only blue I saw was in the star-strewn sky above. I had never been to a nighttime funeral before. The light from grinning jack-o'-lanterns flickered in the darkness. Nona, Skip, and several others were gathered around a freshly dug grave. Cruiser was there, too, looking silly as ever in his Sherlock Holmes costume. Everyone was costumed for the occasion. Were these mourners or trick-or-treaters?

I realized this was definitely a funeral when Reverend Ramseth spoke the words, "Ashes to ashes, dust to dust." I felt my throat constrict. I began to cry. Rosie had died, and this was her funeral. We were here to bury her. At least that's what I assumed, until I saw her standing among the group gathered around the gravesite. The sensation in my throat grew more pronounced until it felt like I was wearing a cravat knotted too tightly around my neck. Then Rosie emerged from the group and pointed to the stone at the head of the empty grave. Suddenly, a meteor blazed across the sky, igniting the darkness like fireworks on the Fourth of July. In the flash of light, I saw there was something etched in the polished granite. The words on the stone read: *Rest in Peace, Elsinore MacBean.*

19

"No, no! This can't be!" I heard myself say. "This is some kind of sick joke."

As I leaned sobbing against my own gravestone, I felt something tug hard at the end of the blue plastic cord that hung from my neck. I gasped for breath, and everything went black. When I awoke, I was enveloped in darkness. I couldn't move. Couldn't breathe. I was suffocating. Then I heard sounds from somewhere above me. Where was I? The sounds grew louder. Was someone crying? No, it was something else. It was a dog whining, and it sounded familiar. It was Cruiser. "Cruiser! Cruiser, where are you?" I heard a scrabbling sound and something like dirt clods falling on wood. Then I saw the light from a meteor shower in the heavens, silhouetting Cruiser as he dug the dirt away from the glass cover of my coffin. "Hurry, Cruiser. Hurry, boy! Save me."

I jerked awake when I felt Cruiser

pawing at my arm. My scarf had snagged on one of his dewclaws, and he was trying to free himself. I unhooked my scarf from Cruiser's claw, surveying the damaged silk. He nursed the offended paw.

"We'll have to get Doc Heaton to trim those claws for you, Cruiser. I'd do it, but you're such a crybaby about pawdicures."

Nona stepped out on the deck, along with Rags and Lang Po, who must have heard Cruiser whining. "You awake, Mom?"

"Yes. Why didn't you wake me up? Were you going to let me grill like a Ballpark Frank out here?"

"Sorry. You were sleeping so soundly I didn't want to wake you. Looks like you-know-who wants to go for a walk."

"So, what else is new? My life is just one extended dog walk."

"And now we have two more to exercise. Maybe you should apply for a kennel permit."

I rubbed my throbbing temples. Napping in the sun sometimes had that effect on me, especially when I dreamed I was being buried alive. Shades of Edgar Allan Poe! I was thankful to be awake and that it was only a dream.

"Is anything wrong?"

"Just a slight headache is all."

"It's more than that. You seem kinda down or some-thing this afternoon. Sure there's nothing else bothering you?"

I shook my head, but Nona wasn't convinced. "You're not coming down with that flu bug, are you?"

"I don't think so. I guess it's just the visit with Walter Wiley bearing on my mind."

Nona's brow knitted with worry. "Was there some trouble while you were there?"

"Oh, no. It just didn't go as I expected is all. I thought I had this case all wrapped up, but now I see that I don't."

Nona sighed. It was the same sigh I'd heard from Tom when he was exasperated with me. "I wish you weren't involved in this, Mother. Why can't you just stick to freelance writing?"

"Because I can't let Rosie down."

"I understand that, but I worry about you. You should always take Skip along with you when you pay visits to murder suspects."

"I usually do, but he already questioned Wiley about this. I thought perhaps the old man might open up more to a woman. And he did."

"Yeah? What did he tell you?"

"More than I ever expected he would."

"Well, why don't we put all that aside, at least for now? It's Sunday, and you know what that means."

"No, what?" I was relieved Nona didn't press for details.

"I can't believe you don't remember our Sunday sundae, Mom."

"Oh, of course I remember." When Tom was alive, the three of us always went to the ice cream parlor every Sunday, winter or summer. It was a family tradition Nona and I had continued. After baking in the sun on the deck, ice cream sounded pretty good.

"Then what are we waiting for? Let's go."

"You're on, kiddo."

"What about Cruiser and these two?" Rags and Lang Po knew something exciting was about to happen in the day's routine of food, nap, walk, food, nap, walk. So did Cruiser. Dogs always know. Masters at reading our body language and interpreting meaning from our words and tone of voice, they know what's on our minds even before we do. A trio of tails wagged in expectant but varied tempos.

"Sure, I guess we can take them along with us."

"Okay. Let's go!" Nona had said the

magic *G* word. The dogs beat her to the door.

"Cruiser will teach these guys a thing or two about cruising, won't you, boy?" I said.

Roo, roo!

20

I heard an odd sound coming from my car as I drove down Al Tahoe Boulevard. I thought perhaps I'd blown a tire until I realized that the funny flapping noise was the sound of Cruiser's pendulous ears in the breeze from the open rear window. If anyone ever asked me to define pure bliss, I'd tell him to observe the expression on the face of any dog when it's hanging its head out a car window. That was the look I saw on Cruiser's face when I glanced in the rearview mirror. Rags and Lang Po looked happy, too. Much happier than they'd looked in a while. Both had been moping around the house, missing their owners. Lang Po wouldn't eat. I tried to be a surrogate to them, but with all that was going on lately, it was hard to be everything to everyone. Anyway, I was glad we'd brought them along for the ride. It was lifting all our spirits.

Ordinarily, we'd have gone inside the parlor to eat our ice cream, but since the dogs had come along for the ride, we enjoyed our sundaes 1950s drive-in style, in the car. The only things missing were the gum-chewing waitresses on roller skates, Fonzie slicking back his Brylcremed ducktail with an Ace comb, and a serving tray suspended from the window. In fact, I'd picked up a wad of bubble gum on the sole of my shoe as we walked back to the car.

Scraping the sticky gob of goo off my Nikes, I thought of the Tahoe that existed before the arrival of fast-food restaurants and video stores. For a moment I was transported to those "happy days" when I was young and the world I lived in was a simpler, less fearful place. Murder was something you only read about in dime store novels.

"Gosh, you're a million miles away today, Mom. I hoped this outing might take your mind off of work, at least for a little while."

"Sorry, honey. I don't mean to be a drag. I just have a lot on my mind is all."

"I know, I know. My mom, the gumshoe."

"Funny girl." I laughed and cuffed Nona playfully on the head.

She knew me well enough to know that there was no point in trying to distract me with sundaes and silliness when I had a murder case on my mind. "You said you're not sure Wiley's your perp. What will you do now?"

Nona was starting to sound like a gum-shoe herself. I suppose that is what comes of having one for a mother. "I'm not sure. I suppose the best place to start is by talking to everyone who was at the Howloween event, since that's where Abby Haversham was killed."

"That could take forever. Meanwhile . . ."

"I know, I know. Time is of the essence." I didn't tell Nona about the threatening e-mails I'd received. I knew she already worried enough about me.

"Is there anything I can do to help?"

"Maybe there is, honey." I wouldn't dream of putting my daughter in any jeopardy, but I figured she might be able to help out by asking some of my friends and acquaintances who were vendors at the event if they noticed anything odd that day. Skip and I would handle the tougher customers in the anti-dog park faction. "I'd like you to talk to Sally Applebaum at the Haute Hydrant. Ask her if she noticed anything strange at the Howloween event. Since Abby was discovered not far from the vendor area where she was, Sally might have information that could be of some significance."

"Sure. I'd be glad to."

"And while you're at it, why don't you order some treats for this muttly crew in the back seat?" I figured that by having Nona order something from the Haute Hydrant at the same time she questioned Sally, my friend might not think I imagined she could be in any way involved in this case, although in my mind anyone present at the fund-raiser wasn't beyond suspicion.

"You mean ice cream isn't a good enough treat? Don't look now, but I think we're going to have to share our desserts."

Cruiser, the Dairy King, wasn't about to be left out of the Sunday sundae fun. I heard the familiar whine, then the next thing I knew my right shoulder was soaked with drool.

"Oh, all right. You win." I ripped open the paper sack we'd carried our napkins and spoons in, spread it on the back seat, and set my plastic container of melting vanilla ice cream on it. Good thing I'd skipped my usual hot fudge topping this time. Cruiser wasted no time in polishing off the remains of my sundae. Nothing went to waste. I snatched the plastic container away before he started to eat that, too. Basset Hounds — the only true omnivores.

Rags and Lang Po were determined to get their just desserts, too. Supermodel Nona, who is forever watching her weight and considers water a food group, offered spoonfuls of her ice cream, first to one dog, then the other. Lang Po lapped the plastic spoon clean, wasting nary a drop. Rags, on the other hand, wasn't as adept at eating from a spoon. When the ice cream began dripping down his chest, I took my napkin and tucked it in his collar, fashioning a sort of bowser bib. Finally, he got the hang of it and polished off the rest of the ice cream, although his Scottie dog beard was stained snowy white.

"Hey, look, Mom! It's Santa Paws!"

"So it is." It felt good to laugh and have a good time again with Nona.

"What will happen to these two little guys, if Rosie doesn't make it? Will you keep them?"

"I haven't thought that far ahead. I'm praying for her to pull through this, but I admit it doesn't look promising. The odds of her coming out of the coma aren't good."

"People do sometimes, though, don't they? I've heard of cases . . ."

"Yes, miracles happen. I hope there's a miracle for Rosie."

Nona laid her hand on mine. "Me, too, Mom."

21

The next day, I went to visit Rosie at the hospital, but I just missed visiting hours. Since I was so close to Skip's house, I decided to pay him a visit instead. Perhaps he'd uncovered some new evidence on the Sirius case.

Leaves and litter flew past my windshield in the rising wind. Cumulus clouds lumbered across the western horizon like great white bears, signaling an approaching autumn storm. I hoped it would bring some blessed rain with it, to wet the dangerously dry underbrush and wash the last of the summer smog from the basin.

Skip's place was just the opposite of Walter Wiley's. It was the definitive bachelor pad. You'd find no rose bushes or trimmed topiaries in Skip's front yard. He was far too busy for such things, especially with a murderer on the loose. He had been putting in plenty of overtime since all this started, which was probably why he looked like he did when he answered the doorbell. He was clad in a torn T-shirt and sweatpants, and his sandy hair stood as erect as a cockatiel's feathered topknot. I tried not to laugh.

"Sorry to barge in, Skip. Did I wake you?" Stupid question.

The sheriff swept Sandman grains from his eyes. "Yeah, I think I'm coming down with that flu that's been going around. I've been feeling really rotten."

"Sorry to hear that. Should I come back another time?"

"Naw, come on in if you want to. Hope I'm not contagious, though."

"Me, too."

He admitted his uninvited guest, and I sat down in one of the two La-Z-Boy recliners, which were his idea of interior decoration. "Nice to have some furniture to sit on that's not already occupied by a dog."

Skip laughed. "I'll brew us some coffee. That should perk me up."

"Hah, good one." Skip had a joke for every occasion. There were his crime scene quips, his awkward social situation sarcasm, and of course his perfectly pedestrian puns.

He disappeared into the kitchen. A moment later I heard the clatter of pots and pans, then the sound of running water as he filled the coffeepot. I assumed that the kitchen must look like the rest of his place. The inside of Skip's house looked more like a bunch of frat boys lived in it than the county sheriff. Beer cans, pizza boxes, and newspapers littered the coffee table. Wrinkled clothes were draped over the sofa, and a collection of cast-off shoes and socks marked an Arthur Murray cha-cha pattern across the floor. I'd have cut him some slack for sloppiness because he wasn't feeling well, except that his house always looked like this.

In a while, Skip reappeared and handed me a steaming cup of coffee. He even served it in a cup and saucer instead of a mug. Undissolved Folger's crystals clotted the muddy liquid. No wonder he was always bumming my brew, not to mention breakfast, lunch, and dinner.

"Sorry, all I have is instant. I've got sugar, but I'm all out of cream."

"Don't sweat it. This'll do." I stirred in the last of the crystals with a spoon and took a swig.

"Taste all right?"

I nodded and feigned approval. My friend seemed more apologetic than usual about the state of his pad. He picked up a waste can and started collecting some of the litter, but soon gave up the effort. I didn't think there was a landfill large enough to accommodate this collection. "This place could use a woman's touch, Skip."

"You applying for the job?"

"Nope, and neither would Martha Stewart."

"No wonder. I hear she has other lobsters to boil these days. Guess she'll stick to soup stocks from now on."

"It's a good thing. I'm sure she'd pass on this home decorating project, but I can recommend a good maid service."

"Great. Maybe you can recommend someone who'd like to apply for a vacancy at the sheriff's office, too. There may be one opening up before long."

"What's the matter? This case about to get the best of you?"

"If it weren't for everything else I have to do around the office, it wouldn't be. When I wanted to be sheriff, I never imagined all the problems I was letting myself in for."

"What do you mean?"

"Some of the appointments I made in the department after I took this job haven't worked out as well as I'd hoped. I'm beginning to understand what my predecessor had to deal with."

"Dissension among the ranks?"

"I'll say. There's so much backbiting among these guys, I feel like I'm running a women's club instead of a sheriff's office."

"I resemble that."

A wry grin flitted across Skip's dour puss. "There's one guy in particular who's always making trouble. He's like some little kid poking at a wasp's nest."

"There's always a bad apple in every bushel, Skip."

"So I'm finding out. You never know if a guy will make a good sergeant until he's in the job, but by then it's too late."

"Office politics. Who needs it? I've quit more than one job because of it."

"Yeah . . . unfortunately, I can't quit, and I have a few years left until I can retire. Or maybe I can get a nice, quiet state job."

"Government jobs aren't immune from office politics. In fact, I think they're among the worst."

"Too many chiefs, and not enough Indians."

"That's certainly a politically incorrect way of putting it, but I suppose you could say that. I had some of the worst bosses imaginable in the state system. My co-workers and I called one woman we worked under 'The Nazi.' She goose-stepped through our stalag like a storm trooper. She was a miserable harpy who made everyone who worked under her miserable, too."

"People are the same everywhere, I suppose. Until my retirement party, I'll just have to grin and bear it. It'll be tough, though. I mean, considering what these guys have to do on a daily basis, what a bunch of crybabies!"

"You're talking to the woman who owns the worst crybaby in Tahoe. You should have heard Cruiser whining yesterday when he thought I wouldn't share my ice cream with him."

It was good to see Skip laugh. Dark circles under his eyes betrayed sleepless nights and considerable stress.

"How's Mrs. Clark doing, by the way?"

"Not good. She's still in a coma."

"I'm really sorry, Beanie."

"Me too. I hope we find out who's behind this soon, before anyone else becomes a victim."

"Did you find out anything else from Walter Wiley?"

"We had a little chat."

"What did he say?"

"He told me he doesn't have a computer

or even know how to use one."

"So?"

"So, I saw a brand new computer box stuffed in his garbage can. How do you explain that?"

"Maybe he bought it for someone else, a grandchild perhaps. Or a neighbor ran out of room in his own garbage can and used Walter's instead. I do that sometimes, don't you?"

I figured I could fill at least a dozen cans with the junk from Skip's living room alone. I took another sip of his terrible-tasting coffee before I answered. Bitter as the coffee was, what the sheriff was about to tell me would be much harder to swallow.

22

"What do you mean, I'm off the case, Skip? Says who?"

"By popular demand, I guess you could say."

"Is this what you were talking about before, when you mentioned you were having problems with your staff?"

"Well, partly. It's just that this case has become so high profile in the community. People are concerned, and they want professionals to handle it."

"What people?"

"The mayor, for one."

"What you really mean is your boys don't like it that a middle-aged Native American woman might upstage them."

"That's got nothing to do with it. Besides, we do have women working in the department, you know."

"You must mean Pam, the secretary you inherited from Stoddard."

Skip's face flushed. "Don't get mad at me, Beanie. It's not my decision."

"Isn't it?"

"No, I have a boss, too, you know. Mayor Petersen's the main one calling the shots on this case, and he wants us to handle it from here on."

"So, you just want me to sit around and do nothing in the midst of all this? You're forgetting about my friend, who is probably going to die because of this creep."

"I understand how you feel." Skip was starting to squirm, and I was glad. How dare he!

"Do you? Has the mayor already figured out who killed Abigail and hurt Rosie, not to mention the dogs that have been injured? And you're not forgetting about the e-mail threats I received, are you?"

"No, I'm not. That's the main reason I'm asking you to drop out of this case. I don't want you to be the Sirius Killer's next victim. Neither does Nona."

"Sorry. No can do."

"You know you're leaving me with very little choice in this matter."

"Fine. Do what you have to, but it won't keep me from doing what I have to." I stood up and headed for the door.

Skip followed after me and grabbed my wrist. "Please, Beanie. Don't go away mad. Listen to reason."

I jerked my hand away. I was so angry with Skip, my first instinct was to slap him into next week, but of course I didn't. I've never slapped a man, even though I've wanted to plenty of times. As if mimicking my anger, thunder grumbled in the distance. The storm was coming much closer now.

"I thought we were friends, Skip. You've always supported me before, no matter what. I never thought you'd turn against me like this. I'm more disappointed than I can say. Tom would be, too." My last comment stung him more sharply than a slap ever could.

As I drove away, Skip stood in the doorway of his lonely, disheveled bachelor pad. I'd never seen him look that gloomy, not even at Tom's funeral. If I hadn't been so furious with him, I'd have felt sorry for him.

By the time I reached my cabin, the first beads of rain pelted the ground. Nona and Cruiser met me at the door. I slammed it behind me, lynched my jacket on a coat hook, and garroted the hall tree with my scarf. Cruiser read my body language and high-tailed it for his hairy pillow on the sofa. Nona also sensed something was wrong.

"Everything okay, Mom? You look really upset."

"Upset is an understatement."

"What's wrong? It's not another mur . . ."

"No, no. Nothing like that."

"What, then?"

"I'd like to wring the sheriff's neck."

"What did he do?"

"Skip told me to back off on the Sirius case."

"Why?"

"Pressure from the department, or so he says."

"Can he do that?"

"Well, if he can't, the mayor certainly can. I'm so mad I could spit arrowheads." I flopped down on the sofa beside Cruiser and tried to calm myself.

"Maybe he's worried you may come to harm if you get too deeply involved."

"How considerate of him." I stroked my good hound, which did us both good. I could feel my pressure valve slowly start to release.

"He's just showing his concern for you."

"I don't think that's the real reason. I think he's just caving in to pressure from the boys not to let a woman upstage their investigation. Skip was Mike Stoddard's whipping boy for too long. It's affected his judgment, if you ask me."

"Gosh, I've never seen you so mad at him before. I hope this isn't going to affect your friendship. You've been friends for too long. And he and Dad were such good buddies."

A cloudburst drummed a war dance rhythm on the windows as a flash of lightning lit the trees outside. A moment later came the cannon volley of thunder. Nona and I were startled, our conversation temporarily interrupted by the storm's growing ferocity. Cruiser roused momentarily from his nap, then went back to sleep. Not even nature's pyrotechnics can rattle a Basset Hound intent on catching his Zs.

"Well, whatever the case, I can't just turn a blind eye to this, and Skip should understand that. I'm too involved now."

"Yes, I know. Rosie and all. Skip's not the only one who's worried about you, though. I am, too. I've never liked the fact that you put yourself in harm's way all the time, and Dad would have absolutely hated it. Writing books is a much safer occupation for a woman, don't you think?"

My jaw dropped. I couldn't believe my ears. "Why, Wenona MacBean, you amaze

149

me! I never figured you for a sexist."

"I'm not. I just don't want to see you hurt. Maybe Dad would still be alive if he'd had a safer job, instead of being a firefighter."

"Maybe so, but if Tom couldn't have done his job, it would have killed him just the same. Your father was a brave man, Nona. Brave men like him are never content to sit on the sidelines when they can help someone."

"I guess that's why you two were such a good match. You're a lot like him. I might worry about you, but that doesn't mean I'm not proud of you, Mom."

"Thanks, honey. That means more than you know. I'm proud of you, too. Your dad would also be proud." I brushed my hand against Nona's pretty bronze cheek. Her talk of good matches made me think of Addison and what a good one he'd make for my daughter. "Say, Nonie. There's someone I'd like you to meet."

"Yeah? Is he filthy rich or just drop-dead gorgeous?"

"Both."

"I thought we agreed that you were going to butt out of my love life from now on."

"Of course. Unless I find someone filthy

rich and drop-dead gorgeous."

"Never mind the drop-dead part. Just rich and gorgeous will do."

"Rich. Gorgeous. Got it," I said, checking off the imaginary list on my open palm.

Nona laughed and tossed her mane of chestnut hair like she always did when the subject was Men, but she was eager to change the subject from matchmaking. "So, what will you do now?"

"Guess I'll just have to sleuth on the sly like I always have, won't I?"

"With a little help from your friends, I suppose." Nona smiled and gestured first to herself, then the snoring hound at my feet.

"That's right, huh, Cruiser?" I said.

Cruiser woke from his slumber at the mention of his name, gave me a little knowing canine wink, and let out a baritone bark. I didn't need Madame Pawline to translate that response for me. Whenever I needed a friend, Cruiser had never let me down. That's more than I could say for a certain two-faced, sandy-haired sheriff.

23

The storm finally passed. It was safe to get online again, so I brewed a cup of herbal relaxation tea and took it into my office. I was still jumpy from my spat with Skip and the thunderstorm. A storm of another kind loomed on the horizon.

I opened my account and, as usual, found a string of e-mails waiting. More junk mail, along with a reminder from Carla about my article due date, which I quickly answered. I assured her that I was on top of the star search, which of course I wasn't. I hadn't even begun a first draft of the article. In fact, I still had research left to do before I could start writing a draft. I wished I could bounce some ideas off Rosie, but that wasn't possible. I'd visit her tomorrow to see if there had been any improvement in her condition.

I did some Web surfing to see if I could find more information on the impending meteor shower and on the subject of astronomy. Science was far from my best subject in school. I wondered why I'd accepted this assignment in the first place. That's why I was so blocked, I figured. I could still see my high school chemistry teacher, Mr. Vater, peering at me through his nerdy horn-rimmed glasses while I tried in vain to identify those Tinker Toy models of molecules during the final exam. The *pling* of an instant message scattered unpleasant memories of failed chemistry classes. It was Skip.

"You still mad at me?"

I wasn't going to answer him at first, then decided I would. It was preferable to thinking about Mr. Vater. "Yes!" I added a frowning emoticon for emphasis.

"I'm sorry I upset you. You know I wouldn't deliberately hurt you, right?"

"I used to think so."

"I know you have a personal stake in this with your friend, and the threats you received. If you like, I can keep you informed about anything else we uncover on the case. It'll be strictly on the Q-T, though, you understand."

"I understand. Thanks."

"And let me know if you get any more of those weird e-mails, okay?"

"Sure. I've got to get back to work on this article for the *Tattler* now."

"Okay. I'll let you go. I just wanted to be sure we're still friends."

"Friends support each other, Skip."

"I did support you, but when the mayor barks, I have to obey."

"Well, I have to obey someone else's bark right now. Cruiser is barking at the front door. We must have company. Better go."

"Talk to you later, okay?"

"Okay. TTYL."

I logged off and went to see what Cruiser was carrying on about. He never barked at the door unless there was a visitor. Odd that no one had rung the doorbell. It was beginning to get dark, so I was cautious when I opened the door and looked outside. No one was there. Cruiser saw his opportunity to slip out the door and headed for the pine tree to check his pee mail.

As I waited for him, I glanced down at the doormat and saw that someone had tucked an orange envelope under the edge of the mat. Printed by computer in Helvetica Bold was my name. Thinking it was a Halloween card from a friend, I picked up the envelope and opened it. I unfolded the plain sheet of computer paper inside. It was covered with drips of red candle wax, the same as had been discovered in Rosie's den.

This couldn't be a good sign, I thought. I scanned the front yard but saw nothing except my hound dog lifting his leg on the pine. Even so, I had the uncomfortable feeling I was being watched and that danger lurked nearby. I felt a sudden chill and decided it was time to round up the hound. "Cruiser, come on in now, boy!" Cruiser thought about it only a second before trotting back into the house. Perhaps he sensed danger, too. In one swift motion, I shut the door and flipped the deadbolt. I had the unsettling feeling that, like Cruiser's favorite pine tree in my yard, I had been marked. Marked for murder.

"What have you got there?" Nona said, noticing the paper in my hand.

"I'm not sure. I found it on the doorstep just now."

Nona examined it. "What is this?" She held the paper up and sniffed it. "Candle wax. It smells nice, like berries or something. That's weird. Who would drip candle wax all over this paper?"

"Well, it wasn't Liberace."

"Seriously, Mother. Who did this?"

"I'm guessing it's the same person who dripped candle wax all over Rosie's carpet before we found her."

"What's the connection, though? What could it mean?"

"I have no clue."

"Yes, you do, Mom. This paper is definitely a clue."

"I agree, but it's not much of one. A few candle drips aren't conclusive evidence in a murder case, although I know that Pauline and Walter Wiley use candles. Trouble is, so do lots of people. Everyone in Tahoe keeps candles around, in case of power outages during storms. I do, too."

"Not everyone uses them like this, though. I think you're in danger."

"Wrong, honey. We're all in danger."

"What will you do?"

"I'll just have to hurry and find out who the killer is, won't I?"

"How?"

"With a little help from my friends, remember?"

"But I thought Skip said . . ."

"Never mind what Skip said. He can't keep two concerned citizens from trying to protect themselves."

"Incidentally, while you were out I talked to Sally at the Haute Hydrant like you asked me to. She said she didn't know anything. Same with Rub-a-Dub-Dog and the other vendors I called. I'm sure they were telling the truth."

"Me too, dear. I guess we'll just have to dig a little deeper."

Nona cocked an eyebrow. "You're not suggesting I be your partner on this case, are you?"

"Why not? You're my friend, aren't you?"

"Yes, of course I am, but I thought you were talking about Cruiser."

"He's my friend, too."

"You know I'll help any way I can, but Rosie's in a coma, and she's the only one who could possibly identify the killer."

"You're forgetting that we've had other eyewitnesses to both crimes."

"We have? Who?"

"Lang Po and Rags, of course." Rags trotted over to me when he heard his name. Lang Po yawned, looking regally bored on his adopted throne.

"And just how are you going to get these two to talk?"

"I have my methods."

24

"A dog séance? Please tell me you're joking, Mother."

"Not a dog séance. I've been reading Pauline LeBlanc's book on animal communication, and I'm going to give it a try. Maybe I can use her methods to find out who the Sirius Killer is. Who better to ask than a dog, especially one who was at the crime scene?"

"You can't really believe this will work."

"It's unconventional, I admit, and Skip would think I've flipped my beanie, but I have nothing to lose by trying, do I? It might even be fun." That was the magic word for fun-loving Nona, but this might be over the top, even for her.

"Whatever," she said with a wrist flick of dismissal.

"Okay, let's gather the dogs in the living room."

"Cruiser, too?"

"Sure, why not? He was also at the Howloween event. He may know something we don't. You'll probably find him in my room on his Raining Cats and Dogs quilt. He's getting tired of sharing his territory with Rags and Lang Po, I think."

Just then the doorbell rang.

"You go get Cruiser. I'll see who it is."

"Look through the peephole before you answer, Mom."

"Don't worry, I will."

Nona didn't have to fetch Cruiser. The doorbell brought him running on the double. I turned on the porch light to see who was out there. I was relieved to see it was Skip, and he was carrying something. A peace offering, perhaps?

I opened the door, and he gave me a sheepish grin. "It's late, Skip. What do you want?"

"Er . . . I was just cruising the area and thought I'd stop by and say hi."

"Hi."

There was an awkward silence. He shuffled from foot to foot, unsure what to say next. I couldn't let him squirm any longer. Cruiser and Rags were straining to get a whiff of the package Skip had tucked under his arm. Even His Royal Highness Lang Po had abandoned his armchair citadel to get into the act.

"What have you got there, anyway?" I said.

"Oh, this is for you." He handed me an enormous box of chocolates wrapped in seasonal orange and black ribbons. Skip knew how to get at my soft center, all right.

"It's a bit early for Halloween candy, isn't it?"

"Only a little. You can get a head start on the trick-or-treaters."

"That was nice of you, but you really shouldn't have. You know I'm trying to watch my weight."

"Well, Nona can help you eat it."

"String bean MacBean? Are you kidding?"

"I heard that!" Nona yelled from the hallway.

Skip and I laughed, and the ice between us melted like a spring thaw. "Come on in. We were just about to conduct an experiment of sorts."

I bolted the door behind us and put the chocolates out of the tidbit trio's reach. I didn't need any more vet bills for sick dogs, certainly not three at once.

"What kind of experiment?" Skip said, trying to hide the excitement in his voice.

"Better hold onto your Ouija board,

Skip," Nona said. "She's having a dog séance."

"A what?"

"Don't pay any attention to my smart aleck daughter. What I'm going to do is try to communicate with our furry witnesses here, using the techniques I learned in Pauline's book."

"Come on. You've gotta be jerkin' my chain, Beanie. Maybe I *should* have brought a Ouija board. You'd stand a better chance with that than with this phony baloney . . ."

"Be as skeptical as you want, but I'm going to try it. If you want to join in the circle, fine. If not, just leave or be quiet so I can concentrate, okay?"

Skip didn't want to burn the newly reconstructed bridge in our friendship so soon, so he agreed to be a silent observer. "Okay, Madame MacBean, do your psychic stuff."

I struck a match and lit the beeswax candle Nona found in the kitchen drawer where I kept the flashlight, matches, and my assortment of other tools for emergencies. The candle sputtered in the darkened room. The mood was just right for a doggie séance, or even the spirit-conjuring

161

people variety, but I wasn't trying to conjure the ghost of Rin Tin Tin. The goal was to make some kind of connection with one of the four-legged subjects in Madame MacBean's mountain parlor. That didn't seem so farfetched to me. Cruiser and I had a heart connection; of that much I was certain. Whether or not I could actually communicate with these furry fellows remained to be seen.

"So, now what happens, Mom?"

"According to Pauline's book, first I should meditate and try to reach a relaxed state. Then I'll try to tune in to their wavelength and see if I pick up anything. I need complete quiet while I do this. Everyone ready?"

"Ready," Nona and Skip responded.

I closed my eyes and took three deep, slow breaths from my stomach, not shallow puffs from the chest like we do most of the time. I used the relaxation technique I'd learned in yoga, relaxing the muscles, from the top of my head to the tips of my toes until my entire body felt like a big tub of Jell-O. I let my jaw go slack, and focused on any areas that were still tense. My breathing became deeper and slower until I was fully relaxed. The room was so silent you could have heard a deer tick hit the pine floor.

"Beanie to basset, Beanie to basset," Skip imitated radio static sounds. "Come in, Commander Basset. Reading you loud and clear."

Nona started to giggle. Then Skip joined in.

"Please, you two."

"Sorry, Beanie. I couldn't resist."

"Now I'll have to start all over again."

"I'll shut up. I promise."

"Me, too, Mom. Go ahead."

I took a deep breath, and then repeated the process. This time I visualized myself floating on a soft, white cloud until I reached my deepest level of relaxation. When I felt I was ready, I opened my eyes and studied my subjects. First I tried addressing them as a group, but I wasn't getting anything. Then I tried focusing on just one dog at a time.

"Lang Po, can we talk?" I wondered if Joan Rivers ever communicated with her dog, Spike, like this.

Nothing. I repeated the phrase again, but Lang Po wasn't cooperating. I tried it again with Rags. "Rags, is there something you'd like to say?"

I thought I saw Rags' ears perk forward like he'd heard a sound, but it could just as well have been Fred and Ginger Squirrel setting up their winter dance studio in my attic.

Well, if I was going to be able to communicate with any subject in this canine circle, it had to be my own dog, Cruiser. Surely, he wouldn't let me down.

"Cruiser, will you talk to me?"

Again, nothing. Cruiser scratched his ear, making drumming sounds on the floor. Had he heard something?

"Cruiser, do you have anything to say?"

Then it came to me. Not words but an image. Of a Bacon Beggin' Strip. Naturally, Cruiser's first thought would be of food. At least something was happening, though. Cruiser and I were communicating. This was actually working!

Another image came. This time it was of a china plate of petit fours and finger sandwiches. I had no doubt who was sending me messages now. It was Abigail's pampered Pomeranian, Lang Po. No wonder the dog was so fat it could barely walk.

Then a flood of images poured over me. Thoughts of biscuits, trees, peanut butter-filled Kong toys, hissing cats, chattering chipmunks, toilet bowls — too many images to sort out. I could only conclude that some kind of human/animal barrier had been broken and I was communicating with all three dogs at once. The images kept coming — green grassy fields, rabbit, quail, more treats — and I even began to receive scents, very faintly at first, then stronger. Feral scents that my own weak olfactory organ would never normally detect hit my nose like a dose of smelling salts. A plethora of impressions continued to assault my senses until one seemed to drown out all the others. With it came an overwhelming sensation of terror.

25

I blew out the candle and turned on the lights.

"Is the séance over?" Skip said. "I didn't see any ghosts or floating tables."

"Very funny, Skip."

"Did you get anything, Mom?"

"Boy, did I ever!"

"Well, don't keep us in suspense any longer, Beanie."

"At first I wasn't getting much, but then I was overwhelmed. All of them were talking to me at once. I couldn't sort it all out, but I know one thing for sure."

"What?" Skip said.

"One of these dogs knows who our killer is."

"Did he tell you who it is?"

I knew Skip was being facetious, but he hadn't sensed what I had moments ago. "Well, no. Not exactly."

"Too bad you can't put them on a witness stand."

Skip just wouldn't let up with the wisecracks. I guess I couldn't blame him. I had to admit that what I was saying seemed pretty farfetched to the rational mind of a lawman, and I knew his skeptical nature wouldn't allow him to believe anything he couldn't see for himself. Being Washo, I believe in many things that are not visible to the naked eye, but I wouldn't have believed what had happened, either, if I hadn't experienced it myself.

"What did you see?" Nona said.

"It wasn't so much what I saw but what I sensed. It was a paralyzing fear like I've never experienced before, not even when I was up against the Tahoe Terror that winter. One of these two pooches definitely saw his mistress being attacked."

"Poor little guy," Nona said. "He must have been pretty traumatized by the whole thing."

"Remembering how upset Cruiser used to get when Tom and I quarreled, I can only imagine what a dog must feel in such a dire situation. Dogs are such empaths. They read our body language, sense our moods, and, I believe, read our thoughts and intentions before we're even aware of them ourselves."

"I'm sure you're right about that, Beanie. How else can they assist us so well

in search and rescue and function as sei-
zure and guide dogs?"

"Some can even detect the presence of
disease in humans," I added.

"If only we were as sensitive to them,"
Nona said.

"Whichever dog sent me these images
knew of the killer's intent to commit
murder and may even be able to identify
who it is, if given the chance."

"So, what now?" Skip said. "Am I supposed to take these guys along with me on
a stakeout?"

"Better make it a T-bone stakeout."
Nona giggled.

"I think I'll go have a talk with Pauline
tomorrow, tell her what I picked up, and
see if she can offer any suggestions or in-
sights." I wasn't about to tell Skip I was
planning to do more nosing around in the
murder case. What he didn't know
couldn't hurt him, but what I didn't know
could put me in mortal danger. I'd be
sniffing around with Cruiser for further
clues, but I'd also be watching my tail, as
I'd been advised. And Cruiser's, too, after
what had happened to Lang Po and Rags.

It was late by the time Skip left. Gusting
winds signaled another storm was immi-

nent. Perhaps this one might finally bring the first snow of the season. The trees outside clawed at the cabin walls like an angry beast, and it was hard not to think of the killer who lurked somewhere out in the Tahoe night.

I tried to put such thoughts aside as I sat at my desk, drumming my fingers, feeling more distracted than ever. Lying on top of my desk was the letter I'd found on my porch. I opened it again and studied the strange assortment of red wax blobs on the paper. What could it mean? Was there some connection to the stranglings? Or was it just some silly pre-Halloween prank?

It was approaching midnight. I decided if I was going to get this article written, I'd better quit stalling and get busy. The due date was looming. I decided to do a little more research on my article, but once again I got sidetracked. It was no use. I just couldn't concentrate on anything but this case. Out of curiosity, I decided to type in the word *Sirius* in the search field and see what came up. Of course, I already knew Sirius was the Dog Star. The constellation in which it orbits the heavens, Alpha Canis Majoris, also came up, along with some numbers, which I assumed had something to do with the star's position in the constellation.

I clicked on the link. Again, up came the sky chart showing the names of the other stars in the constellation. As before, the stars were connected in a crude dot-to-dot stick figure of a dog. And the eye of the great dog was the largest star in the constellation, the brilliant blue Sirius. I glanced at the open letter on my desk, then back at the screen. Suddenly, the connection hit me like the Scottie bookend had hit Rosie. The dots on the paper exactly matched the dots on the computer screen that represented the stars in Canis Majoris. This was another murderous message from the Sirius Killer.

26

Psychic Paws was located in one of the less affluent areas of South Lake Tahoe, but Pauline kept a tidy place. Formerly a Mexican restaurant, it had been completely transformed from Taco Shop to Trance Shangri-la. A waiting area for her clients and their pets was accented with statuettes of various dog breeds. Her books were prominently displayed on a sideboard, along with an assortment of dog treats and other pup paraphernalia.

"Nice to see you, Elsie," Pauline said. "Have a seat and make yourself comfortable. I'm almost finished with my client. There are some magazines over there to read while you wait. Help yourself to some tea."

"Thanks."

I selected the only black tea in the box of weak herbals, hoping it might have at least a trace of caffeine in it. Formosa Oolong wasn't my preference, but it tasted good enough. I sipped and surveyed the room, taking mental notes.

The décor of the entire establishment was New Age, Earth Mother, Ya-Ya Sister, Mondo Beyondo. From the crystals and angels to the Neo-hippie beaded curtain to the flickering candles in a plethora of colors and scents to the trickling fountains to the meditation music playing softly in the background, it was everything Skip eschewed. But it was perfect for someone who called herself an animal communicator. I wondered if she did much communicating via the PC on her desk; but then everyone uses e-mail these days, I reasoned, from toddlers to senior citizens-to-be like Elsie "technophobe" MacBean. I used it, too, mainly to keep in touch with Nona when she was on photo shoots. Next, she'd be after me to get a cell phone and Palm Pilot.

I had just finished my tea and my inventory when Pauline emerged from her sanctuary. "Sorry to keep you waiting. It's been busier than usual since the Howloween event."

"Lots of new clients, huh?"

"Yes. It was great exposure for my business. I've sold quite a few books, too."

"I'm not surprised. It's an interesting book, Pauline."

"Thank you. Did you try using any of the communication techniques in it?"

"As a matter of fact, I did."

"Were you successful?"

"Yes, I think so. That's what I want to talk to you about."

"Sure. What do you want to know?"

"How do you know which dog you're communicating with?"

Pauline looked puzzled. "I'm not sure I understand your question."

"I was getting lots of responses, but I didn't know which of the dogs was doing the talking."

She laughed. "I find it works best if you communicate with only one animal in the room at a time."

"Oh, I didn't know that."

"No wonder you were confused."

"I imagine they were, too," I said.

"At least it was working for you. Most people aren't that successful at first. You must have an unusually strong connection to the animal world."

"I suppose you could say that. Runs in the family."

"Was there something else you wanted to ask me?" Pauline was reading *me* now. She sensed I had more on my mind than just her book.

I nodded. "I confess that I had another reason for coming here today. I'd like to ask you a few questions about Abigail Haversham."

Pauline's smile evaporated. "What kind of questions?"

"About the day she was murdered."

"What could you expect me to know about that?"

"You talked to her just minutes before she was killed, didn't you?"

"Yes I did." She didn't say it aloud, but her onyx eyes were screaming at me, *So, what's it to you, nosy?*

"From where I was standing, it looked as though you were arguing with her."

"Perhaps you were standing too far away, then. We were having a discussion, that's all."

"Must have been quite some discussion."

"Surely you're not suggesting that I had anything to do with her death?"

"No, of course not, Pauline, but you were one of the last people to see her alive. I'd just like to know what you and Abby were talking about, that's all."

"We were discussing permits."

"Permits? You mean having to do with the dog park?"

"No, having to do with my shop. The

City Council is putting new controls on the kinds of businesses that can get permits in Tahoe. Mine comes under Palm Readers, even though I've never read a palm in my life."

"Just paws, not palms." I was trying to keep things light. When Pauline didn't crack a smile at my puppy pun, I knew this was no joking matter to her.

"I'm in danger of losing my permit, and I was trying to convince Abby to put in a good word for me at the next council meeting."

"Did she agree?"

"No. She didn't. Abby had some pretty strong, preconceived notions about what I do. Probably thought I was the Devil's daughter, with my candles and such. She's not the only one around here who thinks so."

"People can be narrow in their thinking, when it comes to such things."

"I know. That's why I did a free session with her and Lang Po, to try to convince her of the validity of what I do, and that I don't practice Black Magic or Satanism."

"Do you think she was convinced?"

"I thought so."

"Abby was a tough old bird, but she adored her dog."

"That was obvious," Pauline said. "She told me she had to feed the dog with a fork, because it has an underbite. Not many people would go to so much trouble for a dog."

"No kidding, a fork?" No wonder Lang Po was so picky about his food and liked licking ice cream from a spoon. I just hoped he wouldn't expect champagne and caviar, too.

"I think that Abigail left my tent believing I had really helped her and her pet. Most people feel the same when they see what I do isn't hocus-pocus, as your friend put it."

"You mustn't mind the sheriff. He's really good at heart, just a bit skeptical about anything he can't see or touch."

"He has plenty of company," Pauline said, undisguised anger in her voice.

"Tangible evidence is the only thing that will sway him. It comes from being in law enforcement, I suppose. They tend to put their trust in the more traditional methods of collecting information."

"Too bad. There's so much more to be perceived in the world than with our five weak senses alone."

I had to agree with her there. "So you never saw Abby after she left your tent?"

"No, the next time I saw her she was dead."

"Near your booth."

"Uh, huh." Pauline was growing defensive. She didn't need psychic powers to see where I was headed with this. "But Abby was just as close to the other booths as she was to mine. In fact, Rub-a-Dub-Dog even has the same kind of leashes used to kill her. Have you cross-examined them?"

"No, not yet." I sensed it was nearly time to go. Pauline was ready to yank the welcome mat from under me.

Then a cloud of worry further darkened Pauline's countenance.

"Is something wrong?"

She opened the drawer of her desk and pulled out a folded piece of paper. "I found this on my doorstep last night. What do you make of it?"

I unfolded the paper and saw the drops of red candle wax. It was identical to the one I'd found on my own porch. The Sirius Killer was about to strike again, and it looked like Pauline might also be earmarked as a victim.

27

As I drove home from Pauline's place, I was more confused than ever. My list of victims might be about to get longer, but my list of suspects was coming up short. That is, unless Pauline was trying to fool me into thinking she was innocent by showing me the same evidence from the other crimes that she had planted herself.

If she could read Cruiser's mind, why not mine? She may have known I was going to pay a visit to her Psychic Paws parlor before I ever got there, and she no doubt surmised I wasn't there for her autograph. From what she had told me, it sounded like she had an ax to grind with the City Council over the possible closure of her business, and from all accounts Abigail had been the head battle-ax in that organization. Rosie was very active on the council, too. With both of them out of the way, Pauline would be assured of keeping her storefront open. That left only a nosy Elsie MacBean to be dealt with.

Of course, if Pauline did have to close up shop, she could always advertise on the Internet. Perhaps she already had. Could she be the e-mailer known as *dogsbody?* But why would someone who professed to care so much about dogs threaten them and their owners? That would take one pretty twisted individual. Still, everyone has a dark side, and I suspected Pauline had one, too. Perhaps she was just a little better at disguising it than others.

When I walked in my front door, I was met by all three dogs waiting for their breakfast. Of course, Cruiser was at the front of the queue. Nona was still in bed, apparently catching up on her beauty sleep from all those early morning photo shoots.

I went into the kitchen, trailed by the drum of paws on the pine floor in various rhythms and timbres. The familiar plod, scuff, click of Cruiser's easygoing gait was accompanied by Rags' staccato highland fling, accented by Lang Po's labored puffs as he attempted pirouettes on his hind legs.

I felt a little like Goldilocks with her three bears as I filled a large blue, medium yellow, and small red bowl with a blend of high-priced kibble and canned food. I set the bowls down on the floor far enough apart to avoid any competition. Each of my three diners approached his bowl. Cruiser dived right in, just in case one of the others took a notion to sample his food. Rags wasted no time devouring his meal, either. The only one who seemed to be stalling was Lang Po. He sniffed at his breakfast and seemed interested in eating but wouldn't take any. Then I remembered something: his underbite. Sam Spade's spaniel, no wonder he wasn't eating! I hadn't set out His Lordship's silverware.

I took a spoon from the drawer and scooped up a dollop of gourmet grub. I reached down and offered it to Lang Po. He licked it once or twice but still wouldn't eat the food. Then I recalled that Pauline told me Abigail said she fed him with a fork. I didn't know what difference it could possibly make. Perhaps the angle of the utensil made it easier for Lang Po's deformed jaw to get a good grip on the food. Anyway, I shoveled some of the food onto a fork and sure enough, Lang Po took the food the first time.

My back began to ache from bending over to feed the small dog, so I picked him up and held him on my lap like a baby. In spite of myself, I began making baby talk to him, coaxing him to take the next bite.

Once a mother always a mother, I guess.

"Mom! What on earth are you doing?"

My face turned redder than Lang Po's bowl. "How long have you been standing there?"

"Long enough. Don't you think you're spoiling that dog too much? How will you ever place him with someone who will treat him like a human being, feeding him with a fork like that? Why don't you just set him a place at the dinner table?"

"Har de har har. Whoever adopts him will either have to feed him like this or spend big bucks on doggy orthodonture. He has an underbite like a bulldog."

"Good luck finding either. Some people barely spend any time or money on their dogs, let alone hand feed them."

"Well, I know at least two other people who didn't mind giving a dog some extra attention."

"Who?"

"Abby and Rosie."

"Have you heard anything about Rosie? How is she doing?"

"The same, last I heard. I really must get over to see her again soon. In fact, this time I might take someone else along with me."

"I can't go with you, Mom. I have a date."

"I thought you were going to let me introduce you to someone."

"Let's not go there, okay? I gotta run or I'll be late. He lives over in Incline."

"Go ahead. I wasn't thinking of taking you, anyway. I'm going to take Rags with me."

"Do they allow dogs at the hospital?"

"He's small. I should be able to smuggle him in."

"Any new developments on who put her there in the first place?"

"I have a lot of suspicions, but so far, nothing definite. I hope something breaks soon. This could get a whole lot uglier than it already is."

"Well, I'd better go." Nona checked her look in the hall mirror. Perfection, as usual. Clearly, she had more pressing matters on her mind. "I'm late for my date."

"Who are you meeting, by the way?"

"None of your business." Her cinnamon eyes were warm, in spite of her cool response.

"Do I know him?"

"I don't know. Could be." Nona was being evasive, as usual, about her latest boyfriend, which was probably for the best. She knew me too well by now.

"When are you bringing him home to

meet . . ." I hesitated when I caught sight of the masticated kibble circling Cruiser's dog dish on the kitchen floor. "Never mind." I decided she could bring her new boyfriend home to meet the Lord of the Rings and me some other time.

Rags happily occupied Cruiser's usual co-pilot seat as we drove to Barton Memorial Hospital. I had hidden him in a carryall, but when he peeked out the top of it, the nurse at the front desk smiled and gave us the nod.

If it was distressing for me to see Rosie hooked up to noisy monitors and life support devices, it was even more so for poor Rags. At first he was afraid of the whooshing sound of the breathing apparatus and the blipping sound of the heart monitor, but he overcame his fear when he realized it was his owner there in the bed. He began to whine, so I lifted him up so he could see her better. His bright black eyes looked quizzical. I placed him on the bed next to her, being careful not to interfere with the oxygen hose and IV. Rags seemed to understand that he must be quiet and gentle under the circumstances and that something was terribly wrong with his beloved mistress.

He nudged Rosie's hand with his cold, wet nose, but there was no response. That worried Rags even more. True to his tenacious terrier nature, he wasn't about to give up so easily. He nudged her hand a little harder this time and gave her hand a few licks. It was barely perceptible, and anyone not paying close attention at that moment would have missed it entirely, but I didn't. Neither did Rags. He barked when the index finger on her right hand stirred ever so slightly. The steady *blip, blip* of the heart monitor hiccupped.

I buzzed for the nurse. I barely had time to get Rags off the bed before she appeared. I wasn't sure how she'd react when she saw a dog in the bed with her patient.

"Is anything wrong?" she asked when she saw the anxious look on my face.

"Her hand. It moved."

The nurse stepped over to the bed and examined Rosie. She took her patient's pulse, then lifted one of Rosie's eyelids. Her pupils were still fixed and dilated.

"Everything looks about the same, I'm afraid."

"No, no. She moved her finger. I saw it. It must be a good sign, right?"

"Well, it could be, but it could also just be a reflex. Dr. Garrett will be doing his rounds in about an hour, and he'll be doing a full examination of Mrs. Clark then."

"Please be sure he knows about it, okay?"

"Of course. I'll tell him."

"Here's my card. I'm not family, but other than this little dog here, I'm the only family she has. Will you call me if there's any change at all?"

"Certainly. I'll add your name to the list. Mrs. Clark has so many people concerned about her. She's had lots of visitors."

"Really? Who?"

"Several of her friends and neighbors, the young Haversham heir, even Mayor Petersen and a city council member." The nurse smiled, gave Rags a pet, and hurried back to her station. As I led Rags from the room and helped him up into my car, I wondered if Walter Wiley or Pauline LeBlanc had been among Rosie's many visitors. If the Sirius Killer had paid her a visit, how easy it would have been to squeeze off the flow of oxygen through the plastic air hose just long enough to finish her off.

Rags didn't seem as interested in the drive back to my house. I doubt if even one of Cruiser's Beggin' Strips could have gotten any reaction from him at that moment. He curled up in the passenger seat, laid his head on his paws, and uttered a long, heavy sigh. My heart ached for the little dog. How many more times would he be separated from his loving owner under such traumatic circumstances? Cruiser and I would try to fill the empty space in the terrier's life as best we could. As for Rosie and Rags ever being reunited, all any of us could hope for was a miracle.

28

I heard the phone ring over the jangling of my keys in the lock. I managed to open the door and dash to the phone before it stopped ringing. It was Skip. He wanted to meet me for lunch. He was still trying to make up with me, I figured, because he offered to pay. I decided I'd let him. He was into me for more than a few free lunches over the years.

We met at our old haunt, Debbie's Diner. No flirty waitress named Rita Ramirez served us this time, thank goodness. I was glad we'd come on her day off, because I wasn't in the mood for her shameless shenanigans. Skip ordered his usual artery-clogger special, a double bacon cheeseburger with extra bacon. I knew he had something else on his mind besides lunch, though.

"You went to see Pauline, didn't you?"

"Yes, I saw her. Why?"

"I knew it. All right, spill, Jill. Did she tell you anything?"

"Could be." Not only was I going to make Skip pay for any information he got out of me on this case, I was going to make him sit up and beg for it, like Cruiser begs for biscuits.

"Well?"

"Well, what?"

"Come on, Beanie. What did she say?"

"All right, all right. Someone's got to get to the bottom of this case, don't they?"

"Granted. I'm all ears."

"That's Cruiser's line."

"I'm going to sic Cruiser on you if you don't hurry up and . . ."

"Keep your sheriff shirt on. Remember when we were walking over to Pauline's tent that day at the Howloween event?"

"Yes."

"I thought they were arguing before we arrived, and turns out they were."

"Over what?"

"Apparently, Pauline's business permit is about to be revoked."

Skip took a Cruiser-sized bite of his burger. I wondered how his mouth could open that wide. Did he have a hinged jaw like a snake?

"Go on, I'm listening," he said through the mouthful of food. Maybe this was one of the reasons I liked Skip so much. He reminded me a lot of a canine, wolfing his food down that way. My dog, Skip.

"Er, uh, where was I? Oh, yes, she was trying to persuade Abby to intervene for her on the Council."

Skip swallowed before he spoke this time, thank goodness. "Yeah, they've got a regulation about palm readers and weirdo stuff like that around here."

"Pauline isn't a palm reader. She's a pet psychic."

"And that would be different how? It's all kind of the same ball of candle wax, isn't it? They're all charlatans, if you ask me."

"Would you call a psychiatrist or physical therapist a charlatan?"

"Of course not. Those are legitimate professionals."

"Well, that's how Pauline sees herself, as a professional who helps people with their pets' problems, like a trainer or veterinarian."

"Yeah, but those people have to go to school to learn special skills."

"Pauline has special skills, too, Skip. She just doesn't have a diploma or medical license like a doctor. I believe what she does is just as real and beneficial, though."

"I'm from Missouri," Skip said.

"No you're not. You're from Modesto."

"What I mean is you've got to show me more than I've seen so far for me to start believing in pet psychics."

"Why are you always so darned skeptical about everything, Skip? It's really infuriating sometimes."

"I have to be. That's *my* business. I say your Madame Pawline is a prime suspect in this case. She was probably the last person to see Abigail Haversham alive. Her tent was within a few feet of the crime scene, and she's kind of a wacko, as far as I can tell."

"Is everyone who doesn't fit into your Jell-O mold of humanity a wacko? By your standards, I'm a wacko, too."

"You're exempt, Beanie. At any rate, you've confirmed that Pauline had the motive to kill Mrs. Haversham. Rosie was also a likely target, because she was on the same City Council that was threatening to close the LeBlanc woman's business."

"A couple of days ago, I would have concurred with everything you just said."

"So, what's changed your mind?"

"Pauline has also received a death threat from the Sirius Killer."

"She what?" Skip almost spat a mouthful of burger at me, along with his words. He swallowed his food and a little pride with a gulp of root beer float. "Well, looks like that blows my theory. I guess there's still more work to be done on this case, and wouldn't you know I'm shorthanded."

"How come?"

"Most of my staff is out with the flu. I could really use your help, Beanie, especially since you've already been nosing around on this case."

"Gee, thanks a lot. You make me sound like Cruiser. But what about the mayor?"

"I'll fix it with him. We need to get to the bottom of this, and soon, by whatever means necessary."

"So I'm officially back on the crime trail?"

"Yep."

"Cruiser, too?"

"Cruiser, too. Two heads are better than one, even if one is a hound's head."

"So, I guess we're right back where we started when we sat here that winter the Tahoe Terror was on the loose, huh? Only now it's the Sirius Killer we're after."

Skip made loud, slurpy noises through the straw as he drank the dregs of his float. He even sounded like Cruiser when he ate. "Yeah, looks like it's just you and me again, and that slobbery hound dog of yours, of course."

29

I had a lot to think about, with a murderer still at large and a death threat hanging over my head. The threats were escalating, and no dog lover seemed immune to the killer's wrath. Abby Haversham was dead and, as much as I hated to admit it, Rosie might soon succumb, too. Perhaps the nurse was right and the twitch of her finger was only a reflex. She was still deep in a coma, and the prognosis was poor. Now there were new threats to address. Apparently, I was on the killer's agenda and now so was Pauline, who until very recently had been a prime suspect in the case. There was still that old curmudgeon, Walter, but the only thing he'd done to incriminate himself in this so far was damage Rosie's lawn with weed killer. A spiteful act, true, and acts like that can foretell of blacker intentions. Still, he was old, ill, and just didn't seem to me to have the makings of a murderer.

I always do my best thinking while I'm walking with Cruiser, so I decided a walk in the forest might be just what I needed to organize my thoughts and perhaps come up with a new theory or two while I was at it. The only trouble with that idea was that my visiting dog sitter, Nona, wasn't home, so I also had to take Rags and Lang Po along with me. I wondered if I shouldn't be launching a dog walking business along with my kennel. Lately, some people in Tahoe didn't seem to be taking too kindly to anything to do with dogs, whether it was a dog walk park or a dog psychic, and particularly the dirty dog who was being referred to as the Sirius Killer by locals.

These last autumn days were turning out to be truly the dog days in Tahoe. Dog lovers were on high alert, including yours truly. No caring owner left his or her dog unattended anywhere for very long. Dog-sitting services were overbooked. People checked their yards carefully for foreign substances, in case someone might try to harm Spot or Fluffy. The dog didn't get put out at night, or even very much in the daytime. Lonely backyard dogs suddenly became indoor dogs, and dogs stayed firmly attached to their leashes at all times. Dog bites and attacks were virtually non-existent, because dogs were kept under control.

It was ironic that because of the threats from the Sirius Killer, dog owners had been forced to become more responsible and more attentive to their pets. However, that didn't erase the terrible possibility that one of those beloved pets or their doting owners might come to harm.

A cool breeze rocked the pine boughs as I led all three dogs up the trail near the cabin. I kept them on the leash because I not only wanted to keep a close eye on them, but I also didn't know how well Rags or Lang Po were trained to heel off-leash. Either dog was small enough to make a fine *hors d'oeuvre* for some hungry coyote. Even though coyotes aren't usually bold enough to make their presence known to humans, they are always in the vicinity of a potential easy meal. I knew of one woman who was walking her toy poodle in the forest, when a coyote rushed out from the trees and snatched up her dog in its mouth. That was the last she ever saw of her beloved pet. She was heartbroken. I didn't want the same thing to happen to my two small charges.

The only trouble with walking all three dogs on their leashes was that each one had a different idea of where he wanted to go. I had retractable leashes and fed the dogs as much leash as possible. This turned out to be a mistake. Rags trotted along, pausing occasionally to water the scenery. Lang Po was so small and fat that he couldn't cover ground very fast. Cruiser, on the other paw, was his usual scent-obsessed self and wanted to stop at every single pine or shrub to sniff and piddle. His goal, of course, was to water the entire forest before we went back to the cabin.

Rags saw a squirrel run up a tree and gave chase. Lang Po followed suit, but scampered right through a clump of manzanita to reach the same tree. Cruiser looked up momentarily from his sniffing, decided the squirrel wasn't worth the effort, and continued circling a pine tree while he read the daily pee mail. By the time I realized what was going on, all three dogs were hopelessly tangled in the underbrush, their leashes braided like Maypole ribbons.

It was too late to retract the cords of the leashes. I'd end up having to drag Lang Po through the sharp manzanita bushes. Instead, I dropped the handles of the leashes on the ground, walked over to each dog, and unfastened the leash from its collar. I just hoped that Rags and Lang Po would mind me. I didn't really have any worries about Rags, but Lang Po was another matter. He was more accustomed to training his owner than the other way around. Not that Cruiser ever did that to me!

While unwinding the leashes from the tangle of manzanita, yelping and cursing as the thorns poked my fingers, I heard a chorus of yapping in the woods to my right. It sounded like Rags and Lang Po were closing in on Mr. Squirrel. Before they could wander further, I hurried toward the commotion. I discovered that they were focused not on the tree branches but on something out in the forest. I surveyed the area, searching for some movement to signal the presence of the coyote pack I knew roamed this area, but I saw nothing. Suddenly, Cruiser's lips curled in a growl. Then he let out a howl that resonated from his long body like an alpenhorn. Well versed in Cruiser's particular dialect of Dogspeak, I knew this melodious display was a warning that something was watching us from out in the forest, and it wasn't Rocket J. Squirrel or Wile E. Coyote.

30

Ordinarily, I feel at home in the forest, where the wind murmurs through the towering pines and Nature speaks to me through her many creatures. But now, alone, with all three dogs on high alert, I knew something out there meant us harm. I thought I saw something move among the trees a hundred or so yards away — a tall, hulking figure. I was reminded of that terrifying winter when the Tahoe Terror stalked these same woods.

Cruiser growled louder, and his neck ruff spiked in unison with every hair on my body. This was serious. I felt a familiar warning tingle in my gut.

"Time to go, boys!" I said. I quickly tethered the dogs on their leashes and made tracks down the hill in the general direction of the cabin, all three dogs yapping and bellowing in the excitement of the chase. I felt like I was in a foxhunt, only without the horse. Lady MacBean running to hounds, a pack that consisted of a senior Scottie, a baying Basset Hound, and a portly Pomeranian. Of course, what they didn't know was that we were the ones being chased. Or at least that's what I felt was happening. I didn't pause to look. Sometimes you just know it's best to run, don't look back, and keep on running until you're safe. The only place I knew would make me feel safe right now was inside my cozy cabin behind a dead-bolted door.

As I kept on running, zigzagging through the forest, I imagined a slavering beast breathing down my neck, or the mythical Ong of Washo tribal legend ready to descend upon us at any moment. I felt the same awe and fear I felt as a child around the campfire, listening to Grandfather and other tribal elders weave their tales of fearsome creatures that inhabited the woods and hidden caves of Tahoe. Soon, I glimpsed the welcome sight of my cabin sequestered among the pines. I felt the last few endorphins in my body kick into overdrive as we made the final hundred-yard dash to the back door. It was locked! So was the dog door.

I fumbled in my pockets for the key. The dogs, sensing my panic, scratched at the door for entry, yelping and barking hysterically. Then, through the window, I spotted the key hanging on the key holder beside the telephone. Drat the luck! Nona had locked the door behind me. I'd taught her too well. Actually, it was Tom who had taught his wife and daughter always to lock every door and window whenever we left the house or when we were home alone.

There was only one thing left to do. I'd have to break down the door. I rammed my shoulder hard against the door. It didn't budge. I tried again with no result. This would require more drastic measures. I stepped back a few feet, reining the dogs back with me for a running start. Like a team of linebackers, we all rushed the door at once. Rags and Lang Po yelped at the top of their lungs and Cruiser was the cheerleader, bellowing, "Go, team, go! Break that line!"

A split second before we connected with the door, it opened. A mass of surprised fur flew through the back door, toenails skidding and scrabbling on the slick linoleum, dragging an equally surprised middle-aged woman face first across the kitchen floor at the end of three retractable leashes.

"What on earth?" Nona said, looking as surprised as the rest of us.

"Close the door and lock it, Nona!"

Seeing the hectic condition of her mother and the dogs, she did as she was told.

"What's wrong? You look as though you've seen a ghost."

"Hold on a sec. Been running . . ." I panted, along with Cruiser, Rags, and Lang Po. The linoleum was beginning to glisten from the pools of drool from Cruiser.

"Why?"

"Something chased us all the way down the mountain."

"What was chasing you?"

"I don't know."

Nona peeked outside. "I don't see anything. Are you sure? I know it's almost Halloween, Mother, but . . ."

"Of course, I'm sure. The dogs saw it, too." I peered out the kitchen window into the woods. For a second, I fancied I saw the same hideous creature I'd seen leering at me through the window that winter of the Tahoe Terror, but Nona was right. Nothing was there.

"Well, whatever it was is gone now, so you can relax."

"Easy for you to say. You weren't being chased by a Yeti, or whatever it was out there."

"I think you're letting your overactive

imagination run away with you again."

My head told me she was right, but my instincts told me different. So did Cruiser's. He was still growling at the back door. "I thought you'd already left."

"I did, but I came back."

"I was sure I left the door unlocked while I went to walk the dogs."

"You did. I locked it again. You've always told me to lock all the doors when I'm home alone."

"You did right, honey. Why'd you come back, anyway?"

"I was just about to leave when I got a call from my boyfriend. He's taking me to the Bark in the Park Ball. Isn't that great?"

"Yes, great." So much for my hopes of matching Nona with Addison.

"He said he might drop over for a few minutes. He wants to meet you."

"What for?"

"I don't know. I guess he's used to being polite to people he doesn't know." Nona didn't think I picked up on her innuendo that I wasn't usually very polite to her boyfriends. She was right. I knew that someday she would find Mr. Right, and I would see less of her than I already do. Perhaps she might end up moving much farther away from me than San Francisco. At least her newest boyfriend was local, so maybe I should be a little more hospitable to this one than the rest.

"What time is he coming over?"

"He was supposed to be here half an hour ago."

"I'm a fright. If I'm going to be entertaining guests, I'd better go freshen up."

"You don't have to entertain him, I just want you to meet him, maybe offer him a cup of coffee or something." Nona glanced at her Rolex; her modeling career was really starting to pay off. I doubted I'd ever own a Rolex, just a Rolodex. I was ashamed to admit it, but it was hard not to feel a wee bit jealous of my daughter's success sometimes. "That is, if he ever gets here."

Nona is a lot like her mom, at least in some respects. She dislikes tardiness. No-shows are another matter entirely. Unlike some in her profession, Nona is no prima donna. She is always punctual for all her photo shoots. As the hour grew later and later, and Nona's gentleman caller still hadn't shown or bothered to call, she was vexed, but she didn't suspect the same thing I did — she'd been stood up, brokenhearted again. I hoped she wasn't destined to be a loner her whole life, like her mom.

31

When I came out of the bathroom, showered and deslobbered from my adventure in the woods with the pack, Nona was still waiting for her friend.

"He's still not here yet?"

"No, he's not." Nona's pretty brow was crinkled in a frown. She was angry, and she was hurt.

I didn't like seeing my daughter go through this all the time. She met all kinds of interesting men in her modeling work, men from all over the world. Guys with panache and lots of money who don't mind lavishing it on a woman. She'd even dated a prince once. The only trouble was, most of the men she dated were jerks, as she'd found out on more than one occasion. The truth is, most men are intimidated by her beauty and intelligence.

I didn't know whether to be happy or sad that her date hadn't shown. Being admittedly overprotective and possessive of my only child, I dreaded the day she might marry and live abroad with one of the exotic men she was always meeting. I would be happy as a burger-fed basset if she settled down in Tahoe near her mother to live a more sedate life. That was all mist in a crystal ball, though. Right now, I had a daughter who needed some distraction. What better diversion is there for a young, fashion-conscious gal like Nona than a little power shopping?

"Come on, Nonie, you and I are going to the mall."

"Actually, you know where I'd rather go?"

"Where?"

"To The Classic Attic."

"A second-hand store? That's not your usual style, is it?"

"I'm shopping for a Halloween costume, not a designer dress."

"Well, I'm sure you can find whatever it is you're looking for at the Attic. They have tons of costumes this time of year."

"Great! Let's go!"

The dogs were all worn out from chasing squirrels and who knows what else in the woods. They wouldn't miss us for an hour or so. Lang Po had reclaimed his throne on Tom's chair, Rags was curled up on the rug by the hearth, and Cruiser, as usual, was sprawled full-length across his hairy pillow on the sofa, drooling and snoring away. He didn't even blink an eye when the deadbolt clicked. All three dogs were embarking on some serious naptime.

The Classic Attic was always busy this time of year. The manikins in the window were costumed for Halloween, and the store was well-stocked with all kinds of fun clothes and accessories, including wigs, jewelry, makeup, and even some used stage costumes. Those were rental only, though, and expensive. There was also the standard assortment of pre-packaged disguises: witches, pirates, devils, and French maids. Most shoppers preferred to pick and choose items to make up their own Halloween costumes. It was more fun to be creative, and Nona and I were getting into the spirit. So had the clerk. She was total Goth from head to toe, even to her black lipstick and fingernails. Knowing today's youth, though, this was probably everyday attire, not a Halloween costume. Nona decided to try on some of the black lipstick the clerk was wearing. Then she streaked on some silver glitter eyeshadow.

I wasn't going to the ball like my pretty young daughter, but Cruiser and I always wore costumes on Halloween for the benefit of the trick-or-treaters. I never get too elaborate with his costumes, though, because one good shake usually dislodges everything, as it had at the Howloween contest.

The Classic Attic isn't the only place that gets into the spirit of Halloween every year. Local pet stores like Petropolis and the Haute Hydrant cash in on the holiday, too. They had sold out nearly every canine costume in their stores to the Howloween doggie dress-up contest contenders.

I had planned to use the same Sherlock Bones and Watson costumes we wore for the Howloween event, but while costume shopping with Nona I soon found myself in the mood for more dress-up fun. I was prepared to burn a little credit card plastic in the Attic; what I wasn't prepared for was another pre-Halloween fright.

I had collected an assortment of costumes and slipped into one of the dressing rooms to try them on. The person who'd been in the stall before me had left some costumes hanging on the hook, so I grabbed all of them at once to move them to the other hook and make room for mine. I'm not a screamer, except when I see particularly large, hairy spiders, but I couldn't suppress the surprised screech that brought Nona running on the double, with the Morticia clone hot on her heels.

"Mom, what's wrong?" Nona, dressed in black fishnet stockings and a matching vinyl miniskirt, turned a few male heads and even a few female ones in the shop as she hurried to my stall.

"I found this in here." I held up a blue plastic groomer's leash, the same kind the Sirius Killer had used. "Did either of you see who was in this dressing room before me?"

"No," Nona and the clerk said in unison.

"Is this some kind of prank? If it is, it's not very funny." I looked at Nona. Nona looked at the clerk.

"Actually, we carry those in the store, Ma'am."

"You carry dog groomer leads?" I said. "Whatever for?"

"Oh, haven't you heard? It's, like, a totally hot item this year. Everyone's dressing up as the Sirius Killer, or at least what they think the dude looks like, 'cause nobody really knows, but, like, they all buy the leashes, you know? You'll find more of them over there on the rack by the front door. They're only two dollars and ninety-nine cents. I put them right up front and

207

the manager thought it was, like, really cool I did that because, like, everyone's been asking for them the minute they come in the store, and . . ."

I'd had enough of this Heavenly Valley Girl jabber. My temples were beginning to throb. I had to get out of the store quick, before my head exploded. "Nona, go get changed, will you?"

"But . . ."

"Gotta go. Hurry up, now. I'll meet you in the car."

She knew my "don't mess with Momma" tone. "Okay. I'll just be a minute."

As I walked to the car, I had that same strange feeling I'd experienced while walking the dogs in the woods. I sensed it, as clearly as Cruiser senses the presence of wild creatures in the forest. I was being watched. Followed. Targeted.

32

I sat in my car outside The Classic Attic, growing more impatient by the minute. Where the heck was Nona? What was taking her so long? As I waited for her, I saw someone else leave the store. It was Pauline. I hadn't seen her in the shop. How had I missed her? Had she been in one of the dressing rooms? The one next to mine, perhaps? Had the blue leash really been left by another shopper or was it some kind of warning? Could Pauline and the Sirius Killer be one in the same? I don't know if she had spotted me or not, but she quickly disappeared into the Candlewick, a New Age store that carries incense, meditation tapes, and, of course, candles. My mind was swimming with questions, and I had answers for none of them. Finally, I spotted Nona dashing from The Classic Attic, still dressed in the costume she'd been trying on in the store and carrying a large paper sack. For a moment, I pictured the innocent little girl in a Cinderella gown, toting a bag of candy twice her size. Could this be the same girl I remembered from years ago? Several bystanders stopped to gawk at the spectacle of what appeared to be the Happy Hooker pulling a Halloween heist.

"Why didn't you change? People will think you're a prostitute."

"I don't care what they think."

"Get in, smarty hotpants!" I shifted the car into drive and rolled away from the parking space. "What took you so long in there, anyway?"

"I had to pay for my costume. I hurried as fast as I could, but that checker was so slow."

"Her mouth sure wasn't. I never heard anyone talk so fast but say so little."

Nona checked out her black lipstick in the car mirror. "You can say that again. I thought she'd never shut up."

"That lipstick is grotesque. You're not going to wear it all the time, are you?"

"Relax, Mom. It's just for Halloween. I'll leave it for freaks like that clerk to wear every day. By the way, why were you in such a rush to leave?"

"I suddenly got a really bad vibe in there."

"Because of the leash?"

"Partly."

"It was only a costume accessory."

"Maybe that's what bothered me. People dressing up like a murderer who is still out there killing people. How creepy is that?"

"Creepy is what Halloween is all about."

"I can understand dressing up as fictional movie monsters like Dracula, Freddy Kruger, or Michael Myers, but I really don't want to see some little kid dressed like Charles Manson or Ted Bundy or the Sirius Killer on my doorstep shouting, 'Trick or treat!'"

"I'd have to agree," Nona said. "But these days anything goes."

"I guess you're right. Nothing is beyond good taste at Halloween or any other time."

I cruised through the parking lot, waiting to see if Pauline came out of the Candlewick. I wanted to follow her next move, but now it was Nona who was getting impatient to leave.

"I thought you were in a hurry. Why are we circling the parking lot?"

"I saw Pauline come out of The Classic Attic."

"So?"

"If she was in there, it seems strange that she didn't come up and say hello."

"Maybe she didn't see you. She might

have been in a dressing room, like we were."

"Yes, that's what worries me."

"Why should that . . . ? Oh, I see. You think she left that blue leash in your stall to scare you or something? But I don't get it. Are you saying you think Pauline's the Sirius Killer?"

"She's certainly not above suspicion. Besides, she just went into a candle shop. The killer uses candles, remember? Seems too coincidental to me."

"Pauline's a dog psychic, Mother."

"Animal communicator."

"Whatever. The point is she cares about dogs. Why would she want to hurt them or the people who love them?"

"Some folks will pretend to be anything, especially if they stand to profit from it — even dog lovers. Why do you think people are in the dog breeding business?"

"Because they're crazy about dogs, I guess."

"That's true, and reputable breeders truly care about the animals they raise, or at least I like to think they do. But as you well know, there are plenty more who just breed them for the money and don't care a whit about the health or welfare of the dogs."

"I see what you're getting at. What better front could there be for someone who wants to do harm to people and their pets than a business like Pauline's?"

"Exactly."

"That is a pretty creepy thought."

"Well, it's like you said, honey."

"What's that?"

"Creepy is what Halloween's all about."

33

When I drove up to the cabin, I heard Cruiser barking. It wasn't his usual welcome home bark. I recognized it right away as his intruder bark. I was immediately concerned that something might be wrong and ran for the front door. Nona was hot on my heels in her Halloween hooker hot pants. I fumbled for my keys, then dropped them, trying to aim for the keyhole.

"May I be of any assistance?"

"Huh?" I hadn't noticed the young man sitting on my porch.

"Addison!" Nona and I spoke in unison.

"You two know each other?" Nona said.

"Yes, we've met before," I said.

"You have? Where? When?"

"Your mother and I met at the Howloween event earlier this month," Addison volunteered.

"Under the most unfortunate circumstances imaginable," I added. What a shock Abby's death must have been for him, and to find her *that* way.

"Unfortunate, indeed," Addison affirmed, studying me through a flaxen forelock.

"Anyway, this worked out perfectly. I've been wanting to introduce you two." I was glad Cupid had shot his arrow for me.

"What happened to you, anyway, Addison?" Nona said.

"I'm terribly sorry I was late. I had to make a stop on the way over." A sharp dresser, the crease in Addison's gray gabardine slacks could slice butter. And the butter wouldn't have melted in his mouth. The collar of his white shirt was so stiffly starched, it could have served for a boomerang. "Here, Nona. These are for you." Addison presented Nona with a dozen long-stemmed red roses.

"Oh, thank you. These are lovely. How did you know I adore roses?"

"Because you are as lovely as a rose." Addison was busy surveying Nona's own long stems. "That's quite some outfit."

"Oh, this is my costume for the Ball."

"Indeed."

"Come on in, Addison. It's cold out here."

"Oh, uh, all right. Your dog doesn't bite, does he?"

"Only biscuits and bad guys." I unlocked

the door and Cruiser did the welcome home, where have you been so long dance, with backup performances by Rags and Lang Po.

Nona grabbed her boyfriend by the hand and led him past Cruiser, who gave him a good going-over, smelling the cuffs of his pants and working upward. Rags sprang up like a jack-in-the-box, pawing at Addison's leg. Addison shook Rags off and nudged Cruiser aside as discreetly as possible, while trying his best to avert the embarrassment of a nose poking at his crotch. He never stooped to pet or fawn over any of the dogs, as most of my visitors would when met by such an enthusiastic greeting. Cat person, I surmised. The only time he gave them any attention whatsoever was when Lang Po started to hump his leg. He extracted himself from the Pomeranian's amorous grip.

"Off!" All three dogs obeyed my command and retired to their posts. "Sorry, Addison," I said. "All my guests have to endure the scratch and sniff test. Looks like you passed."

"That's good news." A nervous little giggle escaped his lips. Meeting your girlfriend's mother and her randy pack was enough to make any young man edgy.

"Care for some coffee to take the chill off?"

"Sure. It was getting kind of nippy sitting out on your porch so long."

I scooped some French Roast grind into the coffeemaker and flicked it on.

"How long were you waiting for us?" Nona asked.

"Over an hour, I guess."

"Gosh, you didn't have to wait out in the cold for me. You could have just called."

"I know. I didn't want you to think I stood you up or anything."

"Well, I confess that's what I was thinking, Addison."

"So you two are going to the Bark in the Park Ball, eh?" I interjected. "What are you going as, Addison?" I handed him his cup of coffee. He stirred some cream into the steaming beverage and rang the spoon on the rim.

"I haven't decided yet. Now that I've seen Nona's choice of costume, I may have to rethink mine."

"Oh, you already bought a costume, Addison?" I said.

"No, I didn't buy one. I made it."

"You made your costume?" Nona said. I saw the red flags hoisting.

"Yes," Addison replied. "I studied costume design at University."

"From your accent, I gather you've lived in England," I said.

"Yes, until I graduated. I've only recently returned from abroad."

"Which school did you attend there?"

"Cambridge."

"Really? Cambridge. That's very impressive, isn't it, Nona?"

"Yes, very." Nona knew what I was up to.

"It must be wonderful to study at a place with so much history and antiquity. Much different than universities on the West Coast."

"Not so different, really," Addison said. "They have computer technology there, just like here. In fact, I've designed many of my costumes by computer."

"I should have talked to you before I went shopping for my Halloween costume, Addison," Nona said. "You could have whipped me up an Elizabethan gown or something."

"Actually, I did make an Elizabethan gown or two for some Globe Theatre productions in London," Addison said, unaware of her sarcasm. "I can throw something together for you, if you like. There's still time."

"That sounds like a great idea, Nona," I said. I hadn't really liked the idea of her wearing something so revealing in public. The only thing I would have objected to more was if she wore her Victoria's Secret nothings for Halloween. I wouldn't have put it past my brazen daughter.

"Well, I don't know," Nona said.

"Why don't you come with me to Fabric City, and I'll help you choose the materials for your costume," Addison said.

Nona saw me giving her the eagle eye and relented. "Whatever."

"Say, Addison, have you ever thought of designing dog costumes?" I said. "They sell so fast this time of year, the pet shops can't keep them in stock. You could make a lot of money." Then it occurred to me that Addison probably didn't need the money. He was Abigail's sole heir, after all.

"No, I hadn't thought of that. I really don't think of dogs as miniature people, Mrs. MacBean. They're dogs, not children."

"To some of us they are."

Clearly Addison didn't agree, but he was too polite to argue with me, or maybe it was the fact that he was presently outnumbered by dog people of one kind or another.

"Well, I'd better be going," he said, rising. "Thanks for the coffee, Mrs. Mac-Bean. Pleasure to meet you. I'll see you again sometime, I'm sure."

"I hope so."

"I guess I'm going fabric shopping, Mother." Nona was giving me the eagle eye now. "I'll be back as soon as I can."

"No rush, honey. See you later." Nona looked at me strangely as she walked out the door. I think I already knew what she was thinking. After all these years as her mother, we could read each other like a dog-eared book.

We were both wondering whether Addison's Willcox and Gibbs sewed straight or zigzag.

34

No sooner had Nona left with Addison than my three-bark alarm alerted me to another visitor. It was Skip. I could tell he was a man on a mission when he got out of his car so fast he forgot to set the handbrake. He did a quick U-turn as his Jeep started to roll backward. He hopped back in and gave the brake lever a yank just before the car collided with the pine tree.

I met him at the door before he could ring the bell. The doorbell would only start the dogs barking louder. I tried to quiet the pack as I opened the door, but it was no use until after they saw it was Skip. Cruiser stopped his bugling and sounded the retreat. I had to admit I felt safe having the three dogs around to alert me to unexpected visitors, especially with the killer still at large.

"What brings you here in such an all-fired hurry?"

"There's a new development in the Sirius case. I thought you'd want to know."

"You're darned right, I do. Come on in and tell me over coffee. I just brewed some for Nona and her boyfriend."

The sheriff followed me into the kitchen, with all three dogs trailing him like he had bacon strips dangling from his utility belt. He pulled out a chair, spun it around, and mounted it like a horse.

"Nona has a new boyfriend, eh?" Skip commented. "Who's she dating now?"

"Addison Haversham."

"The deceased's nephew?"

"Yes." Skip had a hard time shutting off his crime scene jargon, even when he wasn't at a crime scene. "He seems like a nice young man."

"Better than her last boyfriend, right?"

"That goes without saying." I handed him a cup and poured it to the brim. "So, what's the scoop on Sirius?" Now I was the one using job jargon.

"I just found out something I think may interest you."

"Go on. Cruiser and I are all ears." Cruiser did his best imitation of the RCA Victor dog, but his voluminous ears wouldn't perk up quite right for the full effect.

"It's about Pauline LeBlanc."

"What?"

"She has a criminal record."

"I don't believe it."

"She's done time in the slammer, too."

"You're kidding!"

"Nope. Don't look so shocked, Beanie. I warned you, didn't I?"

"Warned me about what?"

"About her. Pauline. I know these types. They're all the same. They're just clever con artists with a gimmick, that's all. They don't have psychic abilities any more than you or I do. They can't talk to the dead or read your mind. Or your dog's. They're just crooks out to make a quick, dishonest buck off of vulnerable, gullible people."

"Like me, you mean?"

Skip took a long, slow sip of coffee before answering. He knew he was treading on sacred ground and didn't want to end up in sinking in quicksand. "Well, you bought her book, didn't you?"

"Sure, but I buy lots of books."

"The point is she made money off you, just like she does with the other people she sees in her palm reader's parlor."

"Paw."

"Excuse me?"

"Paw reader. She's a pet psychic, remember?"

At that moment, Cruiser reached out his basset-sized paw and planted it firmly on Skip's lap. I wasn't sure whether he was begging for table scraps or whether he was simply playing peacemaker for Skip and me, like he did for Tom and me whenever we argued and our voices became a bit too shrill. It worked like the magic the sheriff said he didn't believe in. But this was a special magic more powerful than any other. It was Dog Magic. We burst into simultaneous gales of laughter at our furry referee. Cruiser barked happily along with us, then retired to his hairy pillow on the sofa when our conversation turned to other things. His work here was done. Time for a nap.

"Are you going to the Bark in the Park Ball, Beanie?"

"I hadn't planned to. Why?"

"I was just wondering if . . ."

"Yes?" Was Skip going to ask me out on a date? Gosh, this was so sudden. And *so* inaccurate. He quickly clarified his intentions before I could misinterpret them.

"Do you think you could come and help me out with surveillance? As I said before, I've got a lot of people out right now with the flu, and I could sure use your help."

"Surveillance? Are you anticipating

some kind of trouble?"

"Could be."

"Expecting a visit from the Sirius Killer, perhaps?"

"Maybe. I figure if anything will draw this mutt-hater out into the open again, it will be the Bark in the Park Ball, with all the dog park sympathizers conveniently in one place."

"I agree. There may never be a better time to nail the suspect than this. Sure, I'll come." *Even without a corsage.* I should have known it would be strictly business. With Skip, everything is always business.

"I need everyone I can enlist to keep a sharp lookout for this Sirius Killer. Folks are scared. If they know we're there, they'll feel more secure."

"So, am I supposed to wear a uniform or something?"

"You'll wear a costume. It's Halloween, remember?"

"I guess I should have tried harder to find a costume when Nona and I went to The Classic Attic."

"There'll be a couple of deputies there, too. They'll also be disguised."

"If everyone's in costume, won't it be hard to tell who are the good guys and the bad guys? If the killer decides to show up,

225

no doubt he'll wear a costume, too."

"We'll have a secret signal, so we can recognize our own people."

"What kind of secret signal?"

Skip pondered a moment. "We'll use the same one they used in *The Sting*." With his sandy blonde hair, Sundance Skip looked vaguely like Robert Redford as he swept an index finger across his nose. The similarity was a little too vague to get very excited about, though. The mask of freckles across his ruddy cheeks spoiled the effect. I'd had a crush on Redford ever since I saw *Butch Cassidy and the Sundance Kid*. In those days, my hair was as long, silky, and dark as Katharine Ross' was — like Nona's is now.

Skip "Butch" Cassidy downed the last of his coffee and plunked the cup down on the table. "Well, I'd better get back to the office. Work waits." He stood up and headed for the door, along with his three-dog escort. Anytime someone headed for the front door, the dogs naturally assumed it was walkies time. Rags and Lang Po pranced at Skip's ankles and Cruiser slapped the sheriff's khaki trouser leg with his long, thick tail.

"Say, wait a minute, Skip. You never did finish telling me about Pauline."

"Oh, that's right. We kind of got side-tracked, didn't we?"

"What did she do to get arrested and thrown in jail?"

"Assault and battery, for one."

"You mean there's more?"

"Yeah. Plenty more. You're not going to like it much, either."

"Oh? Why is that?"

"She was charged with animal cruelty."

35

Although I understood that Pauline was no Pollyanna and a shrewd businesswoman, I was flabbergasted by what Skip had told me about her. I never dreamed she had a criminal record. Assault and battery? And worst of all, animal cruelty? Why would someone who makes her living helping animals and their owners be accused of such a despicable crime? In spite of Skip's negative opinion of Pauline from the get-go and my own suspicions about her, I hadn't really wanted to let myself fully believe that she could be a prime suspect in this case; however, with this latest information, I had to confess that the planchette of my Ouija board was inching toward Yes.

If Madame Pawline was, in fact, our elusive Sirius Killer, she had gone to great lengths to make herself look innocent, even planting evidence to target others and sending herself death threats.

With all that was going on these days, I

was having difficulty meeting my deadlines for the *Tattler*. I'd managed to send off the story about the meteor shower, but I had committed the cardinal sin with an editor — I had missed my deadline. Carla might cut me loose if I let another one slip by and would choose another stringer next time she had an assignment. I couldn't afford that right now. Between trying to leash the Sirius Killer and doing crime surveillance for Skip, I managed to squeeze in time to work on a department piece about the dogfight over Alpine Paws Park.

I had made an appointment to speak to Councilman Grant, so he could bring me up to date on the ongoing battle for the coveted beachfront property. Who would end up the winner in this Dogopoly game was anybody's guess. In the course of obtaining more information on the dog park issue, I was about to uncover more incriminating information about our Madame Pawline.

A powerfully built man, barrel-chested as a bulldog, Grant looked as though he should be tossing the caber in a kilt, not sitting behind a desk in a suit. I knocked on the open door to get his attention. He looked up from his computer screen and smiled broadly. I hadn't had a man smile at me that way for a long time.

"Elsie, I've been expecting you. Please come in and have a seat."

"Thank you, Councilman." Schools of exotic fish began to swim across the monitor at the screensaver start-up.

"No need for such formality. Please call me Colin."

"I won't take much of your time, Colin. I know how busy you must be with all this furor over the proposed dog park."

"Yes, unfortunately, but never too busy to talk to a pretty lady like you."

I smiled, then rifled through my purse for my notepad and pen. Oh, why did they always seem to drop straight to the bottom? Rosie hadn't warned me that the councilman was so charming, and such a shameless flirt. Finally, I found my tools and poised my pen on the pad. "Can you bring me up to date on the dog park?"

"I get correspondence daily from people adamantly opposed to this project, among other things. Hannah Mencken and Sylvia Boyd are driving me crazy. They think the lake is their own private pond and no one else has a right to enjoy it. They'd rather die than see a senior facility or dog park go in next to them. They worked on Abigail constantly to sway the planning commission in their favor before she was . . . well, you know."

"Yes, I know. Abigail was immovable on that, though. She was a dog person and loved her little Pomeranian more than anything. And once Abby made up her mind about something . . . anything . . . that was end of story."

"I'm well aware that she was a driving force on this issue and others in the community," Grant said. "She was also pushing for new regulations on development in Tahoe."

"Oh? What kind of regulations?"

The Councilman's phone rang. "Excuse me a moment. I need to take this call. Please help yourself to some coffee."

"Sure." I spotted the coffee dispenser on a table and pumped some coffee into a Styrofoam cup. I sat back down and scanned the diplomas, licenses, and merit awards you usually see displayed on a busy, successful man's office wall. The only one I found somewhat unique and rather amusing in this collection was a certificate from the Royal Caledonian Saber and Set Academy of Highland Dance, decorated with Scottish heraldry and a pair of ghillies. I laughed as I was reminded of my first date with my late husband, when he took me to the Tartan Ball dressed in full Braveheart regalia. Tom, as my bunions and I soon discovered, had not attended any dance academy. We later enrolled in classes, to no avail. Tom was hopelessly clumsy when it came to cutting a rug.

Still waiting for the councilman to end his call, I glanced at the notepad on his desk, which looked far more orderly than my own. He has a private secretary to arrange things for him, I reasoned. I'm always reading things upside down. It's an odd sort of game I play with myself when I'm bored, or maybe I was dyslexic in a former life. I read the reminder note he'd written to himself on the pad — *Call Scott Re Par Have Rc Pl Em.*

A golf date with some guy named Scott, perhaps? I tried puzzling it out just to amuse myself, but the hieroglyphics made no sense to me. At least he was organized enough to remind himself of his tasks on paper. Commendable. I wondered if he gave private lessons. A gal in her late forties could do a lot worse than hooking up with a well-rounded guy like Colin Grant.

"Sorry, I had to take that call," Grant said. "It's been pretty busy around here lately, since the dog park battle broke out."

"I'm sure it has." Suddenly I got this

funny image of Councilman Grant standing on a battlefield in the Scottish highlands flanked by an army of dogs ranging in size from Scottish deerhound to Scottish terrier. Dressed in his tartan kilt, a smear of blue war paint staining his craggy face, beating his broadsword on his shield, he shouts the battle cry, "Wal-kies! Wal-kies!" The dogs join in the cry in a cacophony of woofs, barks, and yips, then they're all howling and dashing across the field into battle. Except I realized I didn't really know which side of the dog park battle the councilman was on. Being a politician meant you had to stay on middle ground concerning community issues, or at least appear neutral, even if you aren't.

"Now, where were we?" Colin said.

"You were talking about regulations."

"Oh, right."

"Before we continue, I couldn't help noticing your award on the wall. You do Scottish dancing?"

"Yes, have done for years." He must have been reading my mind when he added, "I'm a lot lighter on my feet than I look. Do you dance, Elsie?"

"I love to dance. I've always wanted to learn the Scottish country dances. My husband had two left feet, unfortunately."

"Perhaps you'd like to come to one of our club's ceilis. There's one coming up next week, in fact."

"Sure, sounds like fun."

"Great, I could use a new partner."

He wasn't the only one. I became aware of Colin's earthen brown eyes studying me from beneath those wooly brows and began to fidget like a teenager in spite of myself. I figured I'd best guide the conversation back to business, before I became too stuck in the manly mire. "I didn't mean to interrupt you before. You were saying something about regulations . . ."

"Hmmm? Oh, uh, yes. Well, Lake Tahoe has a lot of old motels and certain kinds of businesses that are creating a, shall we say, cluttered look in the basin."

"You mean trashy?"

"Yes, I suppose you could put it that way, but not in writing, please."

"No, of course not." I liked a man with a diplomatic way about him. In his line of work, he had to be.

"Anyway, these new restrictions would mandate that some of the older motels be either updated or demolished and would prohibit certain kinds of commerce in the area, particularly along Lake Tahoe Boulevard and, obviously, the shoreline."

"Such as?"

"Oh, like junky souvenir shops, run-down restaurants, quickie wedding chapels, palmistry parlors, that kind of thing. The goal is to maintain more of a Tyrolean resort flavor, as has been done with the new tram and skate rink at Heavenly."

"More Sun Valley instead of Sin City."

"Exactly!" Councilman Grant's furry eyebrows formed a determined unibrow that bisected his broad forehead.

"That would also preclude the addition of Indian gaming establishments, I assume."

"Correct. At least along that corridor."

"Tell me, would a pet psychic business also fall under those new regulations?"

"According to Abigail Haversham, it did. In fact, I heard that someone in the community was trying to keep from having her business license revoked, and Abby was making it very difficult."

"You're referring to Pauline LeBlanc?"

"Yes, that was her name, I believe. There was a bit of trouble over that, I heard."

"What kind of trouble?"

"This LeBlanc woman got into some hot water with the law."

"Do you know what the circumstances were?"

"I heard she assaulted Mrs. Haversham."

"Over losing her license?"

"Apparently. Abigail filed charges against her. It's not that she was against the idea of pet psychics per se, because she liked animals, it's just that she was dedicated to making Tahoe the best it could be. She felt that certain things detracted, you see."

"I understand, Councilman, but it seems a bit unfair. The unemployment rate is high enough in this area. What will people do for jobs, if their small businesses are taken away from them?"

Grant shrugged. "I suppose they'll just have to find other work."

"Easier said than done in the country's current economic climate." I expected more than just a nod of agreement. "Many of the businesses along Lake Tahoe Boulevard have been there for decades. Some are even a part of Tahoe's history. In fact, the building that Pauline occupies was one of the first to be built here. It used to be a Pony Express station."

"Yes, I know," Grant said. "There was some talk from the historical society about preservation, but it's on the shortlist for the wrecking ball. Unfortunately, the old must make way for the new."

"As my ancestors discovered."

My comment was drowned out by the buzzing of the intercom. Grant pushed the button to answer.

"Call for you on line one, sir."

"Thanks, Jeanine. You'll have to excuse me, Elsie. I really must take this call in private."

"Sure, I understand how busy you are. Thanks for your time, Councilman."

"Colin, remember?" He flashed an election poster smile at me. "I'll be in touch with you about the ceili."

"Thanks for your time." I don't think he heard me. My farewell wave was met with a distracted nod as he cued me to shut the door behind me as I left.

36

I drove home from the councilman's office via Lake Tahoe Boulevard, still thinking about what he'd told me about Pauline. Despite the colorful Halloween displays in store windows and pumpkins and cornstalks decorating the sidewalks, I could see the reasoning behind the proposed regulatory changes. Driving eastward, a string of seedy motels and tacky souvenir shops lined the avenue up to Ski Run Boulevard. Once I passed Ski Run Boulevard and neared the glitzy casinos of Stateline, the atmosphere transformed dramatically to the look of a Swiss village. The new tram conveyed tourists to Heavenly Summit on a thin silver cable, affording a view the angels would envy. Even the McDonald's Restaurant looked like a little slice of Switzerland.

I had to admit that a little sprucing up was in order here and there in Tahoe, but I didn't feel that it had to put everyone out of business and on the welfare line in the process. The proposed changes certainly wouldn't affect the casinos, which in my opinion were probably the most offensive eyesores of all and historically had had the worst effect on the community since Lucky Baldwin opened the first casino at Tallac in the nineteenth century. In Pauline's defense, a lone pet psychic seemed to be the least of Tahoe's problems. What I didn't know, though, was how far she was prepared to go to protect her interests.

I had seen Pauline arguing with Abby outside her pet psychic booth that day, just before she predicted someone was about to die. Had her anger over being forced out of her business gotten out of hand and baited her to lash out, or rather "leash out," at Abby? Rosie was also a member of the council. Had she also been a victim of Pauline's wrath? And if Pauline was as psychic as she professed to be, she already knew that I suspected her of the crimes. One thing was certain: I'd been threatened. That put not only me but also my loved ones at risk; namely, Nona and Cruiser. I knew I had to get to the bottom of this soon, before we all ended up victims of the Sirius Killer.

I'd have to pay Pauline another visit, but first I felt I needed to go check on the home front to be sure all was in order. I was getting more and more nervous about leaving Nona and Cruiser unattended for very long. As I drove up to the house and saw Nona's car in the driveway and a giant pumpkin on the porch waiting to be carved, relief swept over me. Unless the Great Pumpkin had arrived early, I surmised that Nona had lugged the scale-tipping gourd home. She'd also planted a handcrafted scarecrow beside the walkway. His straw hair and freckled, grinning face reminded me so much of Skip that I laughed.

I heard the canine chorus harmonizing inside as I stepped onto the porch. Nona was already opening the door by the time I fished my keys from the bottom of my bag. I was relieved that she was home and all inhabitants were accounted for.

"Hey, Mom! You're just in time to help me make my new costume. I picked out this great fabric at the store."

"I thought Addison was going to help you make your costume."

"Nah, I decided I'd rather you and I do it together."

"That's nice, Nona, but I haven't sewn a stitch since you were in diapers. My sewing machine is probably rusted solid by now."

"Oh, don't be silly. It'll still work fine.

Go get it and let's try it out."

"All right." I was disappointed that she'd given Addison the slip, but it had been years since Nona and I had done anything domestic as mother and daughter. I went to the storage closet and pulled out my old Singer Featherweight. Tom had bought it for me when we were first married, and I'd put it to good use making curtains, slipcovers, and the like for our first little house. I'd made all of Nona's baby clothes on it, too. It only sewed a straight stitch, but I had rarely needed anything more.

I had no use for a machine that sewed fifty fancy stitches. The trusty little Featherweight had always been more than enough appliance for me. I had told Nona I would pass my little antique on to her someday when she got married. Since that event didn't seem imminent, I'd decided I might as well go ahead and give it to her. Perhaps she'd eventually settle down with a good man and put it to good use, sewing clothes for her own children. At least a mother could hope. I had a feeling it wasn't going to be with Addison Haversham, though.

The shadows in the room had grown long by the time Nona and I had her pattern cut out and she was ready to start stitching. I had set the Singer up on the kitchen table for her and was making us some cocoa. The machine hummed and the needle bobbed smoothly through the fabric, as though not a day had passed since it was last used.

"How did your shopping trip go?" I asked as I stirred the cocoa.

"Fine," Nona said, pretending to concentrate on her stitching. I knew whenever she said "fine" that meant anything but.

"What's the matter, didn't things go well with you and Addison today?"

"I told you everything's fine, Mother. Say, are you going to stir that cocoa all day?"

I took out Nona's mug I kept especially for her visits and poured her a cup of cocoa. Then I poured one for myself and sat down at the table. I didn't say anything but just watched her sew. She reached for the mug and took a sip, trying her best to ignore me as she guided the fabric beneath the presser foot. She let a curtain of chestnut hair obscure her view of me watching her, as she continued sewing. We both knew the tactic wasn't going to work for long. She was too much like her dad. Silence always wore her down. I sensed she was about to spill, like a spring runoff at

Eagle Falls. She did.

"Okay, here's the thing, Mom. Addison's weird. I'm not so sure I want to date this guy."

"Why, because I like him?"

"No, that's not it."

"What then?"

Nona was grasping for any shred of evidence to sway me in her favor. "Well, for one thing, I think he's gay."

"Let's see, now," I said, check-listing on my palm again. "Rich, handsome, well-connected, educated, costume designer — yep, he must be gay all right."

"Trust me, living in San Francisco I've developed a straight eye for the queer guy."

"Just because he knows how to sew doesn't mean he's gay, Nona. There are plenty of well-known clothing designers who are as straight as one of Grandfather's arrows. You've told me that yourself."

"I'm like you. I just get a gut feeling about people sometimes."

"You didn't get it until today. What's the real reason behind this sudden change of heart?"

"I've told you before, I don't want you meddling in my love life. Don't you have enough to do, poking into every-one else's business around here?"

"Does that tongue of yours come with a Julienne blade?"

"I'm not trying to be mean. I just hate it when you stick your nose in my personal business, that's all. I'm not one of your cases. I don't need solving."

"Guess I can't help it. I'm just naturally nosy, like Cruiser. Must be the line of work I'm in. Or maybe I'm just trying to fulfill the job duties I applied for when you were born."

Just then the phone rang. Saved by the bell. I didn't want to get into another argument with Nona over her love life, or lack thereof. She was more like her mother than I cared to admit.

"Hello?"

"Hello, Elsie?" said a male voice on the other end. "Colin here."

"Oh, hi, Colin." I assumed he must have forgotten to tell me something while I was at his office.

Nona stopped sewing, but I knew it wasn't out of courtesy. It was so she could eavesdrop. Yep, just like her mother. Fortunately, she could only hear my half of the conversation, which consisted of one-word responses. I suppose I was too dumbfounded that I was being asked out on a date.

I hung up the phone and went back to the table to sip my cocoa.

"Who was that?"

"Oh, just Councilman Grant."

"Your face is all red, Mom. Are you okay?"

"The cocoa is too hot, that's all. You'd better finish your sewing."

"Not until you tell me what that call was about. What did the councilman want?"

The moccasin was on the other foot now. "Nothing. He just wanted to ask me a question."

"What kind of question? He asked you out on a date, didn't he? Is he taking you to the Bark in the Park Ball?"

"No, he's not taking me to the Ball. Now who's sticking her pretty little nose in *my* personal business?" I smiled and chucked her under the chin. "Now get busy and finish that costume, nosy Nona."

She smiled and went back to guiding the fabric through the Featherweight's presser foot. I was glad she hadn't pressed me any further for details about my invitation to dance at the ceili with Colin Grant, but it was just a matter of time. I knew that, like Cruiser with a Kong toy, she would eventually manage to get all the goodies out of me.

37

On the way to Pauline's place next morning, I could almost smell snow in the air.
Cozy woolens had already displaced the
airy cottons in my closet, and I had once
more donned my pink plaid deerstalker for
extra warmth. Winter was closing in fast,
like I hoped I was closing in on the Sirius
Killer.

My husband, Tom, had never liked
Tahoe winters, perhaps because he was the
one who had done all the snow shoveling,
but I had loved these snowy mountains
since childhood, when I used to visit my
grandparents. Unlike my ancestors, who
traditionally descended pine-mantled peaks
to the sage-speckled deserts of Carson
Valley before the first snowflakes fell, I ascended to the Lake of the Sky to catch
snowflakes on my tongue, throw snowballs
with playmates, and revel in the wonders
of winter at Tahoe.

When I entered Pauline's paw-reading
parlor, I suddenly felt like I was a castaway

on a tropical island. The sound of trickling fountains and a profusion of plants gave the room a hothouse climate. I wasted no time shedding my coat and hat. The proprietor didn't come out to greet me right away, so I assumed she was doing a reading with a client in the back room. I sat down to wait. After fifteen minutes, I saw Sally Applebaum emerge from behind the beaded curtain with her Yorkshire terrier. I gave Fabian a pet. He licked my hand in greeting.

"Hello, Beanie," Sally said. "How are you?" Her plump apple cheeks were two Washington Reds.

"I'm doing fine, Sally, and you?"

"Great! This woman is a wonder! Fabian told Pauline why he won't eat."

"And why is that?"

"Because I threw away his Buggy Bear."

"I'm assuming Buggy Bear is a favorite toy?"

"Yes, I'll have to order him another right away. Where's Cruiser? Is he going to have a reading with Pauline, too?"

"He's with Nona right now. Besides, he's already had one."

"Well, he must have another. I never knew my dog was thinking all this before. It's just wonderful to be able to read your dog's thoughts! Bye."

"See you, Sally."

"Come along, Fabian." Sally walked to the front door, then paused a moment. "Oh, by the way, the order Nona placed came in. I've included some tasty new treats. Let me know if Cruiser likes them."

"Will do." I brushed a hand over Fabian's silky coat as he trotted after his mistress out the door.

Pauline stepped through the beaded curtain to greet me. She seemed pleased to see me until she noticed I didn't have my dog, and became even less friendly when I started off asking questions again, especially when they turned once more to the subject of the killings. At first I wasn't sure if she was going to ask me to leave, but she invited me into her sanctuary, where other customers who might come in wouldn't overhear our conversation.

"I don't know what you can expect me to know about Abby's murder. You don't really think I'm the killer, do you?"

Despite my growing suspicions, I deflected her direct question with a direct question of my own. "It's come to my attention that you have a criminal record, Pauline."

"Who told you that?" She tried to play

innocent, but the look in her eyes told me I was correct.

I answered her question with another question. "Isn't it true that you were arrested for trespassing and assault?"

"Yes, I was, but . . ."

"And also animal cruelty."

"It was that crazy old Abigail Haversham who was to blame for that. She's had it in for me ever since I opened this place. She was determined to put me out of business. Her, and a lot of others in this town."

"Like who?"

"Well . . . Rosie Clark, for one."

"Did you ever pay Mrs. Clark a visit, Pauline?"

"No, I don't even know where she lives."

"But you admit you did have a bone to pick with both these women."

"Sure, I was angry with them for making trouble for me, but I swear I never hurt either of them."

"Then how do you account for the assault charge?"

"I can explain that."

"I'm all ears, Pauline." If Cruiser had been with me, he would have been, too.

"That had nothing to do with her. It happened a long time ago. I was arrested in a demonstration in college, when I struck a police officer with my protest sign. It was justified, though. He whacked me over the head with his nightstick."

"I guess I can understand that. I'd probably have done the same. So it was self-defense, then?"

"Yes."

"That doesn't explain the incident of animal cruelty, though." I was far less inclined to overlook this offense.

"It was just a silly misunderstanding, really. I was attacked by Mrs. Haversham's Pomeranian. You've met Lang Po, I believe."

"Yes, he is a rather testy little fellow."

"Well, he was nipping at my ankles and I just nudged him away with my foot. He yelped in surprise; she misconstrued it as pain, and accused me of kicking and injuring her dog. I tried explaining to her that I hadn't hurt her dog, but she filed a complaint and it went on record as animal abuse."

"I see. Was that what you were arguing about with her outside your booth the day of the Howloween event?"

"No, I told you before. We weren't arguing. I was just trying to persuade her not to close up my business. That's why I offered her a complimentary reading. To demonstrate that what I do is legit."

I knew very well I was treading in old moccasin prints here, but I was purposely asking her the same questions to see if she changed her story. She didn't. "Yes, but you were the last person to see her alive, Pauline, and Lang Po was poisoned. You fed him something during the reading. I saw you do it."

"It was just a treat stuffed with peanut butter. They're those new ones called Peanut Butter Pups."

"Oh, I've heard of those." That must be what Sally had told me about.

"I know this looks bad, but I swear I had nothing to do with any of what's been happening. You've got to believe me. If I'm implicated in this, my father will never speak to me again as long as I live. He's already practically disowned me. I've been trying to make amends, but this would ruin any chance of a reconciliation."

"I'm a little confused, Pauline. Who is your father?"

"Why, I thought you knew. Everyone says we look just alike. My father is Reverend Paul Ramseth."

"But your name is LeBlanc."

"I use my mother's maiden name. He asked me to, because he doesn't want to be linked in any way with my business. He forgets he named me after himself." Her ebony eyes misted.

Pauline almost had me convinced of her innocence, until I discovered something that could not be so easily explained away. She stood up and walked to a storage cupboard. As she searched for some tissues, she knocked over a box that was stacked precariously on some others. When it tipped over, the contents spilled out. A tangle of bright blue plastic groomers' leashes lay on the floor.

38

Pauline offered a plausible explanation for the groomers' leashes she had accidentally overturned in my presence, but I was unconvinced. Sure, she might have been keeping them for the animal shelter because, as she said, she volunteered there and sometimes fostered dogs for the facility. I was trying my best to believe her, because at a deeper level I empathized with Pauline, a woman struggling to make an honest buck. Even so, the Tarot deck was really starting to stack against her in my mind.

Cruiser went along with me to Skip's office. I had decided we should touch bases, but he was already rounding third base and sliding for home on this case.

"Well, it looks like you and everyone else can relax now. Pauline's definitely our perp. I've given the order to take her into custody," Skip said, gnawing on a pencil.

I'd never tell Skip to his face, because I knew how proud he was of being High

Sheriff, but his new status was going to his head. In trying to outdo his predecessor and prove himself worthy of the job, his judgment was a bit skewed. He'd been an underdog in the department for too long, I guess. In addition to that, he was as eager as the rest of us to mark this case closed. A little too eager, in my opinion.

"Aren't you being a bit hasty? We don't know for sure yet that she's the one."

"How can you doubt it, Beanie? I mean look at the evidence. This woman has a criminal record, she runs a phony-baloney psychic business, and she was at the scene of the crime. That's just for openers. How could the Sirius Killer be anyone other than your Madame Pawline?"

"I know all that, and I certainly agree that she seems a likely suspect, but there are just too many frayed ends in this dog leash murder case. It's my gut feeling that there is still some important detail we're overlooking. We need proof positive before we go arresting people."

"But you were in Pauline's tent with me that day," Skip argued. "You heard what she said, and the murder happened right outside her tent, for crying out loud. What more proof do you need?"

"That's true, but there's something that

keeps nagging at me."

"What?" Skip kept chewing on his pencil.

"It took a lot of force to break Abby's neck."

"Not necessarily. According to the autopsy report, Abigail had osteoporosis. If her bones were weak, it wouldn't require very much force to . . ." He snapped his number 2 pencil in half to illustrate his point.

"I see your point, but Pauline swears she was nowhere near Rosie's house at the time she was attacked. She told me she has never been there before and doesn't even know where she lives."

"Ever heard of a phone book? That presents no problem in a small community like Tahoe. She could find out easily enough where Rosie lived. Anyway, we found the candle wax on the carpet, remember? That's evidence enough for me."

"That could have already been there. I know that she used candles sometimes. It was probably just sealing wax. She uses it all the time. She's old fashioned about her letter writing and loves collecting different decorative seals and waxes."

"It's not sealing wax. I checked with the lab. In fact, they're working on identifying where the candle was purchased."

"Well, even if someone else did put it there, it could have been anyone. I mean, they use candles in church, too. Are you going to arrest Reverend Ramseth for murder?"

Skip genuflected, even though he's not a practicing Catholic. "You're liable to go straight to hell for saying that."

"I don't believe in hell. I could never embrace an anti-dog religion. Dogs are too important to me."

"What makes you think Christians are anti-dog?"

"Because they believe animals don't have souls."

"Who says so?" Skip said, looking like a little boy who'd played hooky from Sunday school, which he probably had. "I'm a Christian, and you know how I feel about dogs."

"Even Lang Po?"

"Well, most dogs," Skip corrected. "Anyone who's ever looked in Cruiser's soulful eyes knows better than to say he has no soul."

I smiled. My soulmate, Cruiser, seemed to understand and let out a woof of agreement. "By the way, did you know that Pauline is Reverend Ramseth's daughter?"

"No, I didn't. How'd you find that out?"

"She told me, that's how. I think I'll go pay the good reverend a little visit."

"When you do, tell him he can visit his daughter in the county jail. I'm pulling her in for questioning."

I hadn't talked to the reverend much since all this mayhem began, simply because I assumed there was nothing to talk to him about in relation to the case. Now that I knew he was Pauline's father, I suddenly wondered if he could somehow be involved. As Nona had said, just because you wear a clerical collar didn't mean you were always good, or perfect. Preachers are human, too. The fact that he had ridiculed his own daughter because of her life choices proved that. Suddenly, I was reminded of Nona and how I'd repeatedly done the same thing to her, my beloved only child. Further proof that we're all human, and fallible.

I had forgotten to gas up the car before leaving for Lakeview Methodist Church, so by the time Cruiser and I arrived, the car's tank was empty and Cruiser's was full. Walking along the beachfront of the Haversham property, I could understand why so many were keen on acquiring it.

The beauty of the grounds was surpassed only by the breathtaking view of the lake. Getting an unobstructed view of Lake Tahoe was certainly something worth fighting over, because there were so few such spots left. However, nothing save the desire to preserve some of Tahoe's history stood in the way of development. In a shrinking nature area like Tahoe there was always far more to consider with land use than pure profit. With so little of Tahoe's gentler past remaining to save, razing the beautiful, historic Haversham estate to make room for more so-called progress seemed a crime of another kind.

To add further complications to the mix, the waters off the beach were protected fish habitat. Whatever new structure was built here would require a special use permit. I doubted if a resort hotel would fall into those parameters. In my way of thinking, the only feasible choice for the property was the dog walk park and restoration of the existing Haversham home for the enjoyment of Tahoe's growing senior population. Someday, but not too soon, I hoped, I might be there myself, looking out on the beautiful lake as the wealthy Haversham family had done.

The gates to the estate were unlocked. I

let Cruiser off his leash to follow his nose while I explored the historic area where, in summers long ago, rich and famous visitors strolled arm in arm on gentle, pine-scented evenings. I could hear ghostly laughter from mirthful garden parties, accented by the clinking of fine silver against Limoges china plates and the tinkling of chipped ice against Waterford crystal stemware. I heard thwacks of wooden mallets on croquet balls in friendly matches upon the expanse of verdant lawn, long since blighted by weeds and decaying leaves.

Hidden now by ragged, overgrown foliage, the secluded old house was a reclusive dowager in her lonely sanctuary. Rotting wood planks on the windows blinded her privileged view of the lake. In some places the wood had fallen away to reveal the panes of milk glass, most of which had been broken by mischievous trespassers. As I circled the perimeter of the house, I felt a strange chill course through my veins that had nothing to do with the wintry nip in the air. I felt the fine hairs on my neck stand erect, as though I were being watched. I fancied there was a presence, or many, inside the old estate and that something peered at me through the gaps in the planks that bandaged the wounded, glassy eyes of that dilapidated house.

I thought about all the people of a bygone day, when the lake was still pristine and unspoiled by the greedy hand of man. Perhaps their spirits still wandered among the towering pines or along the shores of the lake. I wished that time could somehow reverse itself and I could be a part of the early days when my ancestors called Da-Aw, as the Washo named the lake, their own.

As I continued traversing the grounds, my vivid writer's imagination took hold, and I was one of the long-dead inhabitants of this estate, one of the Havershams, summoning a faithful spaniel to my side. My clothing of sweatshirt and jeans was transformed to the attire of yesteryear. A long, silk flapper dress rustled in a cooling summer breeze off the lake as I sipped lemonade in the sheltering gazebo. A broadbrimmed floral bonnet shaded my eyes from the shimmering sunlight reflected on the lake. Suddenly, I was aware of my own faithful Cruiser at my side. His baying interrupted my reverie and scattered daydreams like startled mallards from the lake's mirrored surface. I froze when I heard a booming voice call out my name in the eerie stillness. "Elsie MacBean?"

Was it God? Moses? Charlton Heston? In the corner of my eye, I perceived a black, shadowy figure.

"Oh!" I whirled to face Reverend Ramseth. He examined me through his spectacles as though I were some rare insect. I'd seen that same judgmental glare from the pulpit at Abby's funeral when he addressed the flock. Even now he wore his Sunday-go-to-meeting garb. I wondered if he ever took off that penguin suit. Did it give him some supernatural power, like Superman's cape? "Reverend Ramseth. You startled me. I didn't expect to see anyone out here."

"Sorry to frighten you. I was just gathering some firewood. The weather has gotten rather cold these past few nights. The rectory can be quite drafty when the mercury dips. That old boiler of ours needs some repair."

"So does this house," I said. "If it survives, that is."

"I wouldn't care if they burned it to the ground. I've thought of it myself once or twice. There's a lot of history associated with that old place, some of it not so nice."

"I wasn't aware. Like what, for instance?"

"Didn't you know?" the reverend whispered, as though there were anyone else within a mile around to hear him. "It's a murder house."

"No, I didn't. Abby never mentioned it."

"I'm not surprised. It's not the kind of thing she would have wanted people to know about."

"When did that happen?"

"Oh, it was a very long time ago. Some kind of love triangle."

"Really?" So Abigail had some skeletons rattling in her closet. I don't like to gossip about the dead, but I had to know more. "Do you know the story?"

"The way I heard it, Abigail's grandmother tried to kill her husband but accidentally killed her lover instead. She was so distraught over it, she went insane. Her husband locked her in the attic, went downstairs to his study, and shot himself to death. She remained a captive there until she died, or so the story goes." Evidently, the reverend had a taste for a little gossip, too. He was clearly enjoying the retelling of the tale.

"Why didn't she try to climb out the window?"

"She couldn't have. There are bars on the window, see?" The reverend pointed to the attic. Though the glass had been broken by vandals, or perhaps by the captive herself trying to escape her prison, I saw the iron bars were still intact, though stained red with rust, or at least I hoped it was rust.

"They say that when they found her body, there were bloodstained grooves on the other side of the door to the attic, where she had tried to claw her way out. No one has lived in the house since then."

"What a charming tale, Reverend. I guess we picked the perfect place for a Halloween party, didn't we?"

"Indeed."

"But if it's such a well-kept secret, how do you happen to know about it?"

"This church has been here a long time. Stories get passed down from generation to generation. You know how it goes."

"Yes, as a matter of fact I do." I had heard the stories of my ancestors from my grandfather, which I was sure were embellished somewhat in their retelling through the centuries, no doubt like the tale Reverend Ramseth had just related to me.

"That house has many secrets within its walls. The Haversham line is tainted.

Touched by evil. Murder, greed, adultery, insanity."

"All seven deadly sins, huh?"

"Are you mocking me, Mrs. MacBean?"

"No, of course not, Reverend." I didn't like the direction this conversation was taking, so I decided the time had come to say what I'd come to say. "Are you aware that your daughter is in serious trouble?"

The reverend looked as though I'd run him through with one of the iron fence posts. "I beg your pardon?"

"Pauline is suspected of murder."

"I always knew that girl would come to no good. Time and time again I warned her mother." He sermonized to himself, pounding his palm with his fist, like he pounded the pulpit on Sundays. Just when I thought he might start to flagellate himself, he grew aware of my presence once more. "How did you know that I have a daughter, anyway?"

"Pauline told me that you're her father. That seems to be a rather well-guarded secret, too, Reverend."

"My daughter and I parted ways some time ago. We live our own lives."

"That's a shame. Don't you miss seeing her?"

The reverend paused a moment, as

though searching for just the right words. "She displeases me."

"My daughter displeases me sometimes, too, but I'd never refuse to see her, no matter what she did."

"Pauline doesn't just offend me. She offends God with her lifestyle. Practicing the black arts, living a sinful life, breaking the law, both man's and God's."

"I wouldn't call what she does the black arts, Reverend. She's a pet psychic."

"Pet psychic, indeed."

"You obviously don't understand what it is your daughter tries to accomplish with her readings, Reverend. Animal communication is a gift, like playing the piano or dancing."

"Nonsense! It's witchcraft! They used to burn witches in the Middle Ages for such things."

"You'll forgive me for speaking plainly, but that's absurd. It's not the Middle Ages anymore, Reverend. Besides, no matter what she's done, Pauline is, and always will be, your child. Why, she was even named after you."

"My child has brought nothing but shame on me and her family. And now she's accused of murder! She'll burn in hell."

"Before you condemn Pauline, understand that she hasn't been convicted of the crime. She's innocent until proved guilty, according to the law."

"She's already guilty, according to God's law."

"You really must be more tolerant of your daughter, Reverend. Family is all we have, when the chips are down."

"Wrong!" The reverend's voice boomed like thunder. "God is all we have, when the chips are down. Now, if you'll excuse me, I must finish working on my sermon for Sunday."

"Certainly." I hoped his sermon would be about forgiveness.

The reverend gathered up some sticks of wood he had collected and headed back for the church. As he walked away, his voluminous black robes flapped in the wind like a raven's wings.

Once the sun slipped behind the mountains, the wind gusts began to bite. "Come on, Cruiser. Let's go home, boy. Nonie's waiting for us." Cruiser and I retraced our path around Haversham House to the gate. Never was an open gate such a welcome sight. I'd seen enough of this place for one day. As I shut the heavy iron gate behind us, I heard a strange cry, like the shriek of a peacock. "Help! Help!" But there were no peacocks at the Haversham estate. I felt the same warning tingle in my gut that I'd felt in the woods near my cabin that day with my three amigos, Cruiser, Rags, and Lang Po. The feeling you get when danger is lurking near. I was glad I had Cruiser with me now. I knew he would alert me to any possible menace.

Turning up my collar against the chill of nightfall, I glanced back once more at the house. Gazing up at the boarded attic window, I was momentarily blinded by the red glare of the sunset off the fractured glass. When I shaded my eyes from the light, I thought I saw some movement through the window. I tried to assure myself it was only a reflection. As Nona had said, it was just my overactive imagination.

39

When I got back to the cabin, I found Nona modeling her Halloween costume for her canine admirers. She was excited about going to the Halloween bash, and I didn't have the heart to squelch her enthusiasm.

"Hi, Mom."

"H . . . h . . . hi, honey."

"You're shivering. Is it that cold out? Even Cruiser looks chilled."

Whether it was because of ghosts or gales, I did have the shivers. "The wind was f . . . freezing. I think I even felt a few snowflakes. Think I'll light the fire." I turned on the gas log and struck a match. The flame ignited with a poof, and the heat-seeking Cruiser was beside me in a flash, warming his backside.

"So, how do I look?" she said, dancing a lively Charleston step across the floor in her trendy knock-off of a 1920s flapper dress.

"Well, as I live and breathe, if it isn't

Daisy Buchanan." All she needed was her Jay Gatsby.

Nona had even made a royal blue plumed headdress to match the costume. Sequins on her dress and hat sparkled like a galaxy of stars in the glow from the fireplace. For a moment, I saw again the little girl she once had been, looking adorable in her blue Cinderella dress on Halloween Dress-up Day at school.

I remembered drying bitter tears when she came home crying because a cruel classmate had asked her why she wasn't dressed like Pocahontas instead of Cinderella. If they could only see her now, I thought. They'd eat their words and their hearts out, too. This stunning young woman, who earned a very nice living playing dress-up in front of cameras, would be the envy of all the white kids who poked fun at the Indian girl, just like they had her mother.

"Well, you'll be the belle of the ball in that outfit." I felt almost as excited as I thought she must be, going to the ball with a rich, handsome guy.

"Yeah, unless everyone else has the same idea. After all, the Haversham House heyday was in the Roaring Twenties."

"When is Addison picking you up on Halloween?"

"Oh, I forgot to tell you. I canceled our date."

"I think you're wrong about Addison. Why not give him another chance? He'd be a fine catch."

"I'm not fishing for a husband right now, Mother. I actually enjoy being single. There are worse things to be than single, you know. Anyway, he's just not my type."

"I wish I knew what your type is, girl. I'd take out an ad in the personals."

"Why are you always pressuring me to get married? What's the big hurry? I still have a few years left before I get my AARP card."

Lucky you. I expect mine any day. If only she understood how fleeting youth is. "I don't mean to pressure you, honey. It's just that I'd really rather you didn't go out at night unescorted." That wasn't entirely the truth. I wanted to have grandchildren while I was still young enough to enjoy them.

"Get real, Mom! It's the twenty-first century. Women don't need escorts to go to a social function."

"I know that. I'd just feel better if you went along with someone. Anyone!"

"I can go with you, then."

"Go to a party with your mother?

Sounds like a 'bummer' to me, Nona."

"Well, it's too late now to find another date."

"Then Addison probably hasn't found one, either. He's such a nice young man. Why don't you just give him a call?"

"This is blackmail."

"Please? Make your old mom happy."

"Oh, all right. He'd better not be late, either, or I'm leaving without him." Nona coiled her arms in a perturbed pretzel across her chest. She could be as mad at me as she wanted, just as long as I knew she wouldn't be out alone on Halloween night.

"If he stands you up again I'll ask Skip to be your date. Or maybe I can ask Walter Wiley. I'll bet he doesn't have a date, either."

"Very funny." Like sunshine through a cloud, a smile peeped through Nona's frown. "So, what are *you* going to be for Halloween?"

"Sherlock Bones again, I guess."

"Are you taking Dr. Watson along?"

"No, he's taking the night off from sniffing out crime. Besides this party is for humans only. The dogs already had their Howloween party. Watson can stay here with Moriarty and Fu Manchu."

Nona giggled. "Well, I have to finish hemming this costume."

"Don't hem it *too* short now."

"Oh, Mother, pa-leeze. I'm not sixteen anymore."

"Yes, I know, dear." I remembered all too well. I tucked a stray lock of my daughter's silky chestnut hair behind her ear and kissed her cheek. "I'd better hit that computer keyboard. I have some last-minute research to do on the dog park article."

"I'll bring you some hot chocolate later."

"Thanks, honey. That should help keep the sandman at bay."

"Better not stay up too late, though. Aren't you helping decorate the old Haversham place tomorrow?"

"Yeah, I almost forgot."

Nona resumed her stitching, and Cruiser and I adjourned to my office. Rags and Lang Po seemed content to stay in the living room near the fire. My computer buddy climbed onto his Raining Cats and Dogs quilt, neatly spread at the foot of the bed to protect my eiderdown, scrambled it just right with spatula paws, then curled up for a snooze.

I suddenly remembered I also had a date with a rich, handsome guy. The MacBean gals were really cooking! I hadn't given a moment's thought about what to wear to the ceili Colin had invited me to. I'd long since outgrown the dress I'd worn to the Tartan Ball with Tom years ago, although my old mini would be right in fashion now. I opened my closet. Its contents nearly exploded into the room as I wedged open the door. I stood shaking my head in dismay as I surveyed the dreadfully outdated, rarely worn dresses and suits. The only suit I wore these days was my leisure suit of torn jeans and the old "I Love Tahoe" sweatshirt. My clothes were jammed so tight, I couldn't drag the hangers across the rod. The MacBean Fall Collection of 1969 had encroached on Tom's side of the closet, where his clothes used to hang in a tidy row, one-inch spaces between each hanger. Opposites attract. Oh, well, there had to be something in here that would suffice for tomorrow night, but I'd worry about that later. Right now, I had work to do.

I opened the document to review what I had so far on the article, which wasn't much. I felt as frustrated about this story as I did about the murder case that seemed to be somehow connected to that ramshackle old estate and the grounds it occupied. But what could the connection be? I decided to do a little more research on the

Internet to see what I could bring up about the history of the Havershams.

I Googled the name Haversham, and a long list of links came up. Numerous links on families with the same name came up. After some scrolling, I finally located the Tahoe Havershams. I discovered a surprising amount of information about them, even legends of a treasure supposedly hidden somewhere on the estate. I doubted if there was any validity to the stories, though. Old, abandoned houses seemed to inspire wild tales such as these. They were mostly products of overactive imaginations, just like mine.

This would make for great copy in the *Tattler*, though, and I would be in the editor's good graces again. I even found the Haversham family tree and discovered several of Abigail's ancestors had originally emigrated from England to the United States in the mid-eighteenth century. I imagined there was probably a creepy old castle on some misty English moor that bore the Haversham name.

40

Although I wanted to do some more surfing on English castles and such, I couldn't afford to get sidetracked yet again on this latest *Tattler* assignment. If I didn't get busy, I knew that soon procrastination would be displaced by panic.

I went back to the Havershams' American saga. Great Grandpa Haversham had migrated West during the Gold Rush and made his fortune in the gold mines. I explored the family tree a bit further, looking at the names of their ancestors, looking for any clue that might shed some light on this case. Scanning the branches and twigs of the family tree on Generation.com, I came across Abigail's name. Abigail Adhara Haversham.

"Adhara. Interesting. I never knew Abby had a middle name." Where had I heard that name before? I also found Abigail's father and mother, who had lived in England before returning to Lake Tahoe with their two daughters, Abigail and

Alice. The young William Haversham had been sent away by his father, Horace, to an English boarding school, where he remained until after both his parents died.

Cruiser roused momentarily from his slumber at the sound of my voice, then tucked nose back to tail and went back to his snoring.

I clicked on the link for Abigail's grandparents. There were the names of her grandfather, Horace Haversham, and Abigail's grandmother and namesake, Adhara Haversham, the same woman who had killed her lover and gone insane. Had no passerby heard her calling for help? Then I remembered that nothing else stood near the house in the 1920s, except for Lakeview Methodist Church.

I clicked on a link that took me to a layout of the original parcel of land owned by the Havershams. A portion of the land appeared to have been divided from the rest in the 1920s, the same land occupied by the church. Why would a wealthy man like Horace Haversham have sold off part of his land? He certainly didn't need the money. I had no doubt that Haversham House harbored many dark secrets. I also had the feeling that Reverend Ramseth had shared with me only a small part of its history. Was he hiding something more?

Had it been Adhara Haversham's tormented spirit I heard calling out to me from the attic room? An icy river of fear coursed through my veins as I wondered if I might very well have seen the ghost of a madwoman still haunting that hideous old house.

"Oh, Nona!" I called out to my daughter. "I'm ready for that hot cocoa." I was glad I was not alone in the cabin tonight.

Nona came into my office carrying two steaming cups of cocoa. "Here's your hot chocolate, Mom." She handed one to me and sat down on the end of the bed.

"Thanks, honey. Did you finish hemming your dress?"

"Yep. Are you ready for tomorrow night?"

"I think so." She didn't know yet that I was going to be a double agent for Skip in some Sirius surveillance. Things would go ahead as originally planned, just in case he might be wrong about Pauline. We weren't taking any chances.

"Is Skip going to the party, too?"

"Uh-huh."

"You're going to the Halloween Ball together?"

"Yes."

"Oh, Mom. That's great! Now I know why you didn't want me tagging along with you. I can't believe he finally asked you out on a date."

"We're going together, but it's not what you'd call a date, exactly."

"Then what, exactly?"

"We're going to be sort of chaperones."

"Chaperones? This isn't the senior prom, Mother. What are you two really up to?"

"Nothing. I'm just helping the sheriff keep an eye out for any troublemakers. You know what happens when people drink too much at parties."

Nona gave me the same squinty-eyed look her father used to, when he knew I was stretching the truth by a mile. I felt like a butterfly impaled on Styrofoam for a kid's science project. "Uh, let's see. Let me take a wild guess. You're expecting the Sirius Killer to crash the Bark in the Park Ball, right?"

I searched for the right answer to give my daughter, so she wouldn't stay home alone. I wanted her where I could keep an eye on her. My silence tipped her off.

"I'm right, aren't I?" She was like Cruiser with a rawhide chew. One persistent pup.

"Okay, okay. I admit I'm assisting with surveillance, but I'll be in costume, like everyone else. If the Sirius Killer does show up, he won't recognize anyone. Skip will be in costume, too. There'll also be some other undercover officers there. Or under-costume, in this case."

"Gee, is this going to be a Halloween party or the policeman's ball?"

"You must keep it a secret, Nona. If word leaks out about this, it could ruin everything. We are pretty certain that the Sirius Killer won't be able to resist making an appearance at this event. If he does, we want to be certain that no one is harmed."

"But how will you know whether he's there or not, Mom? Everyone's going to be wearing a costume on Halloween, including the Sirius Killer, if he shows up. What are you going to do, ask every Casper the Ghost to lift up his sheet?"

I laughed. "Don't worry. Skip and his team will keep a sharp lookout for any trouble. So will I. Everyone there will be safe."

"I sure hope you're right."

"I wouldn't be letting you go, if I wasn't sure."

Nona stretched and yawned. "Well, it's late. I need my beauty rest."

"It is getting late. If I'm going to help decorate our haunted mansion in the morning, I'd better get some shut-eye, too."

"Looks like His Slobberness has gotten a head start," Nona said.

Cruiser snored away at the foot of my bed on his rumpled quilt, drooling on my duvet. I slipped a corner of the doggie quilt back underneath his wet jowls. He didn't even flick an eyelash, not even when Nona and I heard the electronic voice on the computer say, "You've got mail." I clicked on the mailbox and found another e-mail from *dogsbody*. We hadn't heard anything from our mystery e-mailer in quite some time. I dreaded reading it, but something told me I had to open the mail. Something also told me I wouldn't like it. How right I was! Besides some badly butchered poetry, I found yet another threat from the Sirius Killer.

> I'm a poor Underdog,
> But beware my bark.
> I'm the great Overdog
> That lurks in the dark.
> Never suppose
> You'll win the fight.
> If you follow your nose,

This dog will bite.
Soon it will be Halloween,
Watch your tail, Elsie MacBean.

41

The day before Halloween began as a perfect autumn morning, Tahoe-style. The sky was a topaz gem. Aspen trees on the grounds of the Haversham estate had amassed a priceless cache of gold leaves that glittered in a bracing alpine zephyr. Stabbing wind gusts made me turn up my collar and turn down the earflaps of my deerstalker as Nature's shimmering ore rained down to gild the forest floor. Cruiser didn't seem fazed in the least by the cold. He reveled in it! And why shouldn't he? He was wearing a fur coat. His pointy little noggin bobbing like a plastic dashboard dog, he left no good scent unsniffed. The wild potpourri of deer, coyote, and squirrel on a bouquet of rotting leaves presented a delectable buffet for the keen nose of a Basset Hound.

We had arrived early, but several volunteers were already busy stringing orange and black crepe paper in the foyer of the old house. Others draped synthetic spider webs between antique furniture and lamps, placing plastic black widow spiders at strategic points to startle any unsuspecting arachnophobes who might pass by. I grabbed a package, tore it open, and began a little web spinning of my own. Too bad the manufacturer hadn't included tiny boogie boards for the spiders, so they could surf the web.

"Morning, Beanie." I recognized that voice as surely as Cruiser did mine. I immediately identified it as belonging to a certain sandy-haired sheriff.

"Skip, what are you doing here so early?"

"Installing surveillance cameras. Hey, Cruiser, old buddy. How are ya?" He gave Cruiser a friendly slap on the rump.

"Wow, the department's going all out for this shindig, eh?"

"Yep. We'll catch this creep in action, if he takes a notion to crash the party."

"Something tells me he's definitely going to crash the party."

"Yeah, what makes you so sure?"

"Because I got another e-mail last night from the killer. I forwarded it to you. Didn't you get it?"

"No, I haven't checked my e-mail yet this morning. Once I got started on that, I'd never get away from my desk. What did it say?"

"Pretty much what the others said, only this one was more explicit. Same bad poetry, same threats, only not quite so vague this time. The killer is definitely planning something big for Halloween."

"He'll never have a better opportunity to put the bite on dog park supporters, that's for sure."

"This warning was meant especially for me. Whoever it is must think I'm getting a little too close for comfort. That's why the threats have resumed."

"I think you're right. I'd better finish installing these cameras. I'm almost done, but I still have to do the upstairs rooms. Want to keep me company?"

"Sure, I think the others have got the crepe paper and spider web department covered."

"Good." Skip didn't say so, but I knew the real reason he wanted me to go upstairs with him. This old place was pretty creepy, even in broad daylight.

I followed Skip up the sweeping staircase, which had *real* spider webs, instead of synthetic ones, strung between the railings. The steps creaked in complaint as we ascended to the second floor. Cruiser followed close behind me, sneezing as he sucked in dust bunnies and sticky spider silk. He'd rather have been chasing real bunnies out in the forest, but my good dog stayed close at my heels. I was glad to have him along, because the house creeped me out, too. Especially after what the reverend had told me about the attic room.

"Say, Skip. You never did tell me what costume you're planning to wear."

Skip talked while he drilled the bolts for the hallway surveillance camera mount. "I haven't even had time to think about that yet. I'll think of something, though. How about you?"

"Guess I'll just wear the same outfit I wore to the Howloween contest."

"Sherlock Bones?"

"Yep."

"Sounds perfect for the occasion."

"At least I don't have to dress up for this shindig. I was checking my closet, and I don't have a thing to wear tonight."

"How many times have I heard a woman say that? What are you doing tonight that you need to dress up for?"

I hadn't intended to let that slip out. "Oh, a friend invited me to a ceili."

"What the heck's a ceili?"

"Sort of a Scottish party. In the old days, the clans gathered together for a celebration. There's food, music, dancing, and so on."

Skip busied himself with his drilling, but it was beginning to feel more like grilling as he kept on with his questions. "So you're going with a friend to this ceili?"

"Yes."

"Anyone I know?"

"The councilman."

"Colin Grant?"

"The same."

He drilled another hole in the wall. "You two an item?"

"Of course not. He just asked me to be his partner for the set dances. His regular partner's got an injury."

Skip let out a guffaw.

"What's so funny?"

"It's hard to imagine a big lunk like Grant prancing around in a kilt."

I had to agree. I had a hard time imagining that, too. "If I didn't know better, I'd think you were jealous."

"Me, jealous of him? Don't be ridiculous!" That shot down the sheriff. He abandoned his grilling and went back to his work. "There, that ought to hold it. We should get some good surveillance shots with this camera."

"Let's hope so," I said.

"You bringing Cruiser along with you to the Ball on Halloween?"

"I can't. It's a people party this time. The pups already had their party. Besides, I can't keep track of Cruiser and the Sirius Killer, too."

Skip glanced down at me from the stepladder and laughed.

"What are you laughing at now?" It had better not be me again, I thought, or that stepladder might be bad luck for Skip.

"You seem to be missing a dog," Skip said.

"What? He was here just a second ago. Where is that naughty dog now? Cruiser, come back here!"

I heard a sonorous howl from somewhere on the second floor. I followed the sound down a rat maze of hallways until I found Cruiser standing at a door at the northeast corner of the mansion. I hurried to see what he was up to.

"Cruiser, what is it, boy?"

Cruiser sniffed at the crack beneath the door as though a room full of Bacon Beggin' Strips waited on the other side.

"Ugh," I said, reaching through a sticky thatch of spider webs to try the door latch. The door was locked tighter than a Scotsman's sporran. In fact, it looked as though the door hadn't been opened since the Havershams had lived here. Could this be

287

the entrance to the infamous attic? I don't know why I did it, but I knocked on the door. "Hello. Anyone in there?"

There was no answer, of course. Or at least I thought not, until I noticed Cruiser's ears perk up like he'd heard something. "What is it, boy?"

"Aaarooooo!" Cruiser pointed his nose to the ceiling and let out a mournful bay that brought Skip running on the double.

"Beanie, Cruiser, where are you?"

I heard the sheriff clomping down the hall, the keys and cuffs on his utility belt jangling. "Down here, Gunga Din!" If anyone had been in there, they were long gone.

By the time he found us, Skip was panting like Cruiser after a rabbit chase. "Anything wrong? Cruiser never howls like that, unless it's something worth howling about."

"I think our hound dog sleuth has found the haunted attic room."

"Huh? What do you mean?"

"The room where the ghost of this house lives."

"Ghost?" Skip's face blanched a bit. "Come on, quit kidding around. I've got work to do."

"The ghost of Adhara Haversham. Reverend Ramseth was telling me a lovely little fairytale of how her husband locked her in the attic. She died there, and he committed suicide in the study downstairs."

"Well, I guess a creepy old house like this would have to have a ghost or two haunting it, right?"

Skip flinched when I nudged him playfully. "Maybe you should have installed infrared cameras, so you could record paranormal activity in the house."

42

By the time I arrived at Valhalla that Halloween Eve, the highland ceili was already in full fling. You could have heard the screech of bagpipes from clear across the lake. I'm sure every dog on the North Shore was howling. I was glad I had managed to find a plaid skirt to wear, because I'd have felt as out of place as I had in a miniskirt on my first date with Tom at the Tartan Ball. Everyone here was dressed in some shade of tartan.

The entire room was a swirling, multicolor sea of plaid as the dancers stepped and reeled to the music of the band called Ferrets in the Trousers, led by Screaming Norman Beheejus. Fortunately for our eardrums, he was the lone piper of this group I'd heard play before at The Emerald Shamrock, one of several Irish pubs in South Tahoe. Despite their name, the group was in great demand at local events, especially around St. Patrick's Day.

At six feet four inches tall, Colin Grant

wasn't hard to spot among the group. He saw me at the door and came over to greet me. "Ah, Elsie. You made it. Delighted to see you."

"Sorry I'm a little late. Have I missed much?"

"Ah, no. We're just getting warmed up. Those shoes of yours are going to be hard to dance in, though. This floor can be slippery, and wouldn't you know they just waxed it today. Did you bring any ghillies?"

"No, I don't have any."

"No matter. We have extras. Some dancers invariably forget to bring their own. I'm guessing you wear about a size eight?"

"Yes."

"Come along with me. I think we have a pair that will fit you."

I followed Colin over near the stage. Thank God the Ferrets stopped playing about that time. Screaming Norman's bagpipes deflated, and the band took five. They could take five hundred, as far as I was concerned. I was feeling one of those headaches coming on.

"Have a seat here, while I get your shoes."

I'd never been inside Valhalla for any social functions other than antique shows and craft fairs. The grand old ballroom was usually reserved for special occasions, like weddings and society banquets. In Lucky Baldwin's day, the rich and famous gathered here from around the world to hobnob at high society parties and celebrations. I imagined very few of my native people had ever been admitted into the great hall of Valhalla, although they would have been more entitled, since it is named after the hall of slain warriors in Germanic legend.

Colin returned carrying a pair of black ghillies. He knelt down. "These ought to be a perfect fit for you. Slip off your shoe and let's have a look-see."

I felt a little like Cinderella as he fitted the slipper on my foot. "There, how does that feel?"

"A perfect fit," I said.

He pinched the toe of the slipper to feel where my piggies were. "Yes, I think this will do just fine." I rested my foot on his knee as he deftly laced up the soft leather dance slipper until my entire leg was trussed like a Thanksgiving turkey.

"Is it supposed to be that tight?" I asked.

"Yes, you want to have them firmly laced when you're out there dancing, or you could twist an ankle."

"Okay, if you say so. I hope my leg doesn't turn blue, though."

Colin laughed as he finished lacing the other slipper. "Okay, you're ready to reel, Elsie. They're about to start up the music again. Let's go take our places for the next set."

I paused a moment to loosen the laces on my slippers, then followed Colin onto the dance floor as the Ferrets started up the music. Now I was the one who felt like I had two left feet, as I tried my best to follow my partner's expert lead. He wove gracefully in and out of the twin lines of dancers just as he had woven the laces of my dancing shoes. He was light on his feet for a man of his size. If Skip could only see this. I understood why Colin had the award displayed on his office wall; this guy was a regular Lord of the Dance.

As we reeled in a double helix pattern through the other dancers, I found myself transported back in time to the Tartan Ball, where Tom and I first danced together. I remembered how handsome he had looked in his red MacBean Tartan and blue velvet jacket, how young we both were, and how much in love. While I reminisced, not paying very close attention to what I was doing, I felt a sharp stab of pain, only not in my heart. This pain was in my knee. I wailed louder than Screaming Norman's bagpipes, then stopped dead in my tracks, clutching my right kneecap. The other dancers piled up behind me, then one fell down, creating a domino effect. Kilts flew up in the air, revealing once and for all what Scotsmen wear beneath their kilts. Oh, for a pair of trousers, with or without the ferrets.

43

Colin was very gallant about the whole ceili mêlée, although I noticed he didn't say very much to me afterward. I supposed it was the last time he'd let an amateur crash a ceili. I felt so embarrassed I just wanted to leave as quickly as possible after the pile-up on the Valhalla dance floor. It was still only the shank of the evening when I departed the ceili.

I told Colin I could manage on my own, but he helped me out to my car anyway. He insisted repeatedly on driving me home, but I finally convinced him I could pedal the gas on the automatic transmission with my left foot instead of my right. Under the circumstances, the drive home with him would have been far too uncomfortable.

Fortunately, no one else had been injured because of my clumsiness, and I figured an ice pack would fix my knee. The pain had already subsided some by the time I pulled into my driveway and found my daughter on the front porch with Rags and Lang Po. She was busy with something, so she didn't notice my slight limp. I was glad I hadn't told her about going to the ceili. I was in no mood for any of her nosy questions or smart aleck comments right now.

Nona had never outgrown carving the Halloween pumpkin. Neither had her mother. She had spread out newspapers and was conducting a post-mortem on Jack O. Lantern with a serrated-edge steak knife. I watched her as she repeatedly plunged the blade into the rotund gourd.

"Have you killed it yet, Nona?"

"Huh? Oh, hi Mom. I didn't hear you drive up."

"I'm not surprised, the way you were stabbing at that pumpkin. Anyone I know?"

"Will Addison do?"

"Now, now. Cut the guy some slack. He's honoring the memory of his aunt by allowing us to go ahead with the party at the mansion to raise money for Abigail's 'pet' project."

"That's true."

"You're carving Jack a little early, aren't you?"

"Yeah, I thought I'd better do it now. I

may not have time tomorrow night. So, did you get the old Haversham place all decorated today?"

"Yep. The halls are all horrified."

Nona laughed. "I hope the ghosts of the Havershams don't turn up for this Halloween party."

"Oooooo, you never know. Hey, save some of the insides for Cruiser. He loves pumpkin guts." Cruiser took his cue and moved in closer for a sample of some of Jack's gooey innards.

"Here you go, Cruiser." Nona pulled a wad of strings and seeds from the pumpkin and tossed it atop the evening news. He snapped up a clump of the stuff, then spit it out, shaking his head in a great ear-flapping, jowl-slapping display, sowing pumpkin seeds in my planter for next fall's harvest.

"Not that part. He likes the meaty part. Cut off some of that for him."

"Oh, I didn't know you were a gourd gourmet, Cruiser."

R . . . R . . . Roo!

"You didn't use today's paper for that, did you, Nona?"

"Yes, all the others went out with yesterday's recycling pick-up. Why?"

"I haven't had a chance to read it yet."

"Sorry."

"That's okay. I wouldn't have wanted this mess on my porch. Anyway, I can read it online." Fortunately for Nona, I wasn't as fanatical about the daily paper as her father had been, and I even write some of the news that's printed in it. No one was ever allowed to touch that paper before Tom. His First Reader Rule was sacred around our house. A virgin newspaper — the last bastion of male dominance.

While Nona kept carving choice bits of pumpkin for Cruiser and creating a scary face for Jack to keep evil spirits away from our door on Halloween, I couldn't help reading the parts of the paper that weren't covered in soggy, seedy squash. The first thing I always read in the paper is the Police Blotter, and that's what I was reading now. I like it better than Dear Abby.

I skimmed through the usual assortment of robberies, drug arrests, purse snatchings, and a suicide. Suicide? Now, that isn't something you read about every day in the *Tattler*. But neither is murder, although we hadn't caught up to Sacramento or Modesto, yet. There was another Blotter item of particular interest to me.

Nona must have noticed me reading the police reports, or maybe she saw my mouth gaping wider than the one she'd just carved in the jack-o'-lantern. "What is it, Mom?"

"Just browsing the Police Blotter."

She sighed. "Why can't I have a mother who reads the Home and Garden section?" She kept dissecting Jack. "Well, any more news about the Sirius Killer?"

"Just that Skip's prime suspect has escaped."

"Pauline LeBlanc?"

"Yep."

"Do you really think she's capable of murder?"

"It's sure beginning to look that way."

"Yeah, I guess if she bolted, she must have something to hide."

"It will only make things worse for her, whether or not she's guilty of the crimes," I said. "People are innocent until proven guilty; at least that's the way it's supposed to go down."

"I really hope they catch this creep soon," Nona said.

"Me, too, honey."

"There now, what do you think of our Jack?" Nona turned the pumpkin so I could see the gruesome face she'd carved.

I grimaced in mock horror. "That should certainly keep the bogey man away. Trick-or-treaters, too, I expect." She put down the knife and started cleaning up the mess. If only the messes this killer had left in his murderous wake could be so easily tidied up.

It looked like Madame Pawline was still top dog on the list of suspects in this canine crime spree. Perhaps Skip had been right about her from the very beginning. I'd had my suspicions about her, too, but I hadn't wanted to believe that someone who ran a business to help people and their pets would also use it as a means to hurt them. If she was the culprit, I only hoped that no one would be in any danger at the Bark in the Park Ball. The Haversham ghosts might be the least of our worries this Halloween.

44

No one else had been attacked since Rosie, but there had been more Sirius threats, and now Pauline had escaped from jail. She'd vanished right from under Skip's nose, or at least that's how it appeared to everyone who read about it in the *Tattler*. He'd never live this one down.

The Sirius Killer was still out there somewhere, killing time until the perfect opportunity presented itself to commit another murder. It seemed as if the killer was employing terrorist tactics by letting the fear in our little alpine community snowball, so that no one in Tahoe would feel safe venturing out the front door. This endless Yellow Dog alert was starting to get to everyone. Sirius was making detainees of us in our own homes; then, when people finally let their guard down, Sirius would strike again when least expected, perhaps with greater ferocity than before.

What better opportunity would there be

to have all of Tahoe's dog fanciers gathered in one place than at the Bark in the Park Ball? One thing was certain: as long as this sick puppy was still up to the same old tricks, this Halloween celebration would be no treat.

Halloween night was black as a Basset Hound's nose. No orange pumpkin moon illuminated the cloudless night, which made for perfect viewing of the spectacular meteor shower that had been predicted. Such cosmic events were always better appreciated at this lofty elevation than in the smog-shrouded valley. From the porch I waved goodbye to my beautiful Betty Boop, who went alone to the ball when Addison didn't show. I was just as glad, since no one was beyond my suspicion at this point. Glancing up, I glimpsed a brief flash of quicksilver in the dark, as a meteor burned through Earth's atmosphere. Chicken Little was right. The sky was falling.

My trusty dog sitter, Scotty, had come down with the flu at the last minute, and all the other pet sitters in town were either in quarantine themselves or booked. I didn't like leaving my charges alone tonight of all nights, but under the circumstances I had no choice. I'd try not to stay out too long, if I could help it.

I fed the dogs, took them out for a poop-poop-a-doop, and had finally managed to get them settled for the night after some difficulty with Cruiser, who kept hanging around my feet, circling my ankles like a cat. He used to behave that way when Tom and I first adopted him. For many months, Cruiser acted terribly clingy and never wanted to let us out of his sight for a minute. I think he always feared that we wouldn't come back. He knew a good thing when he'd found it. Eventually, he settled into his new life with us. I thought he'd finally outgrown his separation anxiety, but he was awfully restless tonight. I marked it off to the trick-or-treaters prowling the neighborhood.

I finally managed to distract Cruiser with a yummy. I left the lights and TV on, so the dogs would be more at ease. It also gave the impression to any mischievous trick-or-treater or would-be intruder that someone was at home. I secured all the door locks, then made my getaway for the Bark in the Park Ball. Cruiser was still whining on the other side of the door as I hurried to my car.

Haversham House looked more gloomy

than ever, with skeletons in the windows and mechanical bats circling the façade for that "unlived-in" look. A Haversham family graveyard had been recreated for the occasion, complete with headstones and a freshly-dug grave with a real coffin and pop-up corpse. A young girl screamed, then giggled, when the spook-in-the-box surprised her.

For the first time in decades, though, the house was filled with gaiety and people who were there to have a good time. A rogue's gallery of jack-o'-lanterns grinned, frowned, and leered at me from the porch as I followed a group of partygoers to the front door. Someone dressed as Lurch opened the door.

"You rang?"

Several people giggled as Morticia Addams guided us into the mansion's dimly lit ballroom, where the party was already in full swing. I could just make out the familiar lyrics of "The Monster Mash" above the lively din of laughter and conversation.

The decorators had gone all-out to create a thoroughly spooky haunted house at the old Haversham mansion. In the basement was Dr. Frankenstein's lab, complete with monster. An ugly witch with a decidedly green cast to her wart-covered complexion stood on the hearth of the fire-place, stirring a "boiling" cauldron of bat's blood and eye of newt, which was really raspberry punch with plastic eyeballs frozen in ice cubes. A gypsy fortuneteller peered into a crystal ball. If only the future were that easy to see. Might Pauline be hiding beneath one of these costumes? Even if she were, we'd never know unless we checked everyone, since there were dozens of people at the party dressed up as the Sirius Killer. So much for originality . . . and good taste.

I looked around to see if I spotted anyone I recognized at the masquerade. I thought I saw a few familiar faces, but it was hard to tell with so many disguises. I searched for Skip among the creepy crowd, but I had no idea what kind of costume he wore. Surely he hadn't dressed up as the Sirius Killer, too. I wandered through the ghouls and goblins, feeling ill at ease in spite of the knowledge that the event was under careful police surveillance. I kept an eye out for anything unusual, as Skip had asked me to. The only unusual thing I spotted was Skip. When I saw him, I burst out laughing.

"Beanie, I've been looking all over for you."

"I've been looking for you, too." I studied his costume. He had strips of silver duct tape and several Barbie dolls attached to his clothes. "I give up. What are you supposed to be?"

"A babe magnet, of course."

I laughed until tears ran down my cheeks. "I didn't know you were a Barbie collector."

"I'm not, smart aleck. They belong to my niece."

I got a grip and glanced around the room. It looked like any other Halloween party. People were laughing, dancing, drinking. "Do you think the killer's joined our little party?"

"Hard to tell, but at least there's been no trouble. Not yet, anyway."

"Let's think positively, Skip. Maybe we'll all just have a happy Halloween, and every-thing will be fine."

"Sure hope so."

"Me, too." Especially with Nona here, I thought.

"Well, it's no good sticking with me."

"Don't you mean sticking ON you?"

"Very funny. Let's mingle."

"Better watch out for all those ghouls."

"Why?"

"You're a babe magnet, remember?"

"Here, Sherlock, take this walkie-talkie with you. Let's keep in touch." Skip winked and disappeared into the crowd.

I spotted Betty Boop MacBean over by the punch cauldron refilling her glass. "How's the punch?"

"Wickedly good," the green witch beverage server answered first with a cackle.

"Oh, hi, Mom. What took you so long to get here?"

"I had to take care of the pack before I could leave them for the evening. Cruiser didn't want me to go. I haven't seen him act like that for a long time. I didn't think he had separation anxiety anymore."

"He certainly shouldn't, with the other two dogs there to keep him company."

"You wouldn't think so."

"He's just spoiled. He thinks he has to go everywhere you go."

"I guess you're right. To tell you the truth, I'm wishing I brought him with me now, even if dogs weren't invited. I can think of worse dates."

"You're such a scream, Mother," Nona said and vanished into the crowd.

As if on cue, I heard a scream. I felt sure it came from somewhere on the second floor. It sounded like the strange cry I had heard as I walked the grounds that day I ran into Reverend Ramseth. I figured it was probably just someone at the party getting too rowdy, but I decided to go check it out, anyway.

Several partygoers on the stair landing glanced at me as I passed, then went back to their conversation. Hadn't they heard the scream I'd heard just moments before? I navigated one hallway, then the next, to where I thought the sound had originated. It didn't take me long to realize I was heading in the direction of the attic. I saw a shaft of light at the end of the dark, narrow hallway. The attic door was ajar!

With a growing sense of dread, I approached the open door. I tried the walkie-talkie, as Skip had instructed me, but I got no response from him. Then I saw the re-charge light flashing. Great, Sheriff Cassidy. Try giving me one of these that works. Where was he, anyway? And what about the rest of the surveillance team? Hadn't they heard anything? I seemed to have been the only one at the party who had heard the scream come from the upper floor. If Cruiser were here, he'd surely have heard it, too. If only I'd brought Cruiser with me. Why had I left my best crime-busting buddy behind when I needed him most? Had he sensed something might happen tonight and tried to warn me of danger with his strange behavior before I left the house?

Rusted hinges screeched like a banshee as I forced open the door. Crossing the threshold to the attic, I discovered yet another staircase leading me onward. Spider webs hung like gossamer chandeliers above my head, tangling in my hair as I ascended the dim passageway toward the topmost attic room. Fear knotted my stomach. What might I find inside that had remained locked up since the Havershams had lived here so long ago? What secrets were in this place where a madwoman had died screaming for help that never came? Why was the door open now? And who or *what* had opened it?

45

When I reached the attic, no one was there, but someone recently had been, because candles in the tarnished silver candelabra atop an ornate roll top desk were lit. In the candlelight, I saw the clutter one usually finds in any attic: antique furniture draped in sheets, trunks stuffed with old clothes, a full-length mirror with seven years' bad luck worth of cracked glass, dust-covered photo albums, bundles of old newspapers, and an oil painting of a beautiful young woman I surmised must be Adhara Haversham. The sapphire eyes of her progeny gazed out from the canvas.

I noticed things had been scattered about the room, as though someone had been searching for something. Drawers in the massive desk gaped open like surprised mouths. Someone had even discovered the secret compartment most roll top desks of that era contained for important papers like birth certificates, deeds, and wills. The compartment was empty.

Had the intruder already found what he was looking for and escaped when my footsteps alerted him? If so, to where had he escaped? I had seen no one as I came down the hall, and no one had met me as I climbed the stairway to the attic. One thing appeared certain; the burglar had not escaped by the window. It was barricaded with iron bars. Perhaps it wasn't a prowler at all that I had frightened away but a malicious poltergeist, Adhara's restless spirit that still inhabited this eerie space in the forgotten attic of Haversham House. What else but a ghost could disappear through walls or iron bars? Was the chill I felt caused by a drafty attic or something else?

A rustling among the papers scattered on the floor startled me. Then I caught a movement in the corner of my eye, something flowing and white as a sheet, arms outstretched to grab me from behind. I whirled around and let out a loud screech when I saw it, then laughed. My attic ghost *was* a sheet, just an old sheet on a chair, flapping in the breeze from the broken window. Then I spotted my noisy little spook, a mouse. Startled by my scream, he skittered across the room, leaving little mouse tracks in the dust, like the woodland creatures do in the snow outside my cabin in winter. In the blink of a shoe button eye, he escaped to the safety of a small knothole in one of the oak floorboards.

Nosy thing that I am, I had to follow the mouse to his hole, like Cruiser tracking a ground squirrel. I poked a finger in the hole, half-expecting it to get mouse nibbled. Instead, I discovered that the floorboard was loose. I tugged on the knothole, and the board lifted up to reveal a space perfect for a mouse house. Only I didn't find the mouse. Apparently, he had a clever trap door in his winter lodging for just such emergencies. What I did find underneath the loose board, tucked behind the cozy mouse nest of rags and paper in a space between the rafters of the floor, was a metal strongbox. Clearly it had been hiding here undiscovered for much longer than any mouse. The dust of a century coated it.

I lifted the heavy box from the subfloor and let it down with a clunk. I brushed some of the dust from the box. A blizzard of dust mites filled the air and my nose. Sneeze spray glistened in the candlelight.

"Okay, the box is locked," I said to myself in a mouse-sized voice. "But every locked box has a key somewhere." I reached under the floorboard and explored every crevice with my fingers, but found no key. Of course, no one would leave the key with the box, especially if the box contained something of value. Why else would its owner take such pains to hide it? There was only one way to get the box open. I'd have to break the lock, but with what?

Attics are full of useful things for cracking locks on boxes, and I found one right away. An old iron doorstop provided the needed force to crack open the lock. I felt excitement at the thought of what I might find inside the old box. Treasury Bonds? Jewels? Gold coins? After all, old man Haversham made his fortune in the gold mines, and there were those stories about a lost treasure. But when I opened the box, all I found were a few worthless trinkets and a stack of old envelopes tied together with a blue satin ribbon.

I untied the ribbon and began leafing through the envelopes. I opened one of the envelopes addressed to Adhara Haversham, which contained several pages of stationery. I began to read. "My beloved Addie, I long for the day we will be together again. I must see you soon or I shall go mad with love for you." Love letters. All I had found were a bunch of old love letters from a lovesick beau of Adhara's. No treasure, at least not to anyone but the person who had hidden them here, no doubt Adhara herself.

I heard the sound of heavy footsteps coming up the stairwell to the attic. Had the prowler who had been here before come back to resume his search? I had to hide, but where? Quickly, I tucked the letters in my pocket, put the box back where I'd found it, and replaced the loose board. The footsteps sounded much closer now. He was nearly here.

I raced for the Queen Anne chair, lifted the sheet, and pulled it back over me to conceal my presence. I had played the game of "statues" many times as a child, but keeping perfectly still and not moving a muscle had never really been vital until now.

I sat still as a wood stump in the old chair, hidden under the sheet, praying not to be discovered by whoever stomped around the attic like an elephant in combat boots. This had to be the noisiest prowler I'd ever heard. His labored breathing from the climb up the stairs convinced me my intruder was a man. No woman breathes like that.

I heard the heavy breather approach the chair where I was hiding. A mini-meteor of bright light from a flashlight rocketed around the room. I held my breath. He was searching for something, all right, but what? Most likely it was the box I'd already found hidden under the floorboards, thanks to a frightened Stuart Little. At the moment, I felt no less afraid than that mouse. But what would anyone want with a bunch of old love letters from people who were long dead?

Why, oh, why wouldn't he leave? He was so close I could smell his aftershave. The scent seemed vaguely familiar. Just when I could keep still no longer, I felt the crushing weight of the intruder's boot come down hard on my big toe. I exhaled all my pain and fear in a single howl that would have caused Cruiser to bay in chorus. I leapt up from the chair and hopped around on one foot, still tangled in the sheet.

When I heard the burglar scream and make tracks for the exit, I knew instantly who it was.

"Skip, wait!" Through the sheet I saw the beam of his flashlight trained on me.

"B . . . B . . . Beanie, is that you under there?"

I tossed off the sheet, and Skip sighed with relief. "Of course it's me, silly. Who

315

did you think? The Haversham Ghost?"

"Hah, good one! Now that you've had your Halloween fun, let's go back downstairs."

"This was no Halloween prank."

"Oh, yeah? Then why were you hiding under a sheet?"

"I thought you were the prowler coming back."

"Prowler? What prowler?"

"Someone was up here searching for something before I got here, and it must have been something important. The room has been ransacked."

"How can you tell? I thought all attics looked like this."

"Because whoever was here left candles burning in the candelabra, and the contents of the desk drawers are all over the floor."

I was still nursing my smarting bunion, but Skip had recovered enough from his fright to survey the room more critically. "Yeah, I guess you're right."

"I tried to alert you, but this contraption doesn't work."

"Sorry about that. I guess the last person to use it forgot to recharge it."

Why did I get the feeling that person was Skip?

"How'd you know I was up here, anyway?"

"I didn't. I saw the light at the end of the hall and came down to check it out. I wonder what our thief was looking for."

"I'm not sure, but I found these hidden under a loose board in the floor." I showed Skip the collection of letters to Adhara.

He shuffled through them. "Old letters?"

"Love letters, to be exact."

"So what? Who would want these? He must have been looking for something else. Maybe there's some valuable antique up here. A rare painting or jewelry or money."

"I haven't seen anything of real value in here. Just some old furniture and antiques. It was probably whatever was in the desk before the drawers were dumped out on the floor. I even found a secret compartment. These old roll tops always had one."

"Did you find anything in it?"

"Nope, empty."

"Could be that what was hidden there has already been found."

"I thought of that."

"So, you didn't see anyone up here?"

"No. But whoever it was didn't even bother to blow out the candles when he heard me coming."

"Then he could still be hiding here

somewhere." ⸰ Skip glanced furtively around.

"Where? He couldn't escape from the window and there's no other exit from the room, other than the stairs."

"Are you sure? Maybe there's a secret passage or something."

"Maybe, but the only living thing I've seen since I've been up here isn't human."

"You're not still trying to spook me, are you?"

"Relax, Skip. The attic has taken on a small boarder for the winter — a mouse."

"Oh. Well, if anyone did come up here looking for something, then the hallway surveillance camera will have recorded it."

"I hope you installed a camera that detects ghosts."

Skip shuddered. "Enough with the ghosts, already. Come on. Let's go back downstairs. This place gives me the heebie-jeebies."

Just then, a strong gust of wind blew through the broken glass of the attic window, snatching the letters from my hand with icy fingers. The missives flew around the room in a mini cyclone, and then landed at the base of the portrait of Adhara Haversham.

Skip would have dismissed what had just

happened in that eerie old attic as just an odd coincidence, but I knew better. Adhara had returned for her lost letters.

An even stronger blast of air overturned one of the candelabra. A lit candle landed upon the stack of letters, setting them ablaze. I snatched them up and extinguished the stationery. Seeing the letters were only scorched a little on the edges, I tucked the letters back in my pocket. I thought the danger was over, but in a sudden flare-up the fire spread to a pile of oily rags and the stacks of old newspapers.

"Help me, Skip! This whole place will go up like a matchbox!" I looked for something to put out the fire. Grabbing an old throw rug, I used it to beat at the flames, but my efforts were futile. The attic of the old house was kindling for a bonfire.

Skip used the sheet I'd been hiding under to try smothering the blaze, but it was too late. In seconds, flames had engulfed the room.

"Get out of here, Beanie! Find a cell phone and call the fire department!"

"I'm not leaving without you."

"Go now! I'll be right behind you."

As I limped toward the door, I glanced back and saw Skip battling the raging inferno. For a moment, I envisioned my Tom fighting his last forest fire and remembered how that killer blaze had claimed his life in the end. I feared now for Skip, as I had each time Tom had answered the call to duty.

I could see the haunted visage of Adhara Haversham through the flames licking up the attic walls, devouring the ugly secrets of Haversham House in a crimson maw of fire. In the shimmer of firelight, her dour expression appeared to transform. I'd swear she was laughing as the door slammed shut behind me.

46

Even if I hadn't borrowed Nona's cell phone to call the fire department, the glow from the burning Haversham mansion would have signaled them. The blazing house shone like a beacon in the moonless All Hallows Eve night and could be seen for miles in the Tahoe basin. In seconds, sirens shrieked a warning as the engines roared down the highway in response to my emergency call. Nona and I had managed to herd everyone safely and calmly out of the house, despite the acrid smoke that billowed from the attic. The Halloween revelers stood outside in the frigid night air gaping at the spectacle, some thinly clad in their costumes, being warmed by a giant bonfire in the forest.

"Is everyone out of there, Beanie?" Chief Bob Baker asked. He and my Tom had been fishing buddies as well as dedicated public servants. Skip made it three men in the tub they took fishing on the lake — Skip's trusty Trout Scout.

"No. Skip's still in there." Why hadn't I dragged him with me out of that burning attic? Why do all the men in my life have to be heroes?

"You sure he's not out here somewhere?"

"I'm sure, Bob. I just finished looking for him. He's probably in the attic. He was trying to put out the fire up there, last I saw him."

"Don't worry, we'll find him." Bob's team trained the fire hoses on the flames, as Bob rushed into the inferno to search for Skip. For nearly an hour, powerful geysers of water pelted Haversham House. At last, it looked like the battle had been won and the fire was extinguished. Smoke wisps drifted up from the smoldering timbers like phantoms in the night. Most of the second floor had been saved, except for the attic room, the last place I had seen my friend.

Bob appeared, face smeared in soot and sweat. "I'm sorry," he said somberly. "I searched everywhere, but I didn't find the sheriff."

"He's got to be in there somewhere," Nona said.

"He must be okay." My voice choked with emotion, I could barely croak the words. "Skip. Oh, Skip." Nona put her arms around me, burying her head in the crook of my neck.

Then we both heard a familiar voice. "Did someone call my name?"

"Skip!" Nona and I howled in stereo. We embraced him like the returning hero he was.

"Down, girls, down!" Skip laughed, relishing the female adulation.

"Are you all right?" I said.

"Of course, I'm all right. Didn't I tell you I'd be right behind you?"

"You scared us half to death. Where were you, anyway?"

"Chasing the Sirius Killer."

"What?" Nona said.

"Wh . . . wh . . . who?" I hooted.

"You sound like an owl, Beanie. I managed to salvage the surveillance cameras on the second floor. It's all on videotape."

"Well, who is it? We're dying to know," Nona said.

"Who I suspected all along," Skip said. I half-expected him to strut around like a peacock, tail feathers at full mast. "Your pet psychic, Pauline LeBlanc. Evidently, she decided to crash our little Halloween party after all."

"So, where is she?" I said.

"She came barreling out of the house. I chased after her, but lost her in the woods."

"Do you really think she came here tonight to kill someone?" Nona said with a shiver-shake.

"It kind of looks that way, doesn't it?" Skip said.

I had to admit it did. "She's probably the one who was up in the attic, Skip. I wonder what she was looking for."

"Maybe she forgot to bring her leash," Skip said with a snort.

"Very funny, Sheriff. No, she must have been in the attic for some reason."

"She was. She was waiting for you to show up, Beanie."

Nona's breath hitched, partly from the cold. "You could have been killed, Mom!"

"If that were true, and she was planning to do away with me, she's had plenty of opportunities before tonight."

"Well, if she isn't guilty, then why did she run away?"

"Perhaps she wasn't running from you, Skip."

"What, then?"

"Maybe something else frightened her."

"Like what?"

"I don't know. A ghost?"

"I don't believe in ghosts."

"You could have fooled me in the attic earlier."

In the light from the dying blaze, I could see Skip's ears turn pink.

"Well, if you ladies will excuse me, this babe magnet has a pretty fugitive to catch, and she's sure no ghost."

47

The excitement was over for the night, so I headed for home to check on Cruiser and the canine crew. Nona wanted to loiter and flirt with the firemen. I didn't want to leave the dogs alone too long; Rags, the Scottish Terrier, would have my whole place torn to rags if I stayed away longer. He still missed his real owner. The last time I called the hospital to check on Rosie, they told me her condition hadn't changed much, except that she had been moving all the fingers of her right hand, the same hand Rags had licked when I smuggled him in to visit. The nurse commented that it looked like she was crocheting an afghan in her sleep. A comatose crocheter. Regardless of what she was doing with her hand, movement like that had to be an encouraging sign. Whether or not she would fully recover was still anyone's guess, though.

As I pulled into the driveway, I didn't hear the dogs bark, as they usually do when I come home. I thought it odd but figured they were asleep or just too lazy to come greet me. Some watchdogs, I thought. And on Halloween, of all nights, when lots of strangers come knocking at your door. Perhaps they'd worn themselves out running to the door barking every time the disappointed trick-or-treaters rang the bell. I only hoped the kids hadn't done any damage to my house for not delivering the goods on Halloween night.

Jack O. Lantern's orange grimace still flickered in the dark. All seemed normal as I walked to the porch and climbed the steps, until I glimpsed a figure hiding in the bushes. He was short and stocky, with a shock of straw-like hair. I let out a yelp of surprise, then felt like an idiot when I saw my mysterious intruder was just the decorative scarecrow Nona had bought for me. I laughed at myself for being so silly. The fright night at the Haversham House still had me on edge. Perhaps a cup of chamomile tea would calm me for a good night's sleep.

When I unlocked the front door, I noticed that the hall tree had been overturned and the room looked disheveled. What had those naughty dogs gotten into now? And where were they? At least Cruiser always met me at the door whenever I came home. Even if I'd been gone for only ten minutes, I was always welcomed home like I had just returned from the Crusades. Someone must have broken in.

"Cruiser, where are you, boy?" No response.

"Cruiser, Rags, Lang Po! Come!" Still no sign of them. Then I heard a noise coming from the hallway. Perhaps the intruder was still in the house! I broke the first rule when you think your home has been invaded. I shouldn't have entered. But I was more worried about the dogs than myself right now. Then I heard a familiar whine. Cruiser appeared. I felt relieved to see him until I saw him responding to my command even more slowly than usual. He appeared to be injured. Someone *had* broken in while I was gone. Holidays were always the best time for thieves, because people are usually out partying. The other dogs must have run off, but trusty Cruiser stayed to defend his territory. What had possessed me to leave them alone tonight of all nights? Bad Dog Mom! I should have tried harder to find a dog sitter.

"Cruiser, come here, fella. Let me have a look at you." I dropped to my knees and coaxed him to me. He rested his chin on my knee. There was some spit-diluted red smeared on his dewlaps, but I didn't know if it was his blood or the burglar's.

"My poor brave boy," I said, stroking him. "We'll have Doc Heaton fix you up right away."

Then I noticed the remnants of a partly-chewed treat stuck under his gums. It was a Peanut Butter Pup, like the ones Sally sells at the Hydrant and Pauline had offered to Cruiser in her booth that day at the Howloween fund-raiser.

I knew there was no time to waste in getting him to the emergency vet clinic. As for the other two dogs, I could only hope they were all right and would find their way back to the house eventually. When my attack basset took a big bite out of crime, they'd probably escaped through the doggie door, which was no doubt the same way the burglar had gained entry. Before I left for the vet, I'd call Skip and let him know what had happened.

I sat on the living room floor, my finger shaking as I tried to punch the numbers on the phone. While cradling Cruiser's front end on my lap, I felt the vibration of a grumble rise from deep in his chest. "What's the matter, boy? Are you hurt?"

He raised his head and bared his teeth at me. I thought the warning growl was meant for me, until I was yanked backwards and felt a sudden and violent constriction of my airway.

I clutched at my throat, trying to free myself from the noose tightening around my neck, but it was no use. Despite his injuries, Cruiser launched himself at my attacker, then yelped in pain when he was booted sharply aside. My assailant dragged me out the open door and slammed it shut in Cruiser's face. For the first time I understood what dogs feel at the end of a leash and choke chain.

It's true that your life flashes past you before you die. My whole life's memories were instantly rewound and played in my brain like a home video — growing up in San Francisco during the hip 1960s, hearing my beloved grandfather's ancient Washo legends around a glowing campfire in the woods, Tom's and my wedding day, holding a tiny newborn Nona in my arms for the first time, finding Cruiser wandering by the side of the road that Tahoe summer, the winter adventure of the Tahoe Terror. And now this! How I wished I had called Skip immediately when I discovered things amiss at home. I thought of Nona

and Cruiser, who I'd never see again because Elsie MacBean was surely about to
become the next victim of the Sirius Killer.

The last thing I saw before everything
faded to black was Cruiser standing atop
the sofa barking at the window, as my assailant bore me away into the star-streaked
night.

48

I thought I was home lying safe in my bed until I tried to reach over to pet Cruiser and realized I couldn't move. Cruiser wasn't beside me, drooling on my pillow. In fact, there was no pillow. If I was not at home in my bed, where on earth was I? That's exactly where I was . . . on earth, or in it.

I gradually realized that I lay in a hole in the ground. Looking up at the night sky, I could see pine branches stirring above me in the night breeze. I heard no sound at first but the wind moaning through the trees. I knew I must be out in the forest. Then I heard a metallic scraping sound above me and felt myself being pummeled with clods of dirt.

No Edgar Poe or Stephen King tale I had ever read could compare to the horror I felt at that moment when the full weight of my predicament fell upon me, even heavier than the mounds of soil which were falling upon me in that hole. I was being buried alive! I screamed for help, but no one would hear me because, like Skip's homemade Halloween costume, my mouth was covered with duct tape. Bound like an Egyptian mummy, I was incapable of freeing myself from this dark, lonely grave.

Who was doing this to me? And why? My first question was answered when the bright flash of a falling meteor lit the sky, silhouetting my captor. It was so brief that for a moment I wasn't sure if my eyes had deceived me. But I recognized the voice.

"Still alive and kicking, eh, Elsie?" The digger paused as though waiting for me to answer, which under the circumstances I couldn't. "No matter. I'll take care of that in no time. I'm surprised it took you so long to figure things out. You were getting close, though. Too close. You were going to spoil everything for me, and I couldn't let that happen. Too much was at stake. There's no way I was going to let that choice piece of property go to the dogs."

I squirmed like an earthworm there in the dirt, trying to free myself, but it was no use. To make things worse, I had to listen to the ranting of a cold-blooded killer while I lay there dying by the shovel load.

"Anyway, I have better things to do than rot in some prison cell waiting for the hangman's noose. I decided I'd give you some real 'noose' to write about." The killer guffawed at the idiotic pun. "Only, I don't think you'll be tattling this to the papers or your sheriff friend," the man said. "Everyone who stood in the way of my deal with Paragon is out of the way now."

So, this whole thing had been about money all along. I suddenly understood the note I'd read on the councilman's desk. Grant was cutting some megabuck deal for a Paragon Resort Hotel on the Haversham property. *Have* was shorthand for Haversham. The rest of it seemed so obvious to me now. He'd written a checklist of his victims, using their initials. And clearly Elsie MacBean was next on his To Do to Death list.

"With you out of the way now, my success is assured. That stupid pet psychic will take the rap with her criminal record, and no one will ever be the wiser."

As he raved on, the dirt piled gradually higher in the hole. My feet were completely covered, and my legs and knees were slowly disappearing under layer upon layer of soil. Grant was working his way from bottom to top, dragging out the inevitable. He relished it!

The earth crept toward my shoulders now, and I felt the weight of it sinking in upon me like the utter hopelessness of my situation. My forest grave was filling fast. I had to shut my eyes when the dirt occasionally spilled onto my face. I shook my head to keep the dirt away from my nose. I had to keep my airway clear as long as I could until help arrived, if it ever did. No one would ever find me here, I thought. Years hence, some hungry coyote would dig up my bones to gnaw on them.

No, you mustn't think this way, Elsie. You must hold out hope that you'll be found. Nona will be returning to the cabin by now. She'll see that something is wrong and call Skip, and they'll come looking for me. And what of Cruiser? Cruiser, my closest companion in this too often lonely world. You know my heart best, don't you, boy? What will you do without me if I die here like this? What will become of you?

I thought of all our wonderful times together since he had come into my life. I remembered all his endearing little quirks that I had come to love so: his typical basset stubborn streak; the slobber stains I was always wiping off my mirrors and walls; how his head bobbed so comically when he was on a hot scent; how he nudged my elbow to get my attention when I sat mesmerized at the computer; the way he liked to tease with a favorite treat, challenging me to try and take it away from him. And most of all, how he had saved me. He'd saved me from loneliness, from heartache, and from peril. If only he could save me now!

As I lay there helplessly awaiting death, I realized that my connection to Cruiser was closer than with any other being in my life, perhaps even Nona. After all, I spent more time with Cruiser than anyone else. I decided to try what I had learned from Pauline about animal communication. What did I have to lose? I didn't have anything better to do at the moment. I would put her psychic claims to the ultimate test.

In such a stressful situation, it would be hard to overcome my feelings of panic and calm myself enough to reach a meditative state, but I had to try. At the very least, I reasoned, it might help me to survive a little longer by slowing my breathing and the need for oxygen. Even if I was buried alive, perhaps I could hold out long enough for someone to find me.

I took some deep breaths, while I still could. I focused on relaxing my entire body, starting at the top of my head, working to my shoulders, and gradually down to my toes. When I reached a meditative state, I began to project my thoughts to Cruiser long distance. I focused on my surroundings, the pine boughs, even the scents on the night air and the configuration of the constellations twinkling in the sky above me. But mostly, I projected my deepest feelings of love and devotion to my canine companion. My heart felt as though it might burst, it was so full of love at that moment for Cruiser.

I lay there listening. Listening for anything that might indicate that help was on the way. I heard only the wind and the steady scraping sound of the shovel as the crazed councilman worked in a murderous frenzy above me. Tears rolled down my cheeks in muddy gullies as the dirt kept piling up in my grave.

49

I was fast losing my battle for breath. It grew harder to keep the dirt cleared from my face. The soil level reached all the way to my chin now. Even though it kept me from calling out for help, the duct tape at least prevented any dirt from getting in my mouth.

I lost consciousness. Tom was alive again. He and Cruiser were sitting with me around a campfire out in the woods on one of our many camping trips. Tom and I were laughing at some silly private joke, the way we used to. Suddenly, I heard a strange sound somewhere out in the woods. Tom and Cruiser went to see what it was, and I was left all alone. A strong wind shrieked through the stand of pines. Then the fire went out. It grew very cold, and I began to shiver violently. I called for Tom and Cruiser to come back, but all I could hear was Cruiser baying far off in the deep woods. They were not coming back for me. I was going to die here alone in the dark.

My shivering from the cold stirred me

back to consciousness, or at least I thought that's what had done it, until I heard a sound. I strained to hear over the grating sound of the shoveling and the howling wind. Was it the wind that howled?

It was distant at first. Then it grew loud and clear — the same sound I had heard while I lay unconscious in my would-be grave. It was a dog, but not just any dog. I knew that mellifluous bay like a mother knows the distinctive cry of her own child.

Roo, Roo, Aroooooo!

Cruiser! It was my Cruiser! Somehow, he had found me.

I flinched as gunfire split the night.

"Freeze!" Skip shouted. "Drop it, NOW!" I heard a thud as Grant dropped his spade to the ground. "On the ground! Face down! Hands behind your head!"

I tried to sit up, but there was too much dirt piled on top of me. I saw a black nose pop over the edge of the grave, taking in my scent. Cruiser lifted his nose to the starry sky to howl his triumph. Once again, I owed my life to him. Somehow he had gotten Skip to follow and had led him right to me. It was nothing less than a four-legged, tail-wagging miracle.

"Mom, are you okay?" Nona was here,

too. Oh, my dear daughter whom I thought I'd never see again!

"Get me out of here!" I mumbled through my gag. She couldn't understand what I said, but I needed no interpretation. I wanted out of that hole. Nona jumped down into the hole with me. Digging mounds of earth aside Cruiser-style, she freed me and helped me to my feet. She unbound my hands and feet and ripped the tape off my mouth, like I used to rip a Band-Aid off her knee after the latest roller-skating scrape had healed.

"Ouch!"

"Sorry, Mom. Are you all right?"

"Yes, just get me the heck outta here!" I reached up toward the edge of the hole. Skip, still training the gun on Grant, used his free hand to grab one of my wrists. He pulled, Nona pushed, and a moment later I stood topside, looking down at the hole in the ground that had nearly become an Indian burial site. The bracing wind felt wonderful on my face. The blue leash that had nearly claimed my life still dangled from my neck. I pulled it off and threw it to the ground.

"Hey, what about me?" Nona said. It was my turn to help her out of the would-be grave.

"Hands behind your back, Grant." The sheriff straddled the councilman like a hobbyhorse. "And don't you even breathe, man!" Skip tried to lock the handcuffs on his captive's thick wrists, but couldn't get them to close.

"Dang! These things should come in extra large." All at once, Grant broke free from Skip's grasp and snatched up the shovel. In one swift motion, he was armed and on his feet. As though brandishing a broadsword instead of a garden spade, he swung at the sheriff, knocking the gun from his hand. It landed somewhere in the scrub. Grant swung the shovel like Casey at the bat, keeping us all at bay.

Then I heard the wind exit sharply from Skip's lungs as the shovel connected with his back and he hit the ground hard. There were scuffling sounds in the dark as the two men grappled in the dirt, kicking more soil into the hole where moments before I had lain, nearly breathing my last.

Nona and I stood, feeling helpless as the men rolled in the dirt like dogs, growling like two curs in the ferocity of their clash. Cruiser tried to intervene on Skip's behalf by tugging at Grant's pant leg, but when he quickly abandoned the fight, I knew something was wrong.

"We've got to find that gun, Nona. Did you see where it went?"

"Somewhere over there, but how can I see it in the dark?"

"Well, go look. I'll try to think of some way to help Skip."

I tried kicking Grant to distract him, but it was like trying to distract a pit bull in a jaw hold. He didn't even seem to know I was there. My kicks were mere fleabites to the powerful Scotsman. Skip was clearly outmatched.

I spotted a broken branch, one of the ones I'd seen on the pine tree from my pit of death. I tore it loose and repeatedly thrashed Skip's assailant with it. That got his attention. He batted at me with his broad hand, like I was a mosquito. That gave Skip the opportunity he needed. He wrested the shovel from Grant's hand and swung at him. Grant dodged. He was surprisingly agile for such a large man, but I already knew that. The dance academy had paid off, in spades.

Skip missed his mark by only centimeters. Grant grabbed the handle of the shovel but Skip held on. Tugging back and forth on the long vertical handle of the spade, it looked like they were choosing up sides for baseball. Then I had an idea.

While Grant was distracted with his tug of war with Skip, I lassoed the groomer's leash around Grant's tree trunk neck and yanked it with all my might. He let out sharp gasp and a yelp of pain like a dog racing to the end of a too-short chain. The Sirius Killer was at the other end of the leash now.

50

I wound the end of the blue plastic lead around both my hands and held on for dear life, while Grant bucked at the other end of the leash noosed around his neck. He was so powerful, I felt like I was bronco busting in a rodeo. I had begun to lose my grip when Skip gave him a tremendous wallop to the back of his head with the shovel. Grant toppled face-down like an old growth pine, hitting the ground with a mighty thud. Such a powerful blow would have killed a normal man, but Grant's skull was no doubt as sturdy as the rest of him.

The woods were silent except for the wind howling through the trees, the labored breathing of Colin Grant, and the rasp of handcuffs. Skip finally managed to force the cuffs closed on Grant's massive wrists. Using the leash end to bind Grant's ankles, he threaded it through the cuffs to pull up the slack. Knees bent, feet nearly touching his back, Grant lay trussed up like a cowpoke-busted calf, rendered powerless even if he should revive before help came. Nona had finally managed to locate Skip's revolver in the light of an especially bright shooting star that reflected off the gunmetal.

What little air I had left in my lungs escaped in a sigh of relief. Skip had things under control and not a moment too soon. He trained the gun on the deadly doggy lying at his feet while he called for backup.

"I nearly ended up eating a dirt sandwich, Skip."

"You're lucky we found you when we did."

"How on earth did you know where to look for me?"

"We didn't. Your dog did."

"He was acting really strange when I got home from the party. Then, when I saw the state of the place, I knew something was way wrong. I called Skip and he came like a shot," Nona said.

"Cruiser, what a good boy you are." I summoned Cruiser, but I could see he still wasn't acting right. Exhausted from my own ordeal, I sat down on the ground and coaxed him to me. He slowly ambled forward. He was just inches from the comfort of my lap and the reward of a caress when his sturdy basset legs folded under him.

51

Nona and I sat in the waiting room of the veterinary emergency clinic. After my near-fatal ordeal in the woods, I now faced the possibility of losing my beloved dog. In my wildest dreams I could never have imagined a scarier Halloween than this one was turning out to be.

We rushed Cruiser to Doc Heaton right after he collapsed. Grant had slipped him something, so he would be incapacitated and make my abduction easier. Rags and Lang Po had high-tailed out the dog door into the woods at the first sign of trouble, so they had escaped further harm.

Grant had misgauged the doses of poison he gave Lang Po and Rags. I could only hope he hadn't corrected his error this time and given Cruiser enough of the substance to kill him. Doc Heaton had been working over my boy for over an hour. I feared the worst.

"What can be taking so long?" Nona said.

"I don't know. I guess Cruiser got a pretty good dose of whatever that creep Colin gave him."

"Is Skip coming back?" she asked.

"He assured me he'd check in on us later, after he got Grant booked."

"I guess this means Pauline is off the hook, huh, Mom?"

Off the leash, in this case, I thought. "Yes, she's innocent. I just couldn't believe that someone who does the kind of work she does with animals would be capable of something so heinous."

"But why didn't she warn anyone about this, if she's as psychic as she claims to be?"

"She did, Nona. The day of the Howloween event. That warning was meant for Cruiser and me, not just for Abby. I think that's why she showed up at the party tonight, even though she knew she might be apprehended."

"You mean she did come to warn us?"

"I'm certain of it. Speaking of danger, young lady, it's a wonder you weren't hurt out there with all that going on."

"What did you expect me to do, just sit at home and wait for you to show up? My mother was missing. I've told you before, you don't have to worry about me. I can handle myself. Anyway, I thought we were sort of partners on this case."

"I did ask for your help, didn't I?" I hugged my daughter and kissed her cheek. How grateful I felt to be with Nona again. "Now, if someone will just help our Cruiser."

The waiting room was empty, except for Nona and me. I could hear the barking and meowing of other furry patients from the end of the hallway, but I couldn't hear Cruiser. How I longed to hear that familiar howl rising above the others. All I heard was the tinkling of the bell over the door as Skip entered the clinic.

"I got here as fast as I could. How's Cruiser doin'?"

"We haven't heard anything yet. Doc Heaton is still working on him. It's been over an hour already. If anything happens to Cruiser, I don't know what I'll do." I felt my eyes pool with tears.

"Try not to think about that now. I'm sure Doc is doing everything he can for our basset buddy."

"Did you get Grant all taken care of?"

"Yep, we took his statement. He's behind bars. That was some pretty expert lassoing you did, Beanie."

"You didn't do so bad yourself, Cowboy Cassidy."

"I guess the Sirius Killer finally found out how it feels to be at the end of a leash, didn't he?" Nona said.

"Sure did, honey." I touched my throat, the pain of the abrasions on my own neck acute.

"You'd better have that seen to," Skip said.

"I will, just as soon as Cruiser's taken care of."

"I don't understand it," Nona said. "Why did Grant do all those terrible things he did?"

I let Skip do the explaining while I did the worrying. I'd already heard Grant's whole evil plan from the ground up, so to speak.

"He was working out some kind of shady multi-million-dollar deal with the Paragon Hotel chain. He wanted that precious parcel of land, and so did they, but Grant was prepared to do anything to get it, even commit murder," Skip said. "He felt confident he could sway the council in his favor with a little unfriendly persuasion. He put a scare into all the dog park supporters with the pup poisonings to steer them off the project, and it was working. People were becoming too terrified to even leave their homes. The only real obstacles left to claiming the property were the Haver-shams. He killed Addison, too, and made it look like a suicide."

"Addison's dead?" Nona said.

Skip nodded. "Suicide wouldn't have been too much of a stretch. The kid had some problems."

"What a terrible way for Addison to end up, even if I didn't like him," Nona said.

"So that's what Grant was ranting on about, while he was burying his last bit of evidence like an old dog bone."

"What evidence was that, Beanie?"

"Me!"

"But what about Rosie?" Nona asked. "How does she figure into all this?"

"Mrs. Clark was suspicious of Grant, and he knew it," Skip said. "She'd worked with him before on council projects and thought he wasn't entirely aboveboard in the way he'd handled some of them. She suspected he had deep pockets, and she was right. She just didn't know how deep. He knew he had to take her out of the picture for his plan to succeed."

"He almost succeeded at that," I said. "Rosie's still in a coma. She made some disparaging comments about him once, but I never paid it any mind. Now I wish I had."

"You're not a psychic, Beanie. You couldn't have known all this would happen."

"Well, Mom may not be a practicing pet psychic, but she definitely has the pet connection," Nona said.

"Thanks, honey."

Nona looked puzzled. "There's something else I don't understand."

"What?" Skip and I said in duet.

"Why did the councilman try to implicate Pauline in the crimes? Seems kind of farfetched to me that she would do all those horrid things, if she was a pet psychic."

"He knew about the dispute between her and Abby over the new business regulations," I said.

"And he knew Pauline had a police record for assault and animal cruelty, even though they were trumped-up charges," Skip added.

"It was a convenient setup," I said. "That's why he killed Abby near Pauline's tent and planted evidence to incriminate her."

"Right," Skip said.

"But even without his handiwork at the Howloween event, Grant had a whole doggie bag of possible suspects around to throw us off the scent," I said.

"How did the Haversham history figure into all this?" Nona asked.

"Grant told us during questioning that everything is explained in Adhara's letters. That's who was in the attic when you got there. He was searching for the love letters, and you found them for him. He was hiding in a secret compartment in the attic the whole time, watching you."

"So that house really did have a secret passageway?" Nona said.

"A lot of old houses like that did. It came in handy during Prohibition," Skip said. "They probably threw lots of parties and needed to hide the hooch in a hurry if there was a raid. It was the same with Lucky Baldwin's saloon at Tallac."

"I knew I wasn't alone up there in that attic," I said. "I sensed someone was there."

"Tell us more about the Havershams, Skip," Nona said. The curious spark in her eyes reminded me of sitting around the campfire as a child with Grandfather in the forest, listening to my revered elder's captivating tales of Tahoe's history.

"It goes back to the grandparents, Horace and Adhara," Skip said. "Horace was quite a bit older than his young wife and crazy jealous of her. He was even jealous of her affection for her young son, William, and sent him off to a boarding school in England. That broke Adhara's heart. To get even for his cruelty, she had a torrid affair with a minister. She and her lover planned to do away with Horace and she would inherit everything, but what she and her lover didn't know was that Horace planned to do away with *them*. Anyway, things didn't turn out quite as Adhara planned, and it was Adhara's lover and not her husband who was killed. His body was never found. After that, she went off her rocker."

"What happened to her?" Nona said. "Did they put her in an asylum?"

"In those days, wealthy families like the Havershams would never risk such a scandal," I said.

"Right," Skip said. "So Horace locked her in the attic room. She tried to leap from the window to her death, so he had bars installed in the window. He took everything out of the attic that she could possibly harm herself with. He wanted her alive, so she could suffer with her guilt."

"And the loss of her love," Nona said. "It's so sad."

"So Horace got even with his faithless

wife and kept his fortune," I said.

"Well, not exactly," Skip continued. "There was one other little detail."

"What's that?" I said.

"Adhara was pregnant."

"I guess the old dude still had it in him, huh?" Nona quipped.

"It wasn't his baby, though, was it, Skip?"

"No. It was the preacher's child."

"Wait, I'm getting confused by the Begats," Nona said. "So who was this preacher, and who was his kid?"

"I'm guessing it was Reverend Ramseth's ancestor," I said.

"Yes," Skip said. "But it was kept a secret because of the shame it would bring on the church. Horace wasn't talking."

"And neither was his crazy wife up in her attic prison," I added.

"Right. Horace bought off the Ramseths by giving them a share of his land. He later ended up committing suicide after the Crash of Twenty-Nine. Self-inflicted gunshot."

"That's a bit different than the story I heard," I said.

"A tale like that gets distorted after a century of retelling," Skip said.

"What happened to the baby?" Nona asked.

"After she gave birth, the child was quietly put up for adoption, which further deteriorated Adhara's mental condition. Losing both of her children and her lover was just too much for her."

"So she really died all alone up there in that attic?" Nona said.

"Yes," Skip said. "She hanged herself on a rafter with the sash of her dressing gown."

Nona shivered. "How creepy is that?"

"She got even with her husband, though."

"How?" Nona and I spoke in unison.

"She made sure he found several of the letters that she and the preacher had written to each other during their affair. She told him there were other letters that not only incriminated him in the death of her lover but also confirmed that there was another heir."

"What happened to the letters?" Nona said.

"Horace never found them, although he probably drove himself crazy searching. Adhara died, and no one ever knew what became of the letters."

"But the preacher's family must have known of their existence," I said.

"Someone certainly did," Skip said.

"The lost letters grew into a kind of legend, along with a treasure that is supposedly hidden somewhere in the house. No one has ever found that, either."

"Sort of like El Dorado or the Fountain of Youth," Nona said.

"So that's why Grant was in the attic looking for the letters," I said. "Besides the promise of hidden treasure, he wanted to make sure any other possible claim to the Haversham property was eliminated."

"And that's why Grant came after you, Beanie. He knew you'd found the letters. That's why he ransacked your house. He was looking for them. When you showed up, he figured he'd dispense with you and your watchdogs, then go back to your house and search at his leisure until he found them."

"What he didn't know was that I had them with me the whole time." I pulled the letters from my pocket.

"What will become of them now?" Nona asked.

"Enough lives have been sacrificed over these," I said.

"The letters will prove the land belongs to the Ramseths," Skip said.

I was glad the letters hadn't been reduced to ashes, as Haversham House nearly was, along with everyone who had been partying at the old mansion on what had turned out to be an especially frightening Halloween.

52

Doc Heaton finally appeared. The look on his face wasn't the one I had hoped to see.

"How is Cruiser?" I said, fearing the answer I might get.

He paused a moment, as though searching for just the right words. "I pumped Cruiser's stomach. Ibuprofen can be fatal to dogs, if the dose is large enough for the animal's size."

"Is that what it was?"

"Yes," Doc Heaton said. "Motrin tablets were crushed up and mixed with hamburger or something else irresistible. Peanut butter works, too."

I knew that all too well. All food was irresistible to Cruiser, but especially peanut butter. He had polished many a spoonful of Jif whenever I had to pill him. I suspected that was what Lang Po had been given at the Howloween event. In an effort to implicate her in the crimes, Colin Grant had switched the Peanut Butter Pups in Madame Pawline's booth with the drug-laced ones. Lang Po and Rags probably ate only one of the poisoned treats, but Cruiser the chowhound had no doubt begged a whole handful of them from Grant. "Doc, is Cruiser . . . ?"

"Cruiser is still alive, Elsie."

I sighed with relief. "Oh, thank goodness."

"He's been through an awful lot, though. The drug may have had time enough to get into his system. This stuff gets into the bloodstream fast, anywhere from ten to sixty minutes of ingestion. It's broken down in the liver and expelled from the body through the kidneys." Doc Heaton paused again, which worried me. "There may have been some damage done to his organs. He's not a young dog, either. Fortunately, there was no blood in his vomitus, and he hasn't had any seizures. But he was definitely shocky when you brought him in. It could have been from the abdominal pain, though. I'll have to keep him under observation for a while."

"May I see him?"

"Yes, but he's still coming out of anesthesia. He may not know you're there."

"That's all right," I said. "I'll know I'm there."

A young technician appeared in the

doorway. She tried not to look flustered. "Doctor Heaton. We need you in the surgery immediately. There's a problem."

"Coming, Brenda," the doctor said before he raced down the hallway.

I knew instinctively that they were talking about my dog. I began to hyperventilate. I felt like I was back in that grave again being buried alive, gasping for air. Cruiser was in serious trouble! If anything happened to him, they might as well throw me back into that hole and fill it up. I wasn't about to wait out in the reception area while Cruiser fought for his life. I belonged one place only now . . . by his side.

53

Skip and Nona followed me into the surgery. My heart sank when I saw Cruiser lying on his side upon the floor atop a cloud-soft cushion. They had made him as comfortable as possible on the pallet and covered him with a blanket for warmth. Doc Heaton drew a blood sample, while Brenda checked Cruiser's blood pressure and heart rate. She lifted an eyelid. His pupils were dilated, just like Rosie's had been. I feared for Cruiser. I couldn't lose him. I just couldn't.

Doc didn't mind my being present with my dog. In fact, he felt that having a pet's owner nearby in such a crisis was helpful, for the pet and for the owner. The rhythmic *whoosh-whoosh* sound from the respirator filled a heavy silence in the room, much like when I had visited Rosie Clark at the nursing home. A long tube snaked down Cruiser's esophagus to inflate his lungs with precious oxygen. I didn't want to admit it, but as with Rosie, things didn't look too promising for Cruiser.

"Will he make it, Doc?" I said.

"I've done all I can do. The rest is up to Cruiser now."

I sank to my knees and stroked my old friend's paw, the one without the IV inserted in it. I called his name, "Cruiser, Cruiser, come back to me, boy. I need you." There was no response. I just kept on talking to him, like I always talk to him. I told him how much I loved him. Again, no response. I looked back at Nona and Skip. They both had tears in their eyes. My own tears spilled onto the cold linoleum floor as I knelt there, praying for Cruiser to make it through this crisis. I caressed a velvety ear. It felt as cold as the linoleum.

Then I got angry. No one was going to take my dog away from me. Not the Sirius Killer. Not anyone!

"Cruiser, you're going to make it, do you hear me!" I commanded him to obey me, like when we were out in the field and he was being his old stubborn basset self. I thought of all those times he ignored me because he was following a particularly wonderful scent and just couldn't bring himself to heed my command. This was no different. I'd have to get tough with him. "Come back, Cruiser. You come back right now, young man!"

I saw Cruiser's eyelids twitch, as though he dreamed in the REM stages of sleep. But his beautiful cinnamon-colored eyes didn't open. Still, I felt certain that he sensed I was right there beside him. At least I hoped he did.

I tried another method of getting him to respond. At this point, I'd try anything. "Hey, Cruiser! Let's go home, fella. Let's go see Nonie and Rags and that silly Lang Po!" If anything would rouse him, it was the G word. He made funny sounds in his throat, like a ventriloquist. I understood that he was trying to bark in answer to my supplication, but that horrid tube in his windpipe was obstructing the sound. It was the most pitiful sight.

"Please, Cruiser. Come back to me, boy. Please." When the pink hue of his gums paled, the battle appeared lost. I rested my cheek against a broad brindled forepaw, so well designed for digging holes in my yard, and sobbed like a child. Nona knelt beside me, weeping, and rested her hand gently on mine to comfort me. There wasn't a dry eye in the room. Macho man Skip was bawling like a baby. Doc Heaton was misty-eyed, too, although he continued to work tirelessly over the patient, using everything in his veterinary bag of miracles.

Cruiser ranged far afield, tracking that glorious golden scent that beckoned to him from the other side of the mountain, just beyond Rainbow Bridge.

54

The sunset on that March evening was spectacular. A rainstorm had blown through earlier in the day, and the lingering clouds in the western horizon ignited the sky. It was one of the most beautiful Sierra sunsets I'd seen in a very long time. The icy crust of winter had all but melted from fields and marshes, which were an impressionist's canvas of yellow and lilac, the mantle of a glorious Tahoe spring.

Many months had passed since my ordeal at the hands of the Sirius Killer, and Tahoe dog owners felt secure in the knowledge that they and their pets were safe from harm. Colin Grant had been tried and convicted of homicide. He was also charged with felony animal cruelty. He had received life imprisonment for his crimes. He would never see a cent of the money he'd hoped to make from the sale of the Haversham property. I guess you could say most of it went to the dogs, as Abigail had originally intended. Unknown to anyone,

Abby had put her money in a trust for animal welfare causes, including the dog park. She had also bequeathed a large portion of her fortune to the care of Lang Po, should he survive her.

With the discovery of the long-lost love letters of Adhara and her lover, Peter, and proof of kinship with the Havershams through the birth of a child, the Ramseths inherited the property. Though the reverend was not pleased about the stain of sin upon his family that brought him the inheritance, he accepted it nevertheless.

The reverend mellowed some after that. He sold back half of the acreage he had inherited to the city to get enough money to fund his newest church project and also to help his daughter keep her business. Even though he still did not approve wholeheartedly, he and Pauline made peace with each other. Henceforth, he seemed less judgmental of his daughter and her unconventional beliefs.

In return, Pauline helped him with his plans for church expansion, which included Elysian Fields, a new lakeside funeral chapel. She even persuaded him to include a smaller chapel for pet owners, the first of its kind in Tahoe. His funeral chapel was assured of continued prosperity, since he would never run out of customers from seniors checking out of the retirement home right next door.

As I strolled along the beach, I paused in front of Haversham House. It looked nothing like it had when I had walked these grounds the previous autumn with Cruiser. It could never pass for a creepy haunted house now. The Grand Old Lady had risen like a phoenix from the ashes and had enjoyed a reincarnation as the centerpiece of Alpine Haven Retirement Community.

The sad, sagging veranda of the house had been reinforced and repainted, broken windows were replaced, and even the Haversham crest on the iron gates had been recast. The interior had been completely refurbished; even the attic had been rebuilt, including new floorboards to replace the ones that had hidden Adhara's secret love letters. In tearing up the old flooring, a man's skeleton was discovered. DNA tests on the remains revealed it to be the body of Peter Ramseth. Horace had imprisoned his errant wife in the attic with the corpse of her dead lover. No wonder she went mad! One could only hope that their ghosts, and any others in the Haversham House, had taken up residence elsewhere.

That old attic had contained not only a ghost or two but a treasure as well, as the legend claimed. During reconstruction, a fireproof compartment was discovered in an interior wall that contained a sizeable cache of gold coins, enough to support the estate for the next century. The other relics of the Haversham legacy, which consisted mostly of antique furniture and paintings that had not been destroyed in the fire, were cleaned, restored, and displayed throughout the house.

I felt a sense of satisfaction that I had in some way helped to bring all this about. The articles I wrote swayed Tahoe public opinion in favor of the dog park. Perhaps it wasn't all my doing, though. In the wake of the Sirius Killer's frightful chokehold on the community, attitudes toward dogs and their owners had softened considerably. Dog lovers and their canine companions were barking for joy. Neighbors seemed more tolerant of one another, not just in this but in all things.

Even curmudgeonly old Walter Wiley stopped complaining about his neighbors' dogs. His cancer had gone into remission after he'd adopted a dog from the local shelter where his wife had volunteered. Having a dog had improved his disposition and kept him from being so lonely.

Several seniors walked their dogs along the stretch of sand now known as Alpine Paws Park. Some rested on teak benches while their dogs cavorted and socialized off-leash with other dogs. A Labrador and two Goldens bounded into the freezing cold lake as though it were midsummer.

Suddenly, Rags and Lang Po were at my side. "Having fun, boys?" I said. Rags barked and did a joyful Highland fling. Lang Po was a bit more reserved in his response, but the smile on his little fuzzy dog face told me all I needed to know.

"Hey, Beanie, wait up!" Rosie hurried to catch up. She was getting around pretty well on her cane now. A few more weeks of physical therapy and she wouldn't need it at all. Her coming out of the coma in December had been a wonderful Christmas present for all who knew and loved her, especially for Rags. Her amazing recovery had surprised everyone but me. Having observed the effect of Rags' dog magic on her, I had a strong feeling that she might eventually recover.

We sat down on one of the benches to rest and take in the view of the lake. Nothing was quite as restful or healing as that, except perhaps the presence of a good dog or two. Rags leapt into Rosie's lap and Lang Po perched between us.

"How is Lang Po adjusting to his new home?"

"He's doing fine. He and Rags get along great. Rags seems much calmer, having another dog around."

"That makes sense. Dogs are pack animals by nature."

"I never dreamed they'd get along so well together, though."

"I didn't think Cruiser would be so keen on having other dogs around either, but he seemed happier with some canine company in the house, even these two little troublemakers."

Rosie laughed. It was so good to hear my friend's laughter again. It had been too long absent. "Well, it's obvious that these two are plenty content." She reached down to pet her small charges, who looked up at her adoringly, panting pure joy.

"It could be because they were introduced on neutral ground, living with me while you were in the hospital, Rosie."

"You're probably right. If I had tried to bring another dog onto Rags' turf without a proper introduction, it might not have worked out so well."

"I think the same goes for Lang Po. He's used to being boss dog. Abby had him badly spoiled."

"Yes, I know. She really loved her little dog, to the exclusion of just about everyone else in her life, including her own nephew. She raised Addison alone after her twin sister, Alice, died, but Abby wasn't the motherly type. He wasn't too fond of his aunt, either."

"Why?" I said.

"Abby could be quite harsh to people who displeased her."

"That's true and the reason why people avoided displeasing her."

"No one displeased her quite like Addison did. When she was mad at him, she used to lock him in the spooky attic of that old house to punish him. He once told me he used to bang on the door for hours until his hands bled."

"Abby did that? That's awful. I can't believe it," I said. "She was a pillar of the community."

"I guess Abby had a lot of people fooled," Rosie said.

"People's public and private personas can be like night and day," I said, thinking of Colin Grant, who also had fooled a few people, including me.

"Abby had already lost both her parents. When Alice passed, too, I think she went a little crazy."

"I think the whole Haversham family was a little crazy, Rosie."

"You're probably right. Abby somehow blamed Addison for her sister's death, but I think she really blamed herself. She just transferred her anger to him."

"Poor kid."

"I know," Rosie said. "If only Abby could have forgiven her nephew, both of their lives could have been so different."

"Abby loved dogs. How could she have been any less forgiving than the creatures she loved so much?"

"Dogs give us all daily lessons in forgiveness and selfless love, right, Beanie?"

"Right." I thought of my own dog, who had risked his life to save mine. Only a faithful fellow like Cruiser could have endured the pain from a deadly poison coursing through his body to lead Skip and Nona to me.

I hadn't told Rosie about my ordeal in the woods. I didn't like to talk about it. I was trying hard to put the terrifying experience behind me, but I still awoke some nights in a panic, gasping for air, thinking I was being buried alive. Some things were better left in the past where they belonged, just like the Havershams. After he viewed the surveillance tape, Skip concurred.

The video had clearly captured the image of Colin Grant disguised in his Sirius Killer garb making his way down the second-floor hallway to the attic room. Then Pauline appeared on camera, also heading for the attic. Sometime later, the tape showed Pauline being dragged from the room by the killer, struggling for her life as I had. Then something very strange happened. Skip swears to this day a faulty video cartridge was to blame for the phenomenon, but I knew better when I saw a weird, phosphorescent mist leak through crevices in the attic door, engulfing Grant in an eerie fog bank. He screamed, released his captive, and hurtled down the hall in terror.

As I sat there with Rosie, thinking of Cruiser, a familiar, melodious baying echoed in my ears and warmed my heart with love. *Barooooooo!* As in days past, I saw sand kicked up in small clouds from his massive paws as he raced joyfully toward me down the beach, ears flying in the wind. I heard myself call out his name. "Cruiser! Cruiser!"

Rags and Lang Po ran out to greet my beloved companion, who had wandered a bit too far from me in the way a Basset Hound will do, given half the chance. It was so good to see him his old scent-sniffing, pine-piddling self again. He'd been through a lot, but Doc Heaton had done his finest work in sparing Cruiser's life, and without any residual effects from the poison. My best buddy was just as good as new. Perhaps it was a bit more than Doc's skill alone that had brought my companion back to me, though. For once, my stubborn basset had obeyed a command.

"Come here, fella." Cruiser sailed along the lakeside toward me, jowls flapping and ears flying in unison, a spray of slobber in his wake. I'd swear he was laughing. So was I. Surely such a moment had inspired Beethoven's "Ode to Joy," I thought, kneeling open-armed to greet my faithful hound. He bowled me over on my back in the sand, planting his paws on my chest.

"Stop, stop!" I protested as Cruiser drenched me with kisses. He knew I didn't really mean it, though. I righted myself and gave my big, brave dog a fierce hug. He responded with a tongue swipe on my cheek.

As we continued our twilight promenade

along the scenic shores of Lake Tahoe, the first star of the evening appeared in the heavens.

"Look, Beanie!" Rosie said, pointing skyward. "It's Sirius, the Dog Star."

I gazed up to see Canis Major frolicking on hind legs, a merry twinkle in its eye. The brilliant star sparkled like a rare sapphire in the ether.

"Seriously, Rosie," I said, smiling as I stroked my beloved Basset Hound. "You should know by now that Cruiser is the only Dog Star in my universe."

About the Author

Sue Owens Wright is a writer of both fiction and nonfiction about dogs. She is a fancier and rescuer of Basset Hounds, which are frequently featured in her books and essays. Sue is a three-time nominee for the Mighty Maxwell, which is awarded annually by the Dog Writers' Association of America (DWAA) for the best writing on the subject of dogs. Her first nomination was for *Howling Bloody Murder*, the debut novel in the Beanie and Cruiser mystery series. She won the Maxwell Award in 2003 and received a third Maxwell nomination and special recognition from the DWAA in 2004 for the Humane Society of the United States Compassionate Care Award. For more information about the author, please visit www.beanieandcruiser.com.